C0-BWZ-221

Leah on a Leash

& Other Stories

·3 in 1·

Leah on a Leash

& Other Stories

·3 in 1·

Jim Studer

© Copyright by Jim Studer 2020

All rights reserved. No part of this publication may be reproduced, stored in a retrieval system or transmitted in any form or by any means, electronic, mechanical, photocopying, recording or otherwise without the prior permission of the publisher or in accordance with the provisions of the Copyright, Designs and Patents Act 1988 or under the terms of any license permitting limited copying issued by the Copyright Licensing Agency.

This book is a work of fiction.
The characters and plots are the
creation of the author's dream
of a better world.

"The Old Man" was first published in *The Mystery of Tony the Goat and Other Tales* (2018).

ISBN: 978-0-578-75888-6

Also by Jim Studer:

The Road Taken
and
*The Mystery of Tony the Goat
and Other Tales*

To Kate, I hope
you enjoy the stories as much
as I enjoyed writing them.

Jim

Dedication

To Bianca Heller
and
all the speech
and
drama team members
of the last fifty years.

Author's Note

Thank you for opening up a copy of Leah on a Leash. I hope you will find the stories uplifting; I hope they provide you with something to feel good about. Today amidst a world of killer virus, religious and racial bigotry, we need hope. As I see it, hope can be found in people helping people. I have faith in today's youth. They will find ways to counter the illnesses that plague us.

My short stories are not great literature, but they feature hope. They are positive; most have happy endings. I like feel-good stories; I like underdogs who rise above the odds. Most of all, I like those who offer a helping hand.

So many of the stories I read or see on TV feature antiheroes, or the plots give us ugly pictures of divisiveness. A couple of recent ones fed me stories that had not a single character I could cheer for, empathize with, or feel compassion for. They painted a naturalistic world of dog eat dog. I've written a collection of stories that I feel give us hope. Hope for the future depends on individuals who will stand up for and do the right thing. We are all in this together. Only by working together can we survive.

I've tried to give you a glimpse of this kind of hope by writing stories that come out of what I know. My world lies mainly in coaching and teaching. Thus, Stuart August emerges. His stories are grounded in the stories of Jesse Stuart, the Appalachian schoolteacher of sixty years ago. His book is entitled A Jesse Stuart Harvest. The Stuart August stories were also inspired by Margaret Ryan, my eighth grade teacher. I hope you enjoy reading these stories at least half as much as I enjoyed writing them.

As I approach my seventy-sixth birthday, I've reflected on the stories of my grandparents, whom you can find in The Road Taken, and The Old Man featured in the last story in The Mystery of Tony the Goat and Other Tales. I've found a new voice in The Old Man to further explore the world of an old fogy. In spite of his curmudgeonly nature, he is meant to inspire hope. He interacts with those far younger than he. He survives in a world of technology that has convinced him a form of voodoo does exist. How else can the world of computers and their relatives be explained? If I am successful, The Old Man shows us hope and furnishes us with some fun at the same time. He is old, but he is still useful.

Then there are four very good stories that don't fit into the life of either character. I hope you can find some goodness in each of them. One is just pure fun; one provides a belief in a rainbow with a pot of gold at the end. The other two are more realistic but provide us with a form of reclamation. I hope you will find enjoyment in each section.

As in my first two books, I have had much help in making the stories better than they would have been if I were left on my own. Gary Stroeing has been with me for all three books. He has been there with encouragement; he has been a good sounding board and researcher, especially when it comes to cars. He is a muse.

Also along for the third go is Miranda Rice. She has provided sound editorial advice, provided research, and supplied clerical help to a technological illiterate. In spite of her youth, she has been my main muse in creating The Old Man stories.

Joining those two on the third go-round is Bianca Heller. She has given me much-needed clerical help and research. She inspired the characters in some of the stories. She assured me that a few of the stories I was doubting were good. She did what a muse does.

The final preventative medicine for me comes from Kristen Vosberg, who provides the final quality control as a talented proofreader.

Any mistakes in the book are mine.

I owe so much to all four of them. Thank you.

Thanks to all of you who have purchased copies of my books. A special thanks goes to all of the over 400 speech and drama team members who made fifty years of coaching and directing a pure joy. These young folks are tomorrow's positive future.

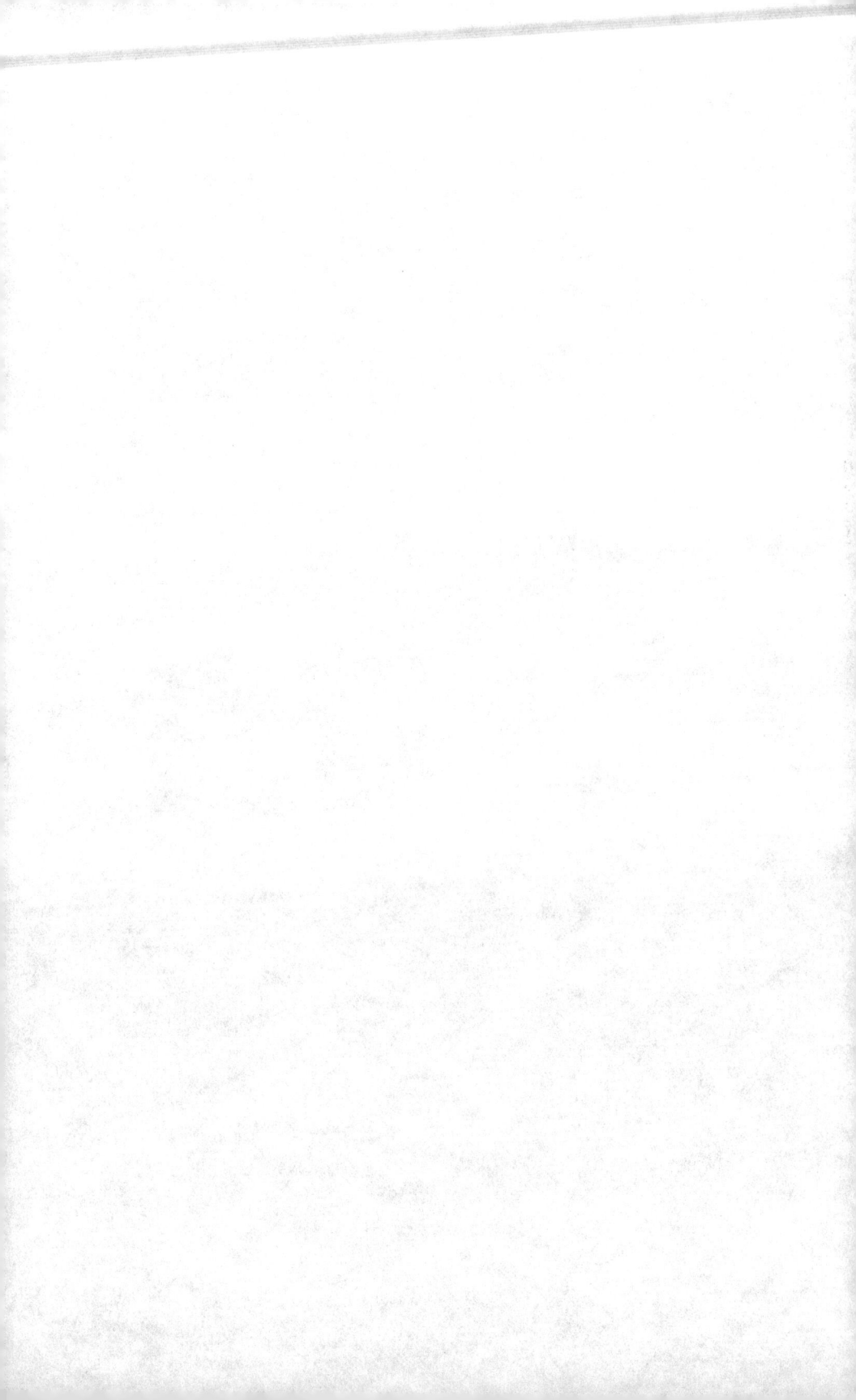

Contents

Stuart August

Classroom Stories

Leah on a Leash

"Phone for you, Gus," said Mary Jo.

Gus took the phone. "This is Gus."

"Hey, Augie, it's Leah. How are you doin', big guy? I'm havin' a riot."

"Slow down a minute. Who is this?"

"Oh man, you must be aging fast. Memory gone in just three weeks."

"Look, tell me who you are and what you want, or I am hanging up."

"Okay, okay. I will take it 'slowly,' an adverb, you know." She preceded ever so deliberately. "This is Leah Gould from Aparecida, you know, just three weeks ago. That's who I am.

"What do I want? I want you to take pen in hand and write this down. Ready? Okay, here goes. Elwood Arnison; that's E-L-W-O-O-D A-R-N-I-S-O-N. He's a lawyer my dad keeps on a string. He will fill you in, and I know you won't let me down, and no, you are not in trouble. Trust me."

Leah babbled on at length, ever more rapidly. "Augie, how do you like my new name for you? You aren't my teacher anymore. You resigned to go back to the North Star State. I looked it up; those good ol' reference books do come in handy, like you said. So, no more Mr. August. From here on in it's Augie, but you are welcome to refer to me as Ms. Gould. See, I learned that non-sexist terminology from you."

"Leah," Gus interrupted. "Where are you and what is this about?"

"I am in . . . wait, hey, what city am I in?" A pause. "Lima, Ohio? Thanks. Augie, I'm in Lima, Ohio. Not Peru, Ohio. I know you won't let me down. See you soon." She hung up.

Stuart August, high school English teacher, had just completed his second two-year contract at an American school in São Paulo, Brazil. Leah Gould had been one of his students for the last two years. She was a senior-to-be as of August 1986. Augustus, Gus to most of his friends, had taken a five-year leave from his Minnesota high school position to teach overseas and attend grad school. He was now returning to his old school.

Leah Gould was a one-person entertainment program. She loved to talk, or perhaps it wasn't love so much as a habit she couldn't break. Her vocal chords vibrated nonstop. She was bright, impatient, and desperately lonely. Her parents were divorced. Aaron Gould, her father, was a wealthy Texas oilman. Her mother was a Central American Catholic beauty who snared a Jewish oil tycoon. Leah inherited her mother's motor mouth and penchant for high jinks. The Texas oilman never listened to anyone, much less to his wife. The marriage ended before Leah was eight.

Two years ago, when Stuart August was teaching his sophomore class at Aparecida how to use library reference books, Leah shouted across the room to him. "Hey, Mr. August, come here and look at this." He walked across the library to her. "Here, see this?" She pointed to the picture of a man in full military regalia. The article in a volume of Current Biography told of the twice-deposed dictator of a Central American country. "That's my abuelo."

"Twice deposed?" An incredulous Mr. August said way too loud.

"Yup, the second time it was his brother, my great-uncle, who said there would be no third time. He shot him dead."

"I am so sorry, Leah," Mr. August said in a consoling attempt.

"Oh, I never knew him. All I know is that he left mi madre with a huge wad of cash in some bank in the Bahamas. That's how she snagged my dad in Nassau. He didn't need her money since he had too much of his own. He must have figured she wasn't after his money because she had so much of her own. He always had an eye for the ladies. My mom was pretty hot stuff, even hotter than me, and that's hot. So here I am."

Stuart August wasn't surprised that one of his students had a claim to notoriety. One of last year's senior girls posed for the cover of Vogue. A few years before, one of the school's students was the granddaughter of the wealthiest man in South America. The grandfather had been successfully ransomed after two separate kidnappings. The sums were staggering. Two of the present-day students were from the family of the founder of one of

4

Brazil's water pump manufacturers, who made a few billion when its jet pumps became a worldwide hit in water recreation.

Escola Aparecida was a K-12 American school with students representing thirty-some countries. Such American schools were in demand as stepping stones into American colleges and universities. Seniors often weighed acceptances from schools that ranged from Cornell, Harvard, Julliard, Stanford, and Vanderbilt all the way down to lowly Western State College of Colorado.

Leah was not seeking prestigious university acceptance; she sought a family. She was a lonely girl. Her mother and new boyfriend lived in São Paulo. They had little time for her. Her oilman daddy was sometimes at home in Texas, but spent more time in the Middle East, Norway, Indonesia, or Alaska, extending and securing his empire.

Stuart August was Leah Gould's prescription for alleviating loneliness. Several times each week she extended both of their school days. She was there to chat. She wanted to know about him, his background. Why wasn't he married, or had he been? She was also there to educate him. She told him about her life, all the places she lived, went to school. She showed him lists and pictures of all of Daddy's girlfriends for the last seven years. Mom seemed more stable, as her list and pictures of boyfriends were fewer in number.

Leah came equipped with pictures over the two years Mr. August knew her. He lost count of the number of thick albums she showed him, page by page, with a detailed script for each. "Hey, Mr. August, look at my dad's houseboat in Waco."

"Waco, Leah, that must be the Brazos River then," responded Mr. August. His heart went out to the girl. She needed someone to listen to her, to ask about her dreams.

"Oh, you know it. Most people I talk to never heard of Waco. My dad wants me to go to college there, Baylor. I don't know why he wants that, he's not there much. I'd just as soon be alone in a place I like. He can afford to keep his spies abreast of my actions no matter where I am."

Another day it was, "Here's a picture of my mom. Some body, yes? Here

5

are twenty-five more pictures of her. Notice that she does not appear in the same outfit more than once. Maybe that's how I got hooked on fashion."

On another day it was, "See these pictures of my cousins? They have a boutique in Philadelphia. I spent my last two summers there working in the store. I am scheduled to go back once more."

"Lucky you," Mr. August replied when she mentioned Philadelphia. "I've been there. I really liked the Ben Franklin Museum and all the Walt Whitman stuff. I saw a Phillies game, too."

"Well, maybe you liked being there. All I want is a place to call home. Philly is not it. I'm just a migrating bird expected to fly to another perch at season's end."

Week after week Leah came after class with stories, pictures, dreams, and shards of broken dreams. He knew that his responses to her pictures and stories only encouraged her. He felt sorry for her. When he took interest and asked questions, he could see her eyes light up. She got excited; someone was actually listening to her. He did care for her and felt as if he was fulfilling a useful purpose beyond teaching her about the library, grammar, and literature. After one session with her he was reminded of the words from a Sherwin Linton song, "Lucky little rich boy, got everything, he's the son of a cotton king." This was the case of the lucky little rich girl, the daughter of an oil tycoon. In both cases the stories were of unhappiness.

When Stuart August had returned from São Paulo to Minnesota, he stayed with his friends Mary Jo and Carl in Minneapolis. He had taught with Mary Jo for years. He had given his students in Brazil the address and phone number of his parents in Middleton, Minnesota. He told his students they could always find him through his parents. His parents were aware of this.

Leah was a determined detective. By the end of the first week with her cousins she had the Minneapolis phone number for August. She was tired of being ignored by her relatives. She thought the only reason they kept her there was to work in the boutique. Leah knew fashion and could charm customers. Her sales figures were top in the shop. After calling Gus's parents, she made repeated calls trying to catch him in Minneapolis. Gus was not at Mary Jo's place very much as he was apartment hunting, catching up with old friends, and attending Twins games.

"Gus, who's this chick in Philly who keeps calling for you? She won't give me her name, but says she must talk to you. You old dog, what have you been up to?" Carl asked him one evening.

At that time Gus didn't know it was Leah who was calling. "I haven't a clue about calls from Philadelphia," replied Gus.

It didn't take long after Leah's call from Ohio when another call came in. This time Gus was present. "Yes, this is the Stuart August answering service. Please hold." As Mary Jo handed Gus the phone, she said, "You need to get a social secretary."

Gus took the phone. "This is Stuart August."

"This is Elwood Arnison. I represent Aaron Gould. You taught his daughter, Leah, in São Paulo. I will meet you in Lima, Ohio, the day after tomorrow at the Allen County Courthouse. Be there at nine a.m. There I will turn Leah over to you.

"I have been in contact with Allen County all day arranging this transfer. Mr. Gould anticipated this eventuality. He is usually three steps ahead of his competition and on a good day half a step ahead of Leah. For the past two years Leah has talked much about you. He does listen to some of what she says. He picks up on her themes. As is he, she is also a schemer; she must have inherited the trait from him. When your name kept coming up in her phone calls to him, he immediately had me hire a firm to have you thoroughly vetted. I see that your ex-wife is doing well in England. The firm declared you safe."

"Wait just a minute, Mr. Arnison," August finally was able to interrupt. "What do you mean about my coming to Lima, Ohio, to have Leah turned over to me?"

"Yes, first of all a cashier's check to cover more than your expenses will arrive at your present address at six a.m. tomorrow so you can be on the road by six thirty. Before you object to that, listen to the rest.

"Leah ran away from Philadelphia four days ago. Since she just turned seventeen in May, she is a minor. Mr. Gould's influence has been able to

7

put out a countrywide alert to find her. He was sure she was headed your way. By bus she got as far as Lima, Ohio. Perhaps she got off the shortest, most direct route. No matter, she was picked up in Lima and placed in the juvenile detention center of the Allen County Jail. Mr. Gould and I have been on the phone with Leah and the authorities in Ohio.

"Leah refuses to return to Philadelphia and insists she will only stay with her father in Texas or with you. Staying with her father is not an option as Mr. Gould will be traveling on business almost the entire summer. This is a critical time for him and his enterprises. Right now he is in Riyadh, Saudi Arabia. His mood is horrible. Because of the time difference he has gotten little sleep. He had to stay up almost all night trying to talk some sense into his daughter.

"Leah says the only alternative is spending the summer with you. Since she is already headed your way, she must have known that being with her father in Texas would never happen. Again, I remind you, Mr. Gould had you thoroughly investigated and has concluded that Leah will be safe with you. We have completed all of the legal paperwork here in Texas to make you her legal guardian until the first of September. By then she will be back with her mother in Brazil. You can sign all the legal paperwork in Allen County. I will also have a contract for you with more than adequate compensation for your inconvenience and effort. You will be in charge of the trust fund for Leah to see that she has all she needs, including rent. Of course this will be less than she will want, but that will be part of earning your salary, keeping her on a leash."

"And if I refuse this mission, Mr. Arnison?" asked Stuart August.

"Leah will be placed in a boarding school for the summer in Houston, Texas. She will, no doubt, run away again and again until she gets what she wants. I have been dealing with her for years. I do know her well. If you refuse this mission, Mr. August, instead of this communication self-destructing, I'm afraid it will be Leah who self-destructs."

With a sigh, Gus said yes, he would accept Mission Impossible. He often wondered if he would regret his promises over the years to his students. "Within law and my ability, I will do what I can to help you." This was certainly a test of that.

Two days later Gus met Elwood Arnison on the steps of the Allen County Courthouse. Papers from Texas were signed, meeting legal requirements for all concerned. Mr. Arnison handed Stuart August a substantial cashier's check. "That should cover your time, expenses, and a little of your upcoming aggravation," said Mr. Arnison. "Now, let's go get Leah."

Before either could move, Leah Gould pranced into the courtroom. She was not dressed in Allen County detention attire as Gus had expected. Instead, dazzling all who laid eyes on her, she sported a red miniskirt, a tight, white, deep V-neck cotton top, and heels. When she located Gus, like a finely trained athlete, she dashed across the room in spike heels that passed for track shoes. She jumped into the arms of Stuart August, wrapping arms and legs around him. "I knew you would come, Augie; I knew I could count on you. Thanks. Now put me down and let's get the hell out of here." The courtroom spectators stood in awe.

Elwood Arnison handed Gus a letter with instructions that would allow him to tap Leah's trust fund as needed. He thanked Gus and said, "Good luck; you'll need it," as he rolled his eyes and looked at Leah.

Gus turned to Leah and said in a parental tone, "We leave in twelve minutes. Now take those two suitcases they brought in for you and find a women's restroom. Change into jeans, a baggy shirt, and tennis shoes. I don't want to be arrested on a morals charge taking a seveneen-year-old across state lines."

"Oh, Augie, everybody trusts you. Besides, I could talk you out of any trouble you get into."

"More than likely talk me into trouble. Now, go get changed, and let's get out of here."

Dressed as instructed, Leah reappeared, and they started the journey to Minnesota. Mr. August told Leah that they would drive the twelve or thirteen hours straight through, stopping only as needed. "That's okay, Augie. Is it okay if I call you Augie? You're not my teacher anymore, I guess it doesn't matter. Even if you don't like it, I'll still call you Augie. I like it." As they headed west on I-80, Mr. August said, "Listen, Leah, I am not your

9

teacher, but I am your legal guardian. You won't be eighteen before you leave for Brazil. Just drop the show you've been staging. Just be you. We have had friendly conversations for two years. You have no need to impress me. I know you are smart and charismatic. I am not blind; I can see that your looks can stop traffic, so let's drop all games. Just be a good kid, you, and a good guy, me."

"Okay, Mr. Augie, I'll behave—well, mostly. Tell me where we are going and what we will do."

On the way to Minneapolis he told her that he had just found an apartment and would move in next week. He said he had to prepare his return to teaching at his old school after a five-year leave. Tonight, he told her they would stay with his friends, Carl and Mary Jo.

"Same room?" Leah chirped.

"LEAH."

"All right, already. I will stop."

The remainder of the drive they chatted. Leah said she was tired of not having a home or a family that did family things. "I am seventeen years old. I feel like I have been an orphan most of those years. I know I am lucky to have all the material things I want, more than I need. College tuition, room and board are not issues for me like they are for many kids. I know I can be a manipulative brat.

"But I want someone to really care. My mom can't wait till this school year is over so she can get rid of me. The only reason she lets me stay on is my Dad pays the high tuition that lets me stay at Aparecida. I want someone to come home to, to listen to my sorrows and dreams. I think you are the only adult who listens to me. I think you care, but I also think you are afraid of me, maybe afraid of what I will do. Don't worry, I would never do anything to embarrass you or hurt you. If you tell anyone else this, I'll deny it, but I would like someone to set limits for me, say no, see to my welfare."

Leah sat quietly for many miles. Then, "You know, Mr. Augie, I think having the likes of me around you will help amend your stodgy image." She smiled as she said this. "People will look at me and then you, and say, 'He's a lucky dog.'"

10

Back in Minnesota after a few days at Mary Jo's, separate rooms, they left for Middelton. August had arranged for Leah to stay with his sister and brother-in-law for a few days as he returned to his old school to find out what he would be teaching, to see how much had changed, and to meet a few new faces.

Over the next week Leah helped him move into his new place in a northwestern suburb of Minneapolis. She helped him prepare his classroom. After exhausting all efforts on those fronts, Leah piped up, "I know you are wondering what you are going to do with me now, and you don't want to bother your sister too much with me. I have an idea. Put me on the phone to my dad or Elly."

"Elly?"

"You know, Elly, Elwood Arnison. I'll talk one or the other into you giving me a grand tour of Minnesota. I want to see it all. Show me this baseball thing, the Twins, that seems to occupy your mind all the time. Are the Twins why you are no longer married? Take me on a tour of the Land of Ten Thousand Lakes. I want to see Lake Superior, Red Lake, and International Falls, the Icebox of the Nation. Show me why they call Minneapolis the Mill City. See, I did my homework. I had your brother-in-law drop me at the library for a few hours one day. All of this will keep us busy, enable you to get some travel expenses out of my dad. You need a new car. This, what do you call it? This Duster is ready for the scrap heap. Doing all of this for a few weeks will get your mind off of my great body." She laughed hysterically as she said the last.

"Don't worry. When we overnight at a motel, Elly will demand receipts for separate rooms. He may not trust me, but for some reason both he and my dad trust you. I bet my dad had you investigated."

When Leah was not at Gus's sister's, they traveled. So it went for the next several weeks. St. Croix Falls, New Ulm, the German capital of southwest Minnesota with its Herman the German and the glockenspiel, Pipestone, the great north woods, and all the lakes. They sailed Lake Superior and viewed the Great Lakes Museum. They met Paul Bunyon and tried to read the Kensington runestone. They visited the museum of the Great

Hinckley Fire and the Mayo Clinic. All was of interest to Leah. Perhaps it was because she had someone who was excited by the showing and telling her of it, or perhaps because someone wanted her to know all about Minnesota.

What Leah didn't know was that during one of his three weekly check-ins with Elwood Arnison, Gus learned that Leah's mother was no longer in São Paulo. She was pursuing a new boyfriend in Mexico City. "Mr. August," Mr. Arnison said, "you know what this means? Leah will be forced into a boarding school in Houston. Mr. Gould will not have her live with him. He is rarely in Houston for more than a few days or weeks at a time. Leah will run again. She has sounded so happy this summer when I have talked to her. She said she loved your nieces and nephews. If you care about the kid, find an answer."

Stuart August gnawed on the problem for days. Meanwhile, Leah pointed out to him that he had ignored St. Paul in her "Minnesota Educational Tour," as she called it. So St. Paul it was. First was the Gangster Bus Tour of the ruthless days of prohibition and St. Paul as a safe haven for the mob. There was an annotated drive down Summit Avenue and a tour of 3M. This was followed by a visit to the James J. Hill House and the St. Paul Cathedral. From there August took her to South St. Paul to see if there was anything left of the famous stockyards. Unfortunately, there was nothing left to see. That's when inspiration hit Stuart August. "Leah, that about does it for St. Paul, but while we are this far south I want to take a look at the school where next year's section speech meet will be held. It's a few miles from here. The school is called the Wittenberg Academy."

They drove over to the school and through its vast grounds. "Why do they have so many buildings?" asked Leah. "Is it a big school?"

"No, it's a fairly small college prep school. It is operated by the Lutheran Church. One building is a chapel, another is a dormitory, another the gym, and then there is the actual school building."

"A dormitory?"

"Yes, the school has a number of Asian students and kids from outstate Minnesota and the Dakotas."

That next week Stuart August was to take a trip he had planned earlier to Cedar Rapids, Iowa. He wanted to take in a few Kernels baseball games. They were a farm team of the Minnesota Twins. He planned to visit a few friends. He was about to cancel his trip because of Leah.

Gus's sister suggested he go and that Leah accompany their family on a long-planned week at a lake up north. His sister's family did that most summers. Two large cabins made it possible for family, extended family, and the occasional friend to spend time together. Leah jumped at the chance.

Leah and Mr. August had a little talk about the invitation and accompanying the family. "Remember, you are not going to Rio; no topless beaches. There will be young children and grandmothers there, including my mom."

"Augie, your mom, now I can really get the dirt on you, but don't worry, Augie. I will behave; I don't even have a tonga with me. Remember, Mr. Augie, I will do nothing to embarrass or harm you. Trust me. I think you are the only one who seems to."

Stuart August trusted her and went to Cedar Rapids. When he returned he found a joyous Leah. She had a great tan with visible tan lines. She babbled about catching fish, bragging, "I caught the biggest pumpkin seed of the week." She raved about canoeing and having a picnic on the lake island. "S'mores, can you believe it? I've never heard of such things." She loved playing with Gus's nieces and nephews. "Outdoor grilling is better than a churrasco. I didn't steal any of your brother-in-law's beer. And, no, I didn't educate your pretty young nieces in the ways of Latin American women. By the way, your mom loved telling stories about how inept you are at most things."

While in Iowa, Gus reviewed the plight of Leah Gould. She would not be happy going to boarding school in Texas. She would not go, even if she was asked, to live in Mexico City with her mother. She was relatively happy in Minnesota. When he got back to Minnesota, Gus got on the phone to Evelyn Huggy. She was a teacher and speech coach at the Wittenberg Academy. He asked her to gather all the information she could on the school: its academics, reputation, mission statement, tuition, dorm fees, and admission standards. He asked her if the students attending there had to be Lutheran or interested in becoming a Lutheran. He asked her to mail all of this information to Elwood Arnison. He gave her the address and suggested she use the DHL delivery service. He would see her later in the day with money to cover all the expenses. Evelyn asked many questions that Gus said he couldn't answer now. He also said that if the school was looking for a new donor, she should make that wish known in the package to Arnison as well.

Then he had even more luck than finding Evelyn at home. He was able to reach Elwood Arnison by phone and told him of his idea of the Wittenberg Academy for Leah. "Mr. Arnison, you will be receiving information ASAP. Meanwhile, will you contact Escola Aparecida and have all of Leah's records forwarded to the Wittenberg Academy? Please do the same for her last two schools. Perhaps a suggestion to Mr. Gould that a worthwhile donation proposal to the Wittenberg Academy might be of some aid in Leah's admission. Meanwhile, I'll break all of this to Leah."

The next day, Mr. August broke the news to Leah about her mother in Mexico City. "I won't go there," she lashed out. "I've been to that smog-choked dump. Worse than São Paulo. I won't go to boarding school in Texas, either."

"Cheer up, Leah, some things are in the works. What if you could stay here in Minnesota? Remember the school in St. Paul, the one with the dormitory? They believe their mission is to provide a Christian education to college prep students who want diversity in their lives. Remember I told you about the number of Asian students they admit each year? Perhaps you could bring to the school the diversity of Texas, Brazil, and Central America. The school is administered by the Lutheran Church, but, I am told, it is not evangelical; they don't try to convert new students, and they welcome Jewish students when they have the opportunity."

"Augie, you scheming devil. I must be rubbing off on you. Now I know why the side trip to that school. By the way, my dad thinks I'm a Jew. My mom thinks I'm a Catholic. I think I am anything I want to be."

"Leah, I will try to set up an interview for you if you are interested. I have already spoken to Mr. Arnison. He and your father seem to be in favor of this."

Word from Texas came in four days. "Try and get Leah admitted."

Mr. August set up an interview. "Now, Leah, some guidelines for the interview. Dress as a young lady, but stay on the conservative side without stunting your personality too much. Don't put on a show. Keep in mind that they like diversity; don't be afraid to draw on your wide background and command of English, Spanish, Portuguese, and Texan. The school is a little ahead of its time for the 1980s."

Leah's interview went well. She addressed the panel of seven and was offered admission to the school and dorms. She would have a roommate from Manila. It did not hurt Leah's chances when the school welcomed a six-figure donation upon Leah's acceptance.

"All that remains, Leah, is your say-so. You can move into the dorm in two weeks. You will have a two-week period of orientation and acclimation. Classes will begin two days after Labor Day."

"Here's the deal, Augie. I will say yes if you promise to visit me every week and take me to dinner. You must come and see all the activities I am in. You must—"

"Stop right there, Leah. Your con game will not work. We both know you want to stay here in Minnesota. So, no negotiation. I promise nothing. You are not my daughter."

Leah smiled. "You can't blame a girl for trying. I had a list of five more things. I don't want to be your daughter. I have one dad already, and other than money he's no dad at all. I'd rather try for you as a boyfriend," Leah said as she broke out in a long giggle.

"I'll get even with you, Leah. Just wait for your first Minnesotan winter."

All was arranged. Mr. Arnison arrived with all the necessary legal papers for Stuart August to continue as guardian and money manager. Mr. Arnison made the Wittenberg Academy happy with checks for tuition, housing, and a generous donation.

Leah moved in. Stuart August attended an orientation open house.

Leah introduced him to her classmates and teachers as her friend from São Paulo. Later in the evening she asked, "Augie, I'm going to try out for a play. Will you come to see it if I get a part?"

"My turn to negotiate. I will come if you agree to be on the speech team. That way I will get to see you at speech meets, too. I am a speech coach, you know."

"Deal," she said as she extended her hand for a shake.

Stuart August attended her play. He learned it was a tradition at the school to present cast members with a red rose at curtain call. He was there with a rose for Leah. He did visit her a couple of times a month and took her to dinner. She treated. She reminded him that she had more money than he did. Mr. August sat in on her teacher conferences. Mr. Gould could not seem to get to those; however, he did manage to show up at the Christmas party with a Star of David in full view on a chain dangling from his neck. He shook Mr. August's hand and pointed to the star. "I am contributing to the diversity."

Leah became a leader on the speech team and placed at several meets. As the year progressed, she looked into colleges in Minnesota. Mr. August took her on a tour of them. She really liked a Catholic liberal arts college for women near Middleton. "Part of my diversified education," she said. "You know, they are a little stuffy, but maybe I can shake them up a bit. Mesh stockings, miniskirts, and a few see-through blouses should do the trick. Not too much; I don't want to get kicked out. By the way, Augie, your Minnesota winter did not drive me out of here. I am tough as well as stunningly beautiful. Winter presents so many more fashion opportunities."

Then she hugged Stuart August and said, "Augie, I think I found what I've been looking for. A place to call home."

Jimmy

During the second week of class, Stuart August had his ninth grade class read Frank Stockton's "The Lady, or the Tiger?" aloud. He announced this to them the day before. August wanted to get an assessment of his ninth graders' reading ability. Just before class meek, soft-spoken Rita stopped him outside the door of his classroom. "Mr. August, please don't call on Jimmy Mills to read today. He is such a nice boy. He will be embarrassed; he can't read. Mr. August, please don't call on Jimmy Mills to read today."

Stuart August, Gus to most, pondered his Jimmy Mills problem. He really had no idea as to what he could do to help the kid, but it was time to do what he had vowed to do when he decided to become a teacher: help kids just as his eighth grade teacher, Miss Ryan, did. He and his classmates hated her at the beginning. She was a retired public school teacher who became the first full-time lay teacher at St. Paul's Grade School. She was the strictest disciplinarian young August had encountered in his eight school years. She assigned more homework than any teacher he had ever known. She said his class was way behind other eighth graders; thus, they had English, math, science, and history twice a day. All the frills were gone, no more art or music. They hated her.

By the end of the year they loved her. She showed them she cared. She prepared them for high school, where they all shined. She was willing to do anything for them and did. She sided with them in a battle with the principal. From the start Stuart August had wanted to repay her by giving to his students what she had given him and all the others. Jimmy Mills was a good place to start, but how?

Gus himself had a tough time learning to read. He didn't remember how he did it, but somewhere along the way he found he liked stories; he liked being read to. He remembered a baseball story Sr. Cabrini had read to them in class, a story about Kingi, a Japanese boy who loved baseball. August remembered that he had read biographies of Babe Ruth, Lou Gehrig, Jim Bridger, and Sacajawea. How could he get Jimmy Mills to read? August didn't know much about teaching reading. He had heard of students who complained about how they hated the new reading classes that some schools were using. "All we do is boring worksheets and read boring articles." In 1969, teaching reading in high school was a new concept. How could students get that far if they couldn't read?

August asked around. An older phy ed teacher said he remembered how a classmate of his became a better reader by reading aloud to his mother for fifteen minutes a day. For want of a better method, August thought he would try this with Jimmy Mills.

After class he pulled Jimmy Mills aside. "Jimmy, you know that each semester I require my students to read an outside book and write about it. I know you have a reading problem. How about this? Instead of the outside book, I want you to make a calendar for the rest of the semester. Five days in each week you will read aloud to someone: mother, sister, friend, grandparent, anyone. You can read whatever you want: sports page, Field & Stream, the back of a cereal box, whatever you want. Whoever listens to you must sign that date on the calendar, five days each week. You need to show me the calendar each Monday.

"I suppose you could cheat on this easily. Just get people to sign and forget the reading. The thing is, you won't be cheating me; you will only be cheating yourself of an opportunity to improve your reading. I think you can see how improved reading can only be good for you."

That night Stuart August phoned Mrs. Mills. She was pleased to hear about Mr. August's plan to help Jimmy. She wondered why it had taken so long to attack the problem. "Yes, I will listen to him and help him with the words and understanding the flow of sentences. His grandma will help, too. He likes her."

18

The months passed. On each Monday Jimmy showed Mr. August his signed calendar. The signatures of his mom and grandma appeared, occasionally supplemented by other names. Some weeks six days with signatures appeared. A few weeks into the second semester Jimmy came to Mr. August's desk well before school. He had a battered paperback in his hand, The Complete Short Stories of Erskine Caldwell. "What have you here, Jim?"

"I found this book in Grandma's attic. I didn't know she had books up there. When I found them, she told me she had always liked to read but hadn't much time for it in her life. She said it was always the kids, the house, baking, the garden, and then the grandchildren. She said she was happy that we could read together. Our fifteen-minute sessions sometimes lasted longer. She says she is now back to reading."

"So, the book, Jimmy?"

"Ya, I found it. It looked interesting." More than likely it was the scantily clad blonde on the cover that caught his attention. "There are some good stories in there. Not all of them are like the cover." Jimmy blushed. "Ya, I did read some of those, too, but not for my mom or grandma. "I found this story called "Rachel." I think the class would like it. Could you read it out loud in class to us? But, don't tell them I asked you to. Only a few kids know what I am doing with the reading."

"And how's that going?"

"I think I'm getting better—no, I know I'm getting better. Pretty soon I will be able to read in class. I'll let you know, but read the story to us."

Erskine Caldwell was one of Stuart August's favorite authors. He was familiar with the story "Rachel." That Friday he told his class he had a treat for them. He was going to read a story by a well-known American author. The story, he told them, was set in the South during the Great Depression. A few people had a lot of money; some had enough but most worked hard to eke out a living. Then, too, there were thousands who could find no work at all.

The story featured a teenage boy who had a paper route that earned him twenty cents a week. Since his parents had no money to spare after the rent, groceries, and streetcar fare to get them to work, the paper route provided his only spending money. If he wanted anything, he had to pay his own way. Of course, the boy had to help around the house and the yard. His mother made him sweep the sidewalk and weed the vegetable garden. He also had to put rat poison in the garbage cans. All the neighbors up and down the alley did it. The rats, too, struggled during the Depression. They threatened to overtake some neighborhoods.

One day in the alley the boy saw a most beautiful girl. She looked to be about his age. She seemed poorer than his family. Her dress was faded, patched, and a little shorter than the modesty of the time required. However, she was clean and had an angelic smile. They talked, and soon the boy would meet her once or twice a week. Some Saturdays he used his entire twenty cents and treated her to a picture show or a malt at the drugstore soda fountain. He never had enough to do both. The girl always wore the same dress and the same smile. The two enjoyed their time together.

One Saturday as the pair passed the drugstore on the way to the picture show, the girl asked him to stop and please, please, get her some water. The boy complied and returned to the sidewalk to find the waiting, pretty teenage blonde. She downed all the water in two gulps. She started to turn pale and shivered. Finally, she collapsed and went into convulsions on the sidewalk. A crowd gathered. The druggist came out of his store and bent over the girl as she took her last breath. Foam escaped from her mouth, emitting a foul odor. "Rat poison," he said.

The class gasped. One ninth grader said, "What a story." A couple of girls cried. All agreed it was some story. The rest of the period was spent discussing the Depression. Many kids related stories their parents or grandparents told about life in the 1930s. Jimmy Mills smiled; he knew a good story.

A few weeks passed. Mr. August was pleased. The Twins baseball season opener was at hand. Even more pleasing, Jimmy Mills stopped Mr. August before school and said, "I am ready to read in class."

That day in August's English Nine class, he announced, "Today we will read in class an Erskine Caldwell story that is in your textbook. You remember he wrote 'Rachel,' the story I read to you a while ago. This story, too, is set in the South during the Depression. We will see that the Depression was especially hard for families of color. The story is entitled 'Daughter.' Today you will do the reading. We will start with Sharon."

As the story went on, Mr. August changed readers after each paragraph or two. For the dialogue he assigned parts. When the story came to a somewhat long narrative paragraph, he asked Jimmy Mills to read. Wide-eyed, the class snapped to attention. Some gasped; some stared at Jimmy. Jimmy Mills began to read. He read the entire paragraph flawlessly. The classroom broke out in cheers, clapping hands, and finally a standing ovation. Humbly hanging his head, a big smile leaked out from Jimmy.

The rest of the class was spent in discussion of the story and whether the father was justified in his action toward his daughter. As the ninth graders filed out of class, Jimmy Mills was congratulated and slapped on the back. "Way to go," was heard up and down the hall.

Stuart August looked up and said quietly, "One payment back to you, Miss Ryan."

Hog Hollow's Delilah

Albion High School valedictorian, Veronica Hannon, stepped up to the microphone to give the class of 1976's graduation speech. "Fellow classmates, faculty, parents, and friends, on behalf of my sister Missy, my parents, and me, I am asking Delilah Vozy, who is a hero to my family and this community, to address us. She is a much better speaker than I can ever hope to be." Delilah left her seat and ascended the stage.

Thank you, Veronica, Missy, and Mr. and Mrs. Hannon. Veronica is so humble and generous. She is an excellent speaker. I have heard her in several classes give fabulous presentations. She is an example of the many points I wish to emphasize today. Her super brain, exceptional talent, and hard work have allowed her to accomplish much. Nevertheless, she has not lorded it over the rest of us who are less gifted. She and all the rest of my classmates have demonstrated special skills to Albion. Each one of us has one or more things that we are more accomplished at doing than others. I hope that each of us has been able to figure out what talents we do have. Some members of the class of '76 can repair a car, a truck, or a tractor engine better than most; some can stitch and sew beyond others' modest skills. Others are the best caregivers in the world for the young and the old. There are talented hunters and trappers who are better than all the rest of the community. Some will become first-class fishing guides. There are gifted athletes among us who can outrun, outhit, or outskate all the rest of us. Some are skilled carpenters or masons; some have the brains to be a surgeon or an engineer like Veronica will become. I believe one or two of us will become religious leaders. Then there are those who may be called animal whisperers who can work miracles with troubled animals.

We all have skills that we need to use, not to make more money than others or to raise our stature above others, but to use these skills to make the world a better, safer, and happier place. We need to recognize those special gifts in others.

Stuart August, who usually avoided graduations, was enjoying this one. Only he and the Hannon family knew about the surprise graduation speaker. He was pleased to see that the new, usually total control freak of a principal was too stunned to step in. The round of applause for Delilah was so great that he couldn't stop the show now.

August was an English and speech teacher who also coached the speech team at Albion. He met Delilah in his ninth grade English class. She was an interesting girl who seldom smiled. Her grades were a little above average in spite of her struggles with grammar and punctuation. He saw flashes of excellence in her work. However, she was inconsistent and had a tendency to be her own worst critic. He was most impressed with her creative writing and oral presentations. She seemed quick to produce answers to his posed questions, with which he loved to pepper the class. Her reasoning abilities put her far ahead of her classmates. In addition, he could see that she was a pretty girl who would one day be a beauty.

She lived in Hog Hollow, a section at the far western end of the school district. Hog Hollow was a scattered collection of run-down shanties and the remains of old farmsteads. The poorest people in the district survived there. Perhaps that was a contributing factor to Deliah's poor self-image. A collection of shanties formed a small community referred to as Hog Town. Hog Hollow earned its name from both words, its geography and the occupation of earlier inhabitants. The area was hilly, with many steep and deep hollows. Years ago it was all pig farms. The farmers were mostly renters, with a few scattered landowners. Since their single farm product, pork on the hoof, was subject to a volatile market, many of the landowners failed, and the renters were in constant turnover, moving in and out with their large families. The poverty was only surpassed by the stench of hog manure, especially in spring as the accumulated piles thawed.

Delilah's mother inherited sixty acres of the Hollow. The land, with its long history of hog manure, was now fertile farmland. Her family had worked an apple and plum orchard and a truck garden supported by two greenhouses that were in constant need of repair. They kept a large flock of hens, which produced eggs that were sold to local stores and to customers who came to the farm. These customers also purchased produce from the orchards, gardens, and greenhouses. A local Christain co-op made regular purchases of all. Delilah's mother was even able to market the chicken manure, good fertilizer. The farm provided for a sparsely livable income.

It was now down to Delilah and her mom. Dakota, an older sister, left the farm when she graduated. She followed in the footsteps of a yet older brother, Darren, who left a year before he graduated. Both now lived in Middleton, some twenty-five miles away. Delilah's father had departed before those two. She still had contact with her sister but little with the two males.

Stuart August looked up at Delilah in her cap, gown, and dimpled smile. He remembered the little girl who wore dresses, skirts, and blouses that always seemed a size or two too large or a size or two too small. She always smelled of Ivory soap, such a pleasant fragrance. She must have taken extra care to rid herself of the stench of the greenhouse, garden, and especially the rankness of the chicken coup. Too bad Ivory soap didn't use her dimpled smile for its ads. She could have used the money, and Ivory soap would have benefited from higher sales.

By her sophomore year Delilah had discovered Mother Seton's Thrift Shop. The Catholic Charities store sold donated clothing, houseware, and a few small pieces of furniture. Delilah used the few dollars she could squirrel away from her mom to shop regularly to see what she could find to augment her wardrobe. She had learned to sew, and with her creativity, she became a fashion designer. She lengthened, shortened, tucked in, let out, dyed, and repurposed apparel to present herself in striking, exotic attire. At first the high school girls made fun of her creations and gossiped about the Hog Hollow fashion model who didn't know her place. By the end of her junior year some of the high school girls tried to imitate her creations. The stinging gossip abated, but Delilah's self-confidence suffered regular blows. August was so proud of her as she spoke about the class of '76's duty to do what is right.

It is easy to identify injustice and mistreatment. It is easier to stand by and watch instead of taking action, taking a risk by stepping in to help. It seems the world is more interested in stray dogs and cats than in helping people, especially children, those who are handicapped, and the elderly who need our help and protection.

August recalled how he had come to her aid early in her sophomore year. He heard that she was in the principal's office because of an altercation with an eleventh grade boy. Apparently the big kid had been harrassing a ninth grade Hog Hollow lad, making fun of his smelly clothes and pushing him repeatedly up against the wall. The skinny kid began to cry and tried to hit the bigger eleventh grader, who then pummeled him to his knees. Delilah saw this and stepped in. "Hey, ox face, if you want to pick on some-one, pick on me. Go ahead, make fun of me; hit me." The eleventh grader looked around at the gathered crowd. "Go ahead, lummox, show us your manhood. Bring it on, big boy." The eleventh grader, all red in the face, took a swing at Delilah. She was a far better athlete than he. She ducked under his punch and gave him a quick one-two in his gut. He gasped for breath. The punches were powered by years of farm work. She spun around behind him, tapped him on his shoulder. He turned to see her bouncing side to side on her toes, fists moving in and out, up and down. "Come on, make me cry if you can." At that point two teachers entered the fracas and marched both to the principal's office. The ninth grade boy was left to himself, wiping tears from his eyes as a smile escaped. Having heard the story, Stuart August headed for the office to support Delilah. The story of what actually happened, his support of her and, the last year before his retirement, the old principal's sense of justice got Delilah only a one-day suspension while the bully got three.

That incident was one of many reasons that Mr. August gained respect and admiration for this Hog Hollow fighter. He knew he had to recruit her for his speech team. She was smart, she had a beautiful voice, and she presented herself well. She was a pretty girl, blossoming into a beautiful young woman. She had the smile of a Greek goddess.

Unfortunately, she didn't smile often. August got her to try the "speech thing," as she called it, "at least for a few weeks." She said she would try if she could read poetry. She had more time now in winter. Her mom might let her, but in the spring there was so much to do at home. The demands of her mom might not allow her the time.

As her speech coach, he learned more about her. Both her older sister and her brother left home. Neither could get along with their mother. Both occasionally sent her a five-dollar bill, Dakota far more often than Darren.

Her mother was a stubborn, demanding woman who hated the world and Delilah. Delilah said she knew her mom hated her because all she ever heard growing up was, "You're no damn good." "You can't do anything right." "You're as selfish as those schweinhunds on the next farm." "Quit trying to make yourself look pretty; you'll only make yourself look like the tramp you will become or maybe already are."

"Mr. August, I couldn't become a tramp. I will not become the Hog Hollow trash I am called. Besides, my mom works me so hard I don't have time."

Just a side note, above all, and this is aimed at all the young women in the audience: own yourself. Don't allow anyone to control who you are; own yourself.

As Delilah developed a stunning figure to complement the beauty of her face and eyes, the males of Albion High took notice. Their thoughts centered on opportunity. The slut from Hog Hollow, a victim of poverty and growing up among the outcasts of the district, would be an easy target. Besides, didn't those shantytown dwellers all lack morals? Twila Delilah, as she was often referred to by those who considered themselves super studs, would be an easy mark. She would be ever so grateful to accept the generosity of someone granting her a date. By the middle of Delilah's junior year she had walked the six miles home from more than one date after doing damage to some swain's ego and manhood. Delilah was always conscious of proving her mother wrong. She was not a cheap tramp.

Of course, when it came to homecoming or prom, she was not considered classy enough to be seen with. For Delilah it wouldn't have mattered. She could not afford the cost of attending prom even in the '70s. The more dignified male citizens of Albion High School would not risk their reputations by asking a Hog Hollow resident to be seen with them at a social gathering.

It was a wonder that Delilah had any positive self-image at all. She must have believed her mother. She often told August that she was not very good at interpreting poetry. If she got a low rank, which didn't happen often, she was quick to say, "It's my fault. I'm just not good."

Still, Delilah had a deep and caring heart. She fought for the underdog. She helped struggling kids with their homework and most of all wanted her family all back together, especially Dakota. She longed for the day, the week, the month that all five of them could be peacefully under one roof. She wanted her mom to love them. She wanted her mom to be happy. "She is so unhappy."

Delilah rarely spoke of her father. The story in the community was that he was a super athlete, but a loner. He had an eye for the ladies and wooed Delilah's mother, who was a beauty from Hog Hollow. She was left with a sixty-acre farm that she had lived on with her father before he died. Delilah never knew her grandfather. He died long before she was born. They said that when all the children were of school age, her dad picked up and left. After that, Delilah's mom became more hateful and mean.

Hard work is another point I wish to emphasize. Most of us have not been and will not be handed things. If we want to get somewhere, be somebody, we must be a worker, a fighter; we can't give up. We cannot accept "no." We must keep at it until we achieve it. Then we must give it to someone else, pass it on. We are in this world to help each other, to make others happier, healthier, and safer. As we learned in American History, potlatch. Only, we must not expect anything in return.

Delilah was a worker. Besides all the hours on the farm, she earned better and better grades each year. She worked on speech. She loved reading poetry, especially Robert Frost's "The Witch of Coos." The story featured a backwoods family that was not living the American Dream. Because of her mom's demands, Delilah missed over half the team's contests. She finaled in the first one she attended. She achieved that again in the second contest her mom allowed her to attend. Then spring weather moved in, and Delilah was barred from further contests for over a month.

Stuart August didn't know how Delilah did it, but she convinced her mom to allow her to come back. August asked how she did that. "I told her you said I was good, that I had talent. Then she said, 'If you're so good, how come you end up fifth or sixth instead of first?' I told her to give me another chance, and I would show her I could do it. So here I am. Maybe she's right. I'm just not good enough. She says I screw up everything I try, but I want to do it. I need to show her I'm not just Hog Hollow trash. Besides, I like speech."

Mr. August responded, "Delilah, you are a wonderful speaker. I admire you in so many ways. I want you back with us, but I can't get you into Saturday's contest. It's too late, but I will register you for the Saturday after. That is the section contest, the last one except for anybody who advances to state. However, Delilah, you must be realistic. You missed a whole month of the season. You can't expect to march into the finals again. You have missed so much."

"No, I haven't," the strong-voiced fighter said. "I've practiced "The Witch of Coos" two or three times a day. My mom kept me home, but I never quit."

While Mr. August gave her a big hug, he said, "No matter what scores you earn next week, always remember you are good, so good. Both of us know that." Delilah's hard work that week, coupled with what she had done on her own for the past month, gave Mr. August hope for her at the section

29

meet. There in the prelim rounds Delilah reported she had done poorly, but Mr. August detected the glint in her aquamarine eyes, or maybe it was just the little green specks that appeared in them. No matter, Delilah was one of six finalists; two would advance to the State Tournament.

Delilah kept pacing before the final round. She kept repeating, "The others are so good. I can't beat them. They're so good. I know I'm not good enough." When the finalists in poetry were called up on stage, Albion's entire speech team watched her release a deep breath when sixth place was called and her name was not attached to it. The same happened after fifth and fourth places were called. Still no Delilah. Now Mr. August saw a look of fear. Delilah closed her eyes and held her breath. "In third place and first alternate to the state tournament, Delilah Vozy of Albion High School." Her shoulders slumped as sadness ruled her face. When she got back to her seat, Stuart August could hear, "My mom is right. I'm just no good."

Mr. August later tried to console her, but she just shrugged him off and would not talk. Later in the week he dragged her into his classroom and told her to sit down. "Delilah, you pulled off a near miracle last Saturday. After the season you have had with interruptions and so little practice, you beat all odds by making it to the finals. One of the three judges had you ranked first. This school has never had a state entry in speech."

"Mr. August, another one of those judges ranked me last. He knew I wasn't any good. Besides being no good, I'm unlucky. The two female judges liked me. Why did I get that last male judge?"

Delilah returned to speech the next year determined to win everything. She made it to more contests, mainly because of an early spring that allowed her to get ahead of the farm's usual spring schedule. The greenhouse was making a profit on seedlings and plants to set in the garden. The hens laid more eggs than usual. Her mother even let her spend a few more dollars at the thrift stores in Middleton. There she bought and altered a dark green corduroy jacket. She found a maroon skirt to go with it. Her sister gave her a pair of high heels that matched her outfit. The skirt might have been a little short, but Mr. August thought that with such an angelic face it would not hurt her chances.

Delilah placed at most of the contests she attended. August liked her chances in the section meet. Three days before the section, Delilah looked like someone just killed her cat. In tears, she said, "Mom says I can't go on Saturday. We've been doing well, and she expects a slew of people on Saturday. She says I have to help her because she can't handle it on her own. I told her that it was the section meet. I had to be there. She told me I was just selfish. 'It's always about you,' she said." Fighting back the tears, Delilah left Mr. August's classroom.

As he heard the words in Delilah's speech about hard work and determination, an image appeared in his mind. He saw a distant figure, running and breathing heavily, headed for the speech team bus on the morning of the section tournament. As the phantom struggled in the pouring rain, the dimpled cheeks of Delilah Vozy emerged. She had an old army pack strapped over her shoulders. Soaked to the skin, she boarded the bus. "I'm here."

She plopped down next to Mr. August. "When I got up at five this morning, I headed for the greenhouse. My mom was already there cursing about the rain that would kill today's sales. She told me it was supposed to rain hard all day. Then she looked at me and said, 'Get the hell out of here. I don't want to see your ugly face today. Go to your damn speech thing, but don't expect me to drive you there.'"

"I knew I had to get here. I packed my speech clothes, extra underwear, makeup, and everything else I would need. I just had to get here. I feel like a drowned rat, but I got here."

"Delilah, you didn't run six miles from home?" a wide-eyed Mr. August asked.

"How else was I to get here? You know I run even though my mom will not let me be in track. I often run several miles to recover my peace of mind after one of her rants. I only hope my dad's old backpack kept my clothes dry."

Stuart August was happy that he had forgotten to drop her from the roster. She was still eligible for the section competition. When the girls on the speech team heard Delilah's story, they dragged her to the back of the

31

bus and started drying her off, especially her long blonde hair. They used towels and blankets, always a staple on speech team trips.

Twenty minutes after the team arrived at the meet Delilah entered the team's home base in the cafeteria looking like a pixie covergirl in her maroon skirt, beige blouse, green blazer, and her sister's heels. Her teammates had given her two long braids to tame her hair.

Perhaps it was more bad luck, perhaps it was the result of a too-demanding day, but Delilah failed to reach the finals. She was crestfallen. She ranked seventh, one rank out of the finals. On the bus ride home Mr. August told her how proud he was of her and how much he admired her drive. He said she was the best. Delilah hung her head down and mumbled, "Yeah, good enough to be not good enough. My mom is right. I am worthless."

Mr. August reached around her shoulders and gave her a hug. "Next year we go to state."

"No, I'm done. There will be no next year." She got up and moved to the back of the bus and sat by herself.

People often ask graduates what they learned in school. What do you think will help you the most: math, science, writing? For me it was none of those things. I think that is the case for most of us. For me, and I hope for all of us graduates, it was the words I've heard over and over again: "Don't give up. Believe in yourself. Believe in those who believe in you."

Stuart August nodded as he heard those words.

The fall of her senior year, Mr. August did not see much of Delilah. Apparently she was sticking by her words that she was done with speech. She was avoiding him so as not to have to reconfirm her decision or risk being talked into returning. Besides, in September and October she missed many school days: apples and plums to pick and sell, gardens to harvest, and produce to sell. Her grades did not seem to suffer. She turned in all her work and sought help on things she had missed, though her top-notch brain didn't need much help.

October fifteenth dawned humid with temperatures already at seventy degrees by 8:00 a.m. This was the beginning of a Minnesota weather phenomenon. By 9:30 the temperature had reached eighty degrees. By 10:30 it had plunged to sixty-five. By 11:30 the temperature had fallen below forty-eight. By noon the snow came down like someone had dumped a truckload of shattered cloud on Wilson County. The winds spiked as the temperature plummeted; the air was still humid. Heavy, wet silver dollar snowflakes blanketed the landscape. At twelve o'clock the announcement came over the intercom: school was closing after lunch, at 12:45 p.m.

At 12:15 the principal was at Mr. August's classroom door with a note. "Please take the Hog Hollow route, bus number 36. You have subbed this route before. Your bus will be out back in the usual place with the keys under the floor mat." August didn't like the idea of driving in these conditions, but what could he do? They evidently needed drivers.

Gus got behind the wheel of a big orange machine and waited for the kids. Only a few got on the bus, among them Delilah. Most high school kids thought that riding the bus was beneath them. Those from Hog Hollow usually had no choice. At the junior high-grade school, twenty more got on, including a few kindergartners. There was much confusion here since several of the buses were parked in different spots because of substitute drivers. Some kids went to two or three buses before they finally found the right one. Gus didn't leave the school until all the children had gotten on a bus.

Delilah sat up front behind Gus. The two chatted about the snow and apples still on the trees as they headed for Hog Hollow. With most of the students having gotten off the bus by the time it passed through Hog Town, only three kids remained. Gus knew that Delilah would be the last stop. He looked in the rearview mirror to the back of the bus. He noticed the head of one tiny kid. That was all he could see. A fifth grade boy had moved up just behind Delilah. He knew him; he was the second to the last stop. His name was Charlie Hemitz. As the bus cleared Hog Town, Mr. August asked Delilah to check on the little one in the back.

When she returned to the front, she told him the girl was a kindergar-

33

tener, Missy Hannon. "She seems terrified. She said she must have gotten on the wrong bus. You were parked where her bus usually was. She said she didn't know what to do so she just got on."

"Delilah, go back and sit with her. Tell her not to worry. I'll get her back to town. I know the Hannon family and where they live just east of town. Take Charlie with you and make her feel safe."

Just as Charlie and Delilah got settled in with Missy, a great gust of wind blasted the wooded glen. August had picked up some speed because he had a hill to climb; he didn't want to lose traction and get stuck going uphill. A fifty-mile-an-hour gale toppled a skyscraping, rotting elm on the right side of the road. August tried to swing the bus to his left to avoid the tree. His actions resulted in the tree, the bus, and a high gravel bank topped with five inches of new snow all colliding. The bus stopped abruptly. August's foot slipped off the brake on impact. He heard a loud pop coupled with a sharp pain as he was tossed off the seat and into the aisle. The engine stalled.

At the same time he heard a scream from the back of the bus. He winced in pain as he twisted toward the back. "Delilah, are you all right?"

"I think so. Ya, I am okay. I got tossed to the floor."

Slightly bruised, Delilah got off the floor and found Missy Hannon in a seat holding her hands over her bloody head, screaming; Charlie was on the floor holding his head, but there was no blood. The bump on the corner of his forehead began to swell. Delilah checked Missy's bloody head. The girl cried harder and harder. "It hurts. Oh my God, blood." Missy had a gash just above her left ear. Blood was flowing, a lot of it. Not panicking, Delilah took off her jacket and then her white blouse. She used it to fashion a bandage by tearing it into strips and tightly binding Missy's head. This helped slow the bleeding. She told Missy that she would be okay as she hugged the terrified elf. "Missy, you must be a brave girl; try not to cry too much."

Delilah then put her jacket back on and tended to Charlie. When she determined that he was not too badly hurt, she told him she needed his help. "We need to stop Missy's bleeding. You have to step up here and be the man." She led him over to Missy.

"Missy, Charlie is going to help you and me. I want him to press very hard on your head. We need to stop or slow the bleeding. Is that okay?" Missy murmerd a yes.

"Charlie, I'm going to put you in charge of Missy. Here, put your hand here and press against her head hard, but not too hard. You must stop the bleeding. Missy, you need to let Charlie do this even if it hurts more. You must be brave and let Charlie help. I'm going to check on Mr. August."

When she returned to the front, she found Stuart August sitting up on the floor. Delilah told him about Missy and Charlie and what she had done. Mr. August had overheard all that and saw what she had done at the back of the bus. He was so impressed with the calmness and maturity of this lately turned seventeen-year-old girl. Perhaps she was no longer a girl but a confident young woman.

"Good work," he said to his favorite student. "Now, you need to get behind the wheel of the bus and get us to the hospital in Albion. I can't drive. I think my right ankle is broken. The first step is to get the engine started. Then back out of the snowbank and turn this thing around."

"Gus," she screamed, "I can't drive this thing. I don't know how. It has a clutch and a shift. The old tractor at home, I only have to let up on the clutch and push a lever to make it go. My mom's truck is an automatic. I can't do this. I'll go get help." She headed for the door. The confident young woman had reverted to the self-doubting girl. "I'm just not good enough. I can't do it."

"STOP," Gus shouted at the top of his lungs. His broken ankle screamed even louder as his body jerked. "Delilah, get your pretty butt back here. We don't have time. Missy needs help, quickly. She will bleed to death if you don't get her out of here. I haven't met many, if any, kids who have the guts that you do. You have the brains to handle what I will tell you to do. You have more than enough athletic ability to handle the clutch and gears. I know you are stubborn enough to keep at it until you make it work. Now get behind the wheel and don't kick my ankle as you cross over me."

Delilah's ashen face stared straight ahead. "DELILAH," August yelled.

Her head snapped up; some color returned to her cheeks as she took a deep breath. She then adeptly stepped over her teacher and eased herself into the driver's seat. After she adjusted it, she said, "What do I do?"

Gus told her to put the clutch down with her left foot and reach over and turn the key while using her right foot to ever so slightly ease down on the gas pedal. The ignition caught. "Listen to all I tell you before you do any more. Now, Delilah, ease off the gas and continue to hold the clutch down. Then we will actually do it as I talk you through it a second time. You know how to slowly ride a bicycle; easy does it, one pedal up, one pedal down. As your left foot comes up slowly off the clutch have your right slowly descend easily, easily; slowly push down on the gas pedal. All of this in sync, slowly, just like riding the slow bicycle. But, before you do that, you put the bus in reverse gear. Keep the clutch down. With your left hand, reach the shift. Imagine an H. Look at the floor; see the H there. Okay, good, now gently guide the stick up and over to the far right as far as it will go; now push it down and out as far away from you as it will go. You will have moved the shift to the right and down on the H just as you have been looking at it. Feel it fall into reverse, I will talk you through it again. This time you will actually do it." She did.

August talked, and Delilah reacted. The bus began to reverse slowly away from the bank, too slow. It jerked, and the engine stalled. "That's okay, Delilah. This may happen a few more times. Don't worry; you will get the hang of it. Relax, just like reading poetry. It has to be subtle and smooth, in rhythm." After she got the bus turned around, August talked her through the forward gears. "Find the H in the middle, first gear down and to the left, clutch up, gas easily down." The bus rolled. "Second gear up to the middle and then up and left." He had her push in the clutch and shift up to the right of the H. The whole process survived three stalled engines.

After the three engine killings, Delilah had the bus humming toward town. When she got into third gear, he told her that there would be no shifting until Albion. They would not drive fast enough to use fourth gear.

Still on the floor, August looked to the back of the bus and asked, "How are you doing back there, Charlie? Missy?"

Charlie yelled back, "My arm hurts, but I'm still holding Delilah's blouse to Missy's head. The bleeding has stopped, I think, but I got blood all over me. Missy looks white and just stares."

"Good work, Charlie. We will be at the hospital soon."

With her confidence returned, a more relaxed Delilah said, "It's a good thing I had a jacket in my locker, or you would be getting quite a show."

"Yeah," Gus chuckled, "just my bad luck. Now, ever-prepared Delilah," he said, "I have all the faith in the world in you, Miss Limo Driver; just before we get into town, I want you to shift down into second gear. You'll do it just the opposite of how you got it into third gear, clutch in, stick up and a little to the left, and up and left again."

Speech coach, now bus driving instructor, Mr. August guided her slowly through the snow-covered streets to the hospital. Delilah brought the orange ambulance to a stop at the emergency entrance. August told her to go back and open the emergency door. As she did, the alarmed door began to scream. Soon hospital personnel came with stretchers and collected Missy and Charlie. The second trip netted Stuart August. Delilah walked in on her own.

Missy was treated immediately. Her parents had been worried and called the bus company about Missy's whereabouts. A few hours later her parents were told that the cut was not life threatening but still required ten stitches. Scans and further tests revealed no serious issues. She would be kept overnight for observation. The doctor told Mr. and Mrs. Hannon, "That young girl and boy saved Missy's life. Without Delilah's bandaging and instructions to Charlie, and Charlie following those instructions, Missy could have bled to death."

Charlie was checked out and was said to have no more than a knot on his head and a headache. Stuart August was X-rayed and his right ankle placed in a cast.

Delilah used the hospital phone and called her mother, informing her of the accident. Her mother told her that the road to their farm was blocked. There was no way for her to get home. The Hannon family heard all of this and offered both Charlie and Delilah a shower, clothes, dinner, and a bed for the night. Charlie's parents were notified and told not to worry.

The Hannons also offered Gus a ride home. As Delilah helped him through the snow to his door, she looked up and said, "I'm back on the speech team." Then as she looked at the snowy step, she humbly said, "Mr. August, I apologize for calling you Gus back there on the bus. I meant no disrespect."

"Delilah, when we are not in public or you are under extreme tension, you may call me anything you like. In public we should remain more formal. Thank you for your concern." He then gave her a hug.

The next day the editor of the Albion Clariion called the Hannon family and asked if they could take pictures and do interviews when the family came to the hospital to pick up Missy. He asked if they could also bring Delilah and Charlie along before anyone took them home.

The following week the Clariion's front page featured headlines, the picture of the heroine, medic, and rescue driver, Delilah, with her aide, Charlie, on either side of Missy Hannon. A second picture featured Missy hugging Delilah. The story had a third picture, Delilah standing next to the dented orange bus. The entire front paged featured the heroic rescue.

The publicized actions of Delilah gave her a new status at school. Now everybody spoke to her. Some of the girls asked her for advice about redoing clothing to gain a more stylish appearance. This new respect enabled Delilah to do what she had longed to do, help others. She wanted more for the kids of Hog Hollow and those like them, the outcasts, the academically troubled. She convinced the student council to organize a tutoring club to help those who needed it. She was able to get an after-school study hall started to help academic stragglers. She organized a National Honors Society clothing drive for the community. In spite of a steadily climbing GPA since her freshman year, she had been bypassed by the National Honors Society in spite of a nomination from Mr. August. Her publicized heroics corrected this as she was made the Society's newest member.

Captain Delilah led the Albion speech team to its most successful season ever. She recruited many kids, including a few from Hog Hollow. Reading Howard Nemerov's "The Pond," she became Albion high schools first-ever state tournament speech participant.

Her popularity led to her having two prom date requests from a couple of her more renowned classmates. She politely turned them down and asked Hog Hollow resident Barry Rickton, one of the nicest kids in school. He was considered a little too slow and too awkward to make the social scene. She easily persuaded Mr. August to go to Mother Seton's and purchase a suit, shirt, and tie for Barry, which she altered to fit him. She convinced her mother to lend her the truck. She went to the greenhouse and made a corsage and a boutonniere. Barry was happy and never had so much fun in his life. The students at Albion treated both with respect and avoided disrespectful comments about a truck for prom transportation.

All of this led to Veronica Hannon, her sister Missy, and her parents to honor Delilah Vozy by asking her to deliver the graduation address. The address was traditionally delivered by the valedictorian. No one in Albion outside of the Hannon family and Mr. August were aware of what was to happen graduation night. Delilah, however, got word to her sister, Dakota. Dakota in turn notified her brother and their dad. Unknown to Delilah, all of her family was in the audience.

Most of all I want to leave the class of '76 with this. No matter what anyone tells us we can't do or tells us we are not smart enough or good enough to do, no matter how anyone treats us, no matter what names we are called to our faces or behind our backs, we must believe that we are okay. Believe that who we are is okay as long as we be the best we can be, give all we can to all we do, strive to be the best, and accept whatever befalls us as long as we can honestly say, and I repeat honestly, I gave my best.

As she said the next, she noticed Dakota and the rest of her family. She had not known all four of them would be there. She smiled.

As usual at a graduation it is important to thank those who have us put here: teachers, coaches, our classmates, the community, and our families. I know that I would not be up here tonight if all of those had not worked hard to help me get here.

As she said this, she looked directly at her family.

I see that my sister and brother are here, along with my mom and dad. I am so happy to see them here. Thank you for coming.

One last thing, be sure to see that those around us are also okay. As people we struggle to be what we want to be. See them all as okay and with a little bit of luck, they will see us as okay.

The audience stood and gave Delilah Vozy loud, heartfelt applause as she descended the stage. Things for Delilah become even better after graduation. She had told Mr. August at the beginning of May that in spite of having been accepted at Middleton State College, she would not go there. She said she didn't really have the money, and besides, she said that in spite of the battles she and her mom had, she couldn't leave her without help on the farm. She said, "Mr. August, my mom can't make it by herself."

Help arrived a few days after graduation. Delilah learned that her father was moving back home. He said he felt obligated. He didn't think Delilah should have to stay home to help her mother. He would move back and help his wife make a go of the place. He would continue to work his automotive fix it shop; he would move it to the farm. His skill with car, truck, and motorcycle engines was well known. He told Delilah he would give the marriage another chance. Her mom agreed, and said she would help to make all things better. Delilah was so happy; family again. Dakota and Darren promised to come home more often and help on the farm.

The second piece of good fortune making Delilah's education a reality came when Stuart August arranged for her to become a nanny. August's old neighbor from when he was growing up needed help. Doctor Koski and his wife, Rose, had five children ranging in age from three to thirteen. Rose had health issues and needed help at home. After a lengthy interview with all of the family present, Delilah was afforded the opportunity. She would receive room and board with additional salary. She would have one

40

weekend off a month. She would have time to attend classes and study. In summer she would work full time and be compensated accordingly. She would be available most evenings. She could also arrange time to do her own thing.

At the end of June, as Delilah Vozy packed her bags to become a nanny in Middleton and prepare for her college education, she thought about the message she hoped she had delivered in her graduation speech.

Believe you are a worthwhile human being and believe those around you are just as worthwhile.

After Dark

Playing mind games to stay awake, he navigated a forested highway in the Upper Peninsula of northern Michigan.

There were at least two priests, and I know where they are. Let me see, how many lawyers? One, two, three, four . . . I guess I can only get to ten. I know where most of them are. Okay, on to medical doctors. I'm not sure but I think I could make it to six.

He enjoyed playing Where Are They Now? This is fun. It should help me stay awake.

His game was interrupted by two deer, with another following closely behind. He had reduced his speed after he saw the first ones some forty miles back. What was he doing driving on such a road in such a place at night this time of year?

He didn't really have to ask. Stuart August, Gus, was in the Upper Peninsula in September. Before he retired he took his scenic drives in the UP in summer. The woods and lakes captivated him. Northern Wisconsin and the Upper Peninsula might as well have been designated one gigantic national park. He knew why he was on this wooded path well after sunset. He had left Marquette, Michigan, at 10:00 a.m. and headed east. When he reached Sault Ste. Marie, he indulged in his usual entertainment at a Native American casino. He was headed for the one on the US side of the two cities with the same name.

How about I try those former students who now reside outside of the United States: Armenia, Belgium, Canada, Denmark, England, Norway . . . . Of course, South American countries take the numbers lead. After all, I taught in Brazil for four years.

Let's see, how about psychologists and teachers? I wonder if I have exact locations for each. They cover most of the US.

He had a good day at the casino in Sault Ste. Marie. He hadn't had a blackjack run like that in a long time. When he cashed out at 5:30 p.m., he planned to head back to his motel, the Blue Superior, overlooking the lake near Marquette. When he saw the buffet sign and since he was already on such a roll, he pushed his luck at the food line. Such a good day demanded he indulge in something he had given up. He needed to avoid buffets because of the overeating that ensued.

After eating in some moderation he tried to head out. He just couldn't resist the last five-dollar blackjack table. Another good run kept him there for two and a half hours, far too long. He should have just stayed at the casino hotel. However, he was determined not to pay double for one night. He hadn't checked out of the Blue Superior.

Another two deer loped out of the trees. Keep awake. I need to get back to the game. Now, how about college and pro athletes? I've got an Olympic bike rider, a few professional baseball players, twelve in college basketball, seven in football, and one, two . . . make it six volleyball players. I'll bet there are at least two dozen coaches, some of them even speech coaches. I keep losing track of the count.

How about a list of those who joined the Peace Corps, or those in politics and government? Where do I start?

When he finally left the casino with the biggest payday he ever had and would likely ever have, it was after 9:00 p.m. He was sure he could easily get back to Marquette at a reasonable time. A stop for gas and a couple bottles of Diet Mountain Dew and he was set for the adventure. Gus was over halfway to his motel as he returned to his game.

Let's see, I have one clown, two actresses, and one LA comedy writer for TV and movies. What about the less noticeable? How many stay at home moms do I know . . . I didn't realize there were so few. Let's see, how many have been in rehab for addiction? How about daycare providers?

As the moon ducked behind clouds and the visibility darkened, he turned to a darker list of the infamous. This will be sad. How many suicides, including death by cop? Oh, yes, then there are those who have served jail sentences or still are. I know of five for sure. I know of two who worked in the sex trade. This is too depressing.

Stuart August jerked his head up and knew he had to change his approach to keeping alert. He started to scan AM radio stations, but after dark that was hopeless, static. He switched to an FM scan. About the third time through the scan he heard some easy listening music. It may not have been conducive to staying awake, but it was something he could listen to, not rock or hip hop, not politics or sports talk hosts harping on the same old stories—fall, NFL, flogging the same dead horse.

After he heard Glenn Miller's "Mood Indigo," the voice of the announcer reminded listeners, "Be sure to tune in tomorrow night for the special full moon edition of 'After Dark with Sherwood Nightingale.'" Stuart August snapped even more awake and pulled to the side of the road, flashers on. That voice, I know that voice, who is it? He waited and listened as the voice recited a verse from a romantic poem that featured a full moon. That voice, that voice. It can't be; it just can't be. He listened some more. That has to be Harold Zenner. He hadn't heard that voice in ages. He was no longer playing Where Are They Now? He was led into a game of I Think I Just Found A New One. Harold Zenner, after all these years.

Harold Zenner had been one of the shyest, most reclusive kids to visit his classroom. However, it was in Stuart August's class, Electronic Media, that Harold enabled himself to make just a little bit of a mark at Albion High School. The class, back in the 1970s, was a nine-week radio and TV study. The highlight was setting up a school radio program that lasted thirty minutes. The kids wrote and read school news, wrote and recorded commercials for school events, and mixed in other features. Harold was a star. He loved the class. He took it three times in two years. The last two times he served as August's teacher's aide. Harold helped kids write, produce, and record their news and commercials.

The Albion principal, Zack Kramer, even allowed Harold to do a few live broadcasts during the half hour lunch period. The program aired in the cafeteria through the school's intercom. For a short while, Harold Zenner was a noted and respected teenager.

Gus was now doing a Harold Zenner special biography to keep awake

45

and avoid the March of the Bambies. I remember how I worked to get Harold to go to radio school. He loved broadcasting. He had a resonating voice that was made for radio, but he was shy, such a recluse. Unless, of course, he was behind a microphone and had shut out the real world. Then he was alive. August had encouraged him to go to Brown Institute in Minneapolis. It was the crown jewel of radio schools in the Upper Midwest. Harold said, "No. I cannot afford it, and you know, I don't do well with other people." Gus had often wondered what happened to that talented hermit.

As he listened to the soft music and the voice of Sherwood Nightingale, he kept going back to Albion High School. Harold was in August's noontime MOD, a twenty-minute break for students to go to a teacher's room for help, to work on a project, or just visit, depending on what was allowed in that room. I can see Harold being grilled about one of his hobbies. Kids had learned Harold liked to visit graveyards after dark. He would sit in them, listen to the birds, take in the moon, and perhaps dream of a life he wanted. Three boys, a year younger than Harold, gave him a rough time about his hobby. They called him gravedigger, goolie, and zombie. They rode him pretty hard, and I was about to step in. I held back hoping Harold would defend himself.

Before I was able to intervene, a senior girl, Lacy Knowles, joined the group. She was new to the school and had not really been a good fit. She was tall, pretty, with long blonde hair, and bright, but she wasn't much of a student. She was into hard rock music and friends from her old school. She wore funky clothes and just didn't seem to fit in at Albion. She sat down among the four boys and said, "Harold, don't let these jerks get to you. Do you guys know that I like cemeteries, too? I often go visit one to think, get my head straight. Harold, I don't think what you and I do is weird."

The kids making fun of Harold sat there in awe and stared. Lacy patted Harold's hand and said, "Come and sit over here with me." They moved to the side of the room. Lacy continued, "Tell me some of your favorite places to go and why you like them." The two spent the next ten minutes taking a tour of some of the county's most fascinating cemeteries. That may have been the only time in Harold Zenner's high school career that he actually

46

had a friendly conversation with a girl. I love the justice of it all. Harold, you put those guys down with Lacy's help.

Before August arrived at the Blue Superior, he learned that the FM station he was listening to was a local Marquette station, KSUP, the Voice of the UP. He planned to visit the station the next day and find out if the Nightingale program was local or syndicated. He was now convinced Nightingale was really Harold Zenner.

The next morning he asked the desk clerk at the motel about KSUP. The clerk told him where it was. Gus found the station. When he talked to the receptionist about the program he had heard the night before, she smiled a big Lake Superior smile and said, "That program is live from here. It's our bread and butter. The program keeps us way above healthy."

Gus smiled, thinking about his continuous run of good luck. "I know you aren't supposed to do this, but I really would like to speak to Sherwood Nightingale. I knew him as Harold Zenner. I was his high school English teacher."

"You are right. I can't put you in contact with him."

Gus studied the name embroidered on her blouse. "Chrissy, I wonder if you would do me and perhaps Sherwood Nightingale a favor. Tell him that Stuart August, his old English teacher from Albion High School, is in town and would like to speak with him."

"Mr. August, Mr. Nightingale does not broadcast out of our studios. He has his own private studio. What I can do is give him your name and how to reach you. It would then be up to him. Does that help you, sir?"

"Yes, thank you, Chrissy." August handed her his card after writing the name and phone number of the motel on it. He then found a Native American casino close to Marquette and spent the rest of the morning and early afternoon rediscovering that Lady Luck is most fleeting.

He returned to his motel to see if he could find a Tigers or Brewers baseball game on TV for that evening. Instead he found a phone message with a number to call before five o'clock. August dialed the number. A female voice answered. August identified himself. "Mr. August, tell me the name of the classroom radio station you think Mr. Nightingale may have

47

been a part of," the woman said.

"KICK radio."

"I guess that confirms that you are who you say you are. Mr. Nightingale will be happy to see you at five o'clock." She then gave him directions.

Following the voice's directions, August discovered a fieldstone mansion on a ridge looking down upon the Great Lake. Cedar trees, flower gardens, and lawns flanked the paved driveway leading to a two-car garage. Gus was met by an attractive forty-something, classically dressed woman. She introduced herself as Maddy Woods. "I am Sherwood's producer and friend. I have known him since he arrived at our station about thirty years ago. My father owns the station. We're so lucky to have had Sherwood stumble upon us. He was a shy young man when he joined us. I am afraid you will not get much time with him. In forty-five minutes he will begin preparation for tonight's highly rated full moon edition of 'After Dark with Sherwood Nightingale.' Come. He is in the Lakeview Parlor, as he calls it."

She led him through the foyer into a sunken living area furnished with easy chairs, couches, a fireplace, and bookshelves fully lined. Classical music softly filled the room. Harold was standing in front of wall-to-wall, floor-to-ceiling windows looking down into the deep wavy blue of Lake Superior. He turned toward Stuart August and stepped forward with his right hand outstretched. Extending his hand in a similar manner, August stepped to greet Harold. As they shook hands, Harold dropped his eyes to the floor and said, "Mr. August, it is so nice of you to stop in. I was told you heard my program last night. Thank you for listening."

Harold and Mr. August chatted awkwardly for about fifteen minutes, Harold asking if Mr. August was still teaching and what was he doing in the UP, Mr. August asking Harold what got him to radio and to the UP.

"Well," said Harold, "I passed the test for the lowest class radio operator's license that would allow me to go on the air. Then I began researching radio magazines for jobs. Sometime in the 1980s I found that KSUP was looking for someone, and here I am."

Stuart August suddenly jumped back forty years. Harold Zenner came to school so sad. He told me that the FCC threatened to fine him or put

48

him in jail. Apparently Harold had assembled his own AM transmitter and had been extending his classroom KICK radio broadcasts into the night. He played easy, slow, romantic music, aired fake ads for supper clubs, dance halls, music stores, and more. His range was far enough that after three months the FCC tracked his private station to his parents' basement. When I heard this I gained even more respect for this radio genius.

"Mr. August, are you okay? You seem to have drifted off. Would you like something to drink?"

"Sorry, Harold, I was just recalling your days at Albion High School. Yes, a glass of water would be nice."

"Please, Mr. August, call me Sherwood. I am now legally Sherwood Nightingale. Those days in high school in your class meant the world to me, but I am still not very comfortable around people."

Just then Maddy Woods came into the Lakeview Parlor with a glass of ice water and handed it to Gus. "Please sit down. The view of the lake is magnificent." Gus sat facing the lake. He looked over his shoulder and found that Sherwood had left the room. "Sherwood tells me that your friends call you Gus. If I may, so will I. As you can tell, Sherwood is as shy as he ever was. I'll tell you his story.

"He arrived at KSUP, my father's station, when I was twelve years old. That was 1983. I used to hang around the station, so I got to know him. When he was hired part time, he did our evening broadcast. We were doing a variety of music in those days. He was still Harold then. He seemed to have a difficult time finding a variety of music to play. It wasn't the music, it was the variety. I began to give him lists of songs I liked to hear. I made sure the variety matched the format of the station.

"It didn't take long and Harold was doing most of our pre-taped commercials. He wrote well. He was a wizard at using music, sound effects records, and producing his own sound effects. He wrote most of our local ads. Before I graduated from high school, I convinced Dad to have Harold become our newscaster. By then he was a full-time employee.

"He lived over the Legion Club downtown in an efficiency apartment. Despite our age difference, we became friends. I realized he was comfort-

49

able with me, a twelve-year-old, but he became unsure of himself around me when he finally noticed I was not a kid anymore. I told him to relax and just be my friend. I expected nothing more of him. It worked. I think he looks to me as a sister or a niece that he never had. I think the word 'sex' still scares him."

"Maddy, how did he get from Harold Zenner to Sherwood Nightingale?" asked Gus.

"I went off to college at Michigan Tech and majored in Business and minored in a program I wrote for myself. I called it Radio Engineering. I continued working for my father during college on some weekends and in the summer. Harold and I remained friends and together we helped my father build a larger listening audience, which increased our revenue. In my senior year I found one of Harold's tapes of an imaginary night owl broadcast that he made in his spare time. I realized that Harold must have listened to programs that used to be broadcast from famous hotels with live orchestras. Some of the programs originated from supper clubs. I love AM radio history. I remember hearing tapes of clear channel AM nighttime broadcasts from such stations as WLS in Chicago and WCCO in Minneapolis. They played easy listening, romantic music with some poetry mixed in. The programs featured congenial hosts. I asked Harold if he had listened to such programs. He said, 'That's what I always wanted to do.'"

Stuart August again drifted. The melodic voice of Franklin Hobbs on WCCO played in his head. "Hobbs' House," in the summer, was broadcast from Hobbs's deluxe cabin on some expensive lakeshore property in north central Minnesota. He could hear Franklin spinning another yarn about his daughter, Missy.

"Gus, you did say you wanted Sherwood's story?"

"Excuse me, Maddy. When you mentioned Hobbs and the type of program Harold wished to do, my mind drifted; I was hearing "Hobbs' House" on WCCOs late-night programming. It was popular and a huge moneymaker in the '50s and '60s."

"Oh, yes, Franklin Hobbs. Harold said he wanted to do a program like his. That made me think, gave me an idea. I convinced my father that since our nighttime programs didn't bring in any money, why not turn it over to Harold? I guess I was always Daddy's girl. He told me to go ahead.

"I talked it over with Harold. His eyes lit up and he actually smiled. He said he would put together a demo tape of two hours for my father and me.

"After we heard the tape, Harold was given the okay and asked to fill the air all night after the 10:00 p.m. news broadcast. That's when Harold Zenner disappeared.

"Come downstairs and I'll show you the byproduct of the birth of 'After Dark with Sherwood Nightingale.'"

Downstairs was a large room much like the one they just vacated. Instead of easy chairs, office chairs, one good-sized desk, and another much smaller one off to the side complemented the room. Everything looked out of wall-to-wall, floor-to-ceiling windowpanes, just like those upstairs. On the east side of the room was a smaller enclosed room, Sherwood's studio. An unlit "On Air" sign was above the door. Through the window into the studio Gus could see the radio host working.

"Every night, five days a week, he spends at least four hours researching, planning his playlist, and reading and rereading the poetry selected for that night. He also records most of the commercials used in the broadcast. His nighttime commercials, at first local and now mostly national, bring in more revenue than all the other hours the station broadcasts. The studio cost several hundred thousand dollars. The equipment is the best. Our KSUP head engineer continually inspects and tweaks as needed. Sherwood and the station shared the cost."

"How does Sherwood generate such revenue?" asked Gus.

"That's where I come in. After the first year of 'After Dark,' the station was making money off the show. The listening audience increased. In summer the population here increases enormously. Even in winter, because of skiing and snowmobiling, we are getting more and more people for the holidays and weekends. Some come for a week or two for a vacation in the snow. So many people wanted to take 'After Dark' home with them to the suburbs of Detroit, Grand Rapids, Chicago, and Milwaukee. I knew it was time. I got a lawyer to represent Sherwood and our station lawyer represented my father. I worked with both to get the program syndicated. We made sure all syndicated contracts would have renewable options based on audience; the larger the audience the bigger the revenue stream. I am paid handsomely. Sherwood and the station have reaped enormous profits. We have grown the syndication each year. We now have affiliates in the snow-bird nests in the Phoenix area, southern Texas, and most of Florida. We are working on the West Coast. 'After Dark' on some stations is live, on some it's tape delayed, and on all of them it may be reclaimed from archives for at least a month after the broadcast."

"You have generated enough income for Sherwood to afford this mansion and studio?" Gus asked.

"I learned a thing or two in my business major. Come over here. Look at the west wall of the office."

Gus looked. He found shelves of merchandise, all with the logo of the moon, a nightingale, and the signature of Sherwood Nightingale. He found over two dozen items, ranging from coffee mugs and pens to t-shirts and blankets. There were scarves and mittens. Gus found plastic and ceramic owls and nightingales on the shelves. There were posters featuring the show's name and pictures of Sherwood. All the pictures of Sherwood were headshots of him wearing headphones and sitting in front of a mic. Other posters featured the many shades of Lake Superior blue and snow-covered ski trails and runs.

"Each year we add new items. We are planning on music packages. Some of them will be the old-style LP vinyls. We are working on a collection of poetry that Sherwood has read on air. These last two involve other companies concerning royalties. Most of the poetry is in the public domain.

"At present we have a warehouse and small staff in Marquette handling distribution. We take out ads in retirement magazines and venues that support a large older listening audience. AARP likes Sherwood.

"Here's a pile of last month's fan mail. We have hired some part-time help to review it and the incoming emails. Sherwood Nightingale has become big business, but Sherwood Nightingale is still Harold Zenner. Look through the window into the studio."

Gus looked as Sherwood held up a page of poetry that he was reading into a microphone. He was now wearing a sky blue t-shirt with white lettering that said "KICK radio" on the back. Sherwood got up and walked to the window for a look at the lake.

"Look on the east wall of the studio." Next to a series of framed awards was a framed blue KICK radio shirt. "It is the original from your classroom. You see, not money, fame, or awards have changed that simple, talented, happy man."

Gus left the fairytale castle on the lake. It was already 7:30 p.m. He decided to check out of his motel and drive toward home in Minnesota. He wanted to listen to 'After Dark with Sherwood Nightingale.'

After a good walleye dinner, Gus was ready for the road and Sherwood Nightingale. He tuned in to KSUP at 10:30 p.m. He figured if he took his time he could listen for at least two hours of the three and a half hour program. However, to be sure he got a good feel for the program, he pulled onto an overlook of Lake Superior and listened. The program began with "Moonlight Serenade" by the Glenn Miller Orchestra. This was followed by the magnetic voice. "Thank you for joining me on this night of our full moon special edition. The music and poetry are of only the best kind. I may even spin a tale of a shy boy who finds happiness through radio, music, a tall blonde, a few cemeteries, and a high school English class. Now as I see the choppy waves sparkling the silvery moon off of Lake Superior, join me in listening to "The Moonlight Sonata" by the Glen Gray Orchestra. Did you know that band played on Mackinac Island here in the UP in 1947?"

The music flowed and Stuart August felt like he had won the grand prize in the biggest game ever played of Where Are They Now?

The Game

Stuart August, Gus, stood outside the door of his first hour class on the first day at his new school. Standing in the hallway before class had always been his practice. At the same time, he kept an eye and an ear as to what was going on in his classroom. His new students filtered in. One voice in particular caught his attention. "He's new; he doesn't know our names. We can raise hell this morning and get by with it." The kid, bigger than his classmates, moved about the room hassling some of the students, leading a few others to do the same. The big kid and his cohorts intimidated some of the boys and most of the girls.

Gus moved down the hall to a veteran teacher's room and asked her to accompany him down the hall and stand outside the door of his classroom. "See the big kid in back?" he asked her. "I need his name."

She identified him as Fred Meckler. "Thanks," said Gus.

When the bell rang, Mr. August called the roll from his class list. As he did so, he assigned seats in alphabetical order. His seating chart would help him learn names. As the seats filled up a few of the students noticed that Mr. August did not assign the center seat front row to anyone. When Mr. August had completed his seating chart, one kid stood in the rear of the room, unassigned.

"What about me?" asked the big kid.

"You, Mr. Meckler, will sit right here in front where I have you at arm's reach."

Fred Meckler slowly moved up the aisle. As he went, he mumbled under his breath, "Geez, he already knows my name."

That week Mr. August kept a tight rein on his first hour writing class. Fred Meckler seemed to be learning to keep his mouth shut. In the first four days he received only one after-school detention from the mean Mr.

August. The rest of the class didn't get by with much either. Their first writing assignment was due on Friday.

Friday morning, as was his custom, Mr. August stood outside the door. As he had instructed them the day before, assignments were to be placed in the wire basket on his desk before class. When Mr. August stepped into the room as the bell rang, he noted an unnatural quiet. He soon discovered why. The front of his desk was dripping from three broken eggs. The cracked shells floated atop the splattered yolks and oozing white of the eggs. One of the eggs had caught his in basket.

Mr. August moved to his desk and removed the scissors. Then he picked up the completed assignment papers and held them over the wastebasket. Bits and pieces of eggshell, yolk, and white ooze dropped into the bin. The silence was broken by the snipping and dripping of egg from the splattered papers as they hit the bottom of the empty basket.

"I'll grade what's left of these essays as they now stand. Lack of introductions or conclusions, parts of sentences and paragraphs that are lost will be penalized. For those of you who wish, you may rewrite your papers during the day and turn them in before you leave. The rewrites will not be considered late. I'll be here until four o'clock.

"Julie, will you please take the hall pass and inform the principal that we need a janitor's help in this room soon?"

The principal, Mr. Kennedy, arrived to check out the situation. By the end of his day Mr. August had an almost complete set of new papers. By the end of Mr. Kennedy's day he had an egg thrower in his office. Eddie Ganz, pressured by a few students, confessed. They told him they were fed up with his antics that caused them trouble. Even if they didn't like school they wanted to graduate. They hated anything like rewriting papers that caused them extra work. They said, "Turn yourself in, or we will."

So ended Stuart August's first week at Little Creek High School. He had taken the new teaching assignment after six years at his previous school. Newly married, his wife was accepted as a graduate student at the state university. His new teaching assignment was thirty miles outside of the Twin Cities. He joined a carpool with another new teacher and two veterans of Little Creek. Gus soon learned that the school had major discipline problems. Many of the veteran teachers were barely hanging on. He also discovered that the area, thus the school, had serious drug issues. Most of the faculty had lost control. Some of them were just too meek and timid; a large number of them were just hanging on desperately hoping for retirement and their pension checks. Survival, rather than educating teenagers, became the mission of the faculty.

This was not the way of Stuart August. As one of his college education professors had stressed, "A classroom with no discipline is not a fertile learning environment." Stuart August did not see himself as a Mr. Tibbs, from the movie To Sir, with Love, but he never respected any of his former teachers who had lost control of their classrooms. That first week marked the beginning of a test of wills with his new students.

The conflict wasn't an all-out war. Over half of his students cooperated; perhaps half of those actually wanted to learn, prepare for post-secondary education. The other twenty-five percent merely wanted to get a diploma with no hassle. The troublemakers who remained saw the classroom as a game. Most were male, but a few females were among the worst of the group. The object of the game was to control the classroom, run the ship, avoid doing any work, and break the teacher. They were often successful in intimidating the teachers into giving them grades of Cs or Ds with little or no work required. Learning had no place in this game.

Daily, Stuart August drudged on. He refused to surrender to their games. Instead of arguing back when the scoundrels challenged him or his ideas, he merely stuck to his rules: all homework had to be completed or no grades would be given; late work would be penalized; tests and quizzes would not be announced, so be ready every day; notebooks were required and would be graded; all homework, assignments, quizzes, and tests would be graded on a point basis; if not enough total points were earned, a passing grade would not be assigned.

Mr. August had an even more important set of rules: respect each other; no put downs of any kind, either racist or sexist; no vulgar language; and only one person in the room was to be speaking at any one time.

Simply put, he told his students, "If you want to learn, I can teach you. Let's have fun doing that. If you don't want to learn," he told them, "I don't get why you are here. I was hired to teach English and speech, not babysit or be a bouncer or jailer."

As the game played on, it took its toll on Mr. August. The principal called him in after school one day during the sixth week of school. "Gus, are you okay? Are you ill? Is everything okay at home?"

"Yes, Mr. Kennedy, all is fine at home. Here at school things seem to be a little harder than they were during my first six years in the classroom. That, too, was a small school in a rural area. I joined the National Guard to avoid a trip to Vietnam, but since I started here, I wonder if I haven't found myself in a war anyway. Lately my stomach begins to turn when I see that tin pole shed at the edge of town. The nice ride with my carpool is about over, I know I have to battle in the classroom. I suppose it would be easier to just go with the flow, but I can't do that."

"Gus, I have a good idea of what you are going through. I know what is happening in your classroom."

"Mr. Kennedy, you may know about a couple of the kids who have ended up in your office, but you don't know the daily struggle."

Mr. Kennedy smiled. "I do know. Kids talk; I listen. You teach with your door open. I spend time in the hall paying attention to your daily battles. I have been looking for someone for the last few years to show this staff that it can be done. They may not be strong enough, or they, like you say, just go with the flow.

"Keep doing what you're doing. I see some change in students and staff already. Just hang in there a while longer."

Stuart August fought on. Just before the end of the first quarter in another English class, his students were wandering about the room evaluating displays that were the culmination of group projects. In lieu of a final test, each student had to write a paper evaluating the projects using the major concepts studied in class. While Mr. August was viewing one of the projects, he heard a scream and turned in its direction. His eyes caught Diana Wenner with her flashy sweatpants around her ankles. Several of the males whistled as they stared at her scarlet panties. Nate Howard, on his knees, had his hands on Diana's sweatpants. There was no doubt about what he had done. As Stuart August instructed two girls to help Diana, he marched up to Nate and grabbed him by the collar of his shirt and hoisted him off his knees. Mr. August then pushed young Mr. Howard out of the room and down the hall toward the principal's office. Nate Howard struggled, swore, and told Mr. August he would get him one way or another. Howard's attempt to escape and his verbal assault lasted all the way to the office.

Stuart August's adrenaline was peaking. He was five foot ten but was able to hold the stocky, muscular five-seven Howard straight up so that the kid was on his tiptoes as his English teacher elevated him higher and higher while he goose-stepped him down the hall.

All the commotion had several students and teachers in the hallway looking on. Mr. Kennedy dashed out of the office, not sure whether to assist his embattled teacher or the struggling student.

Nate Howard had a history of school, local police, and county sheriff's run-ins. Diana's father was the Reverend Mr. Wenner. Many students and a few teachers told Mr. Kennedy they would support Mr. August by telling the school board or the authorities what Nate did and how he threatened Mr. August. The Reverend Wenner and his congregation demanded arrest or at least expulsion for young Howard. A few weeks later Nathan Howard, aged seventeen, joined the US Army.

In the middle of the second quarter things in Mr. August's classroom had settled down considerably. There were occasional confrontations, but they were fewer and of a much weaker nature.

The week before the end of the semester, Mr. Kennedy entered Gus's room after school. He said, "Gus, you know that I have a policy that no student should be forced to take a class from a particular teacher if they don't want to. You also know that I can make that work since we have quarter instead of semester classes and not all required classes are always taught by the same teacher."

"This I do know."

"Good, look at these." He handed Mr. August his class lists for the next

59

quarter. Gus ran his eyes up and down each list, twice. Then he smiled.

"Mr. August, I think the major battles for you are over. Those who prefer open conflict have withdrawn from the field. Almost all of your major pains have transferred out of your classes, while a number of those who want to learn transferred in."

After some thought Stuart August replied, "But doesn't that just transfer the problem to someone else?"

"Yes. It's about time they also take a stand. Keep showing them the way."

During the rest of the school year when Gus saw that tin pole shed instead of his stomach turning, he smiled. Teaching was fun again. On the last day of the third quarter, three of his five classes threw parties with cupcakes, chips, and soft drinks. The students said they wanted to celebrate that school was a lot more fun without a battle for classroom control. When the other two classes heard about the parties, they wished they had done so as well.

Stuart August's eight years at Little Creek High School turned out to be a win-win situation.

All but a Broken Leg

"Oh, God, look, look," came a shout from a terrified high school student. "What's wrong? What is it?"

"Look, that big white thing that scuttled under those boxes next to the costumes."

Rob moved the boxes and exposed a scurrying, oversized albino cockroach. It was about three inches long. Many of the cast and crew of Spoon River gathered to see the creature. A few of the girls screamed as it tried to scamper away. A few of the boys, too, jumped aside while trying to look brave. The Spoon River crew was spending its Saturday morning cleaning up the storage room below the stage at Escola Aparecida, an American school in São Paulo, Brazil. The students were under the direction of Stuart August, who had arrived in São Paulo six weeks before. After fifteen years teaching in Minnesota, this was his first overseas adventure.

One of the cast members ran off to the cafeteria to get a jar. Under Rob's direction, another male and a female cast member led the safari to capture this rare find to present to Mr. Angelo, the biology teacher. The chase lasted ten minutes and ended with a living trophy trying to climb the walls of a glass jar; the lid featured a half dozen holes.

This Saturday task was part of the agreement for Stuart August's foreign teaching position. August was south of the equator in a smog-choked, traffic-jammed, and high rise–packed jungle of some fifteen million inhabitants of São Paulo, Brazil. He signed a two-year contract to teach English and speech, direct plays, and clean up the mess under the stage. It had once been home to a scene shop and a storage facility for costumes, props, and scenery.

The Saturday-morning assignment was not greeted enthusiastically by the cast and crew. "Why us? That junk has been here for years," objected

Megan, a senior who was the school's drama queen.

"Megan, Mr. Milton committed all of us to this when he offered me the job. I did not have a clue about this mess. I am as much a victim here as all of you. Now, let's get this done before two o'clock. We'll save what we can and toss the rest in the dumpster out back," said Mr. August as he swept the corner that had been cleaned out in the securing of the albino cockroach, which already had been baptized El Blanco.

"At least we got some help from the detention kids," Megan tossed in. When sly Dr. Franklin, the new principal, had learned that August had his crew coming in on Saturday to complete the assigned cleaning task Mr. Milton had saddled him with, Franklin told August that since he would be at school on Saturday anyway, he would give him the help of eight kids who had merited Saturday detention in the first six weeks of school. Saturday detention was for the hardcore offenders.

That turned out to be another pain in Mr. August's neck. The stink, mildew, mold, the dozens of friends and relatives of El Blanco, the rotted wood and canvas scenery, plus the moth-eaten costumes weren't enough. During the lunch break August ventured behind the student kiosk near the athletic field only to come face to face with Ricky Hanson and Diego Santos, two of the detention servers, with lit cigarettes in hand, a major school infraction in this land deluged with so much cigarette smoke feeding into the industrial smog. Neither was happy at being caught. August was even more unhappy. He told the boys, both seniors, "You have put me in a difficult situation. I'll have paperwork, parents, and a principal to deal with. I feel taken advantage of by you and the principal. Perhaps it would be a better situation for all of us if by the time I see Dr. Franklin on Monday, he is already aware of this behavior. Turning yourselves in might save you some punishment."

Back in February when Stuart August interviewed for the job, he had no idea that directing a play at Aparecida would present so much pain and suffering. When he signed his contract he immediately considered his plight in terms of directing a play in a school he really knew little about. What did the stage and auditorium look like? What could he expect in terms of constructing a set? Besides being told that the school (grades seven through twelve) had about 300 students, how many were male and would try out, always a consideration in choosing a script in a small school? What was the talent level? He was flying blind.

He reviewed plays that he had read, seen, and wished he had seen. Nightmares caused him as much pain as boot camp at Fort Jackson, South Carolina. Ironically, it was Fort Jackson that gave him the answer. On his only weekend pass he had gone into Columbia. There he ventured to the University of South Carolina campus and saw a production of Spoon River. He always liked the poems and enjoyed their story. The play was based on a collection of poems by Edgar Lee Masters, Spoon River Anthology.

The story was that of a small Illinois town, Spoon River, as told from the graves of its citizens, circa 1900. The set would be black curtains, black boxes, and platforms of various heights, and if possible, a stage of multiple levels. The costumes would be blue jeans, black long-sleeved cotton shirts, and black shoes. Jackets, hats, capes, scarves, canes, and a variety of other props would complement the costumes. Cast members would play many different parts as the deceased citizens of the town proclaimed their epitaphs. The collected stories revealed the history of the town in all its sordidness and a little glory. The script even allowed for background music and singing. How painless it seemed. When Stuart August told his friends about his choice all wished him luck with the theatrical superstition of, "Break a leg." Theatre people, the weird but interesting lot, believed it was bad luck to wish players good luck. As it turned out, a broken leg was all that was missing from August's international debut as a director. He had already directed five high school shows with far less hassle.

Three weeks into his new adventure Stuart August staged auditions. To his surprise only five boys and eight girls showed. This should not have been a major problem. He could assign as many or as few characters to each actor as talent and physical stature permitted. The problem was that of the five boys, four were freshmen and looked it. They were small, skinny, and with no stage experience. The fifth was a six foot three sophomore. He had more talent than the other four combined. All of the girls were far more physically mature than his freshman boys. Two of them looked like twenty-five-year-old women. He thought he would rename the production Women and Boys.

Then there was a new problem for him to solve. A Japanese girl, a senior, approached him in a hallway before school. "Mr. August, I just have to have a part in your play. Please, please. I'll do anything for you if only you give me a part. My father expects it of me. I can't disappoint him." One month into this new culture and Stuart August felt he was being offered a bribe; he just didn't know exactly what was being offered. "Please, Mr. August, I'm afraid of my father if I don't get a part. Anything, anything at all." He told her that he would cast the best people for the parts. She didn't know it, but she had little to worry about. He had little to choose from.

After two days of readings he was ready to cast. Before he did this he had to consider one of the questions he had them all answer on note cards. When were his aspiring thespians available for rehearsal? The questions about rehearsal schedules answered any remaining questions August had. This caused more pain for his yet-unbroken leg. Sports, music, student council, cheerleading, tutoring, and foreign language classes not offered at Aparecida left him with four males and six females who could rehearse some days after school, some evenings, and most Saturdays. His cast featured four fully mature junior and senior girls who towered heads above his three male freshman. He had one six foot three Canadian male giant and two shorter sophomore girls. They represented one each from Brazil, Canada, Japan, Peru, Singapore, and Sweden; he had two from the Netherlands and two from the US.

Three of the groups were talented far beyond the others. Rob O'Bannon, the Canadian boy, could play several instruments, sing, dance, and act. Megan Heath, from the US, was the diva of the group. She was talented and aspired to earn a theatre degree from UCLA or Florida State. Ariane Raymond, also from the US, had considerable talent and looked like she belonged on the cover of Vogue.

Because of rehearsal schedule conflicts, August found himself at school until 9 p.m. far too often. The freshman boys added to his pain, displaying

64

their immaturity by not taking the rehearsals seriously and by being intimidated in the presence of the mature females they had to interact with.

When August got his ensemble on stage in the school's auditorium, which began life as a gymnasium with a stage on one end, a full five feet of which was once a basketball floor, August realized he had another problem. The acting area was too high and too far above an audience to see what he wanted them to see. Ariane, who actually did model clothing in the PTA's end of the year fashion show, told August that they used a runway that extended twenty feet into the auditorium. A light bulb flashed in the director's mind.

After some sleuthing he found the runway and sought permission to use it. That pitted him against the PTA, the most powerful and generous fundraiser for the school, more pain. August, with his master's degree in Speech Communication, put his persuasive skills to work; he convinced a triumvirate of mothers that the runway would remain fully intact and would be covered with protective canvas. Instead of extending far into the audience, the eight-by-twenty-foot pier would run parallel to the stage. It was nine inches lower than the stage. After finding several risers and wooden boxes, Stuart August had an acting space that featured six separate areas of varying heights. Except for the runway turned sideways and the stage itself, all the areas were moveable.

August thought himself a genius, until the next day that is. Someone mentioned lights. When August found the light board and activated it, his heart sank. The bank of lights was set up so that only the original part of the stage was illuminated. His converted runway was mostly in the dark. As he surveyed the light bank, he was convinced that he couldn't solve the problem. The rest of the week he searched for a cure for his newfound ache.

At a TGIF party he stumbled onto a possible answer. The elementary drama director listened to his dilemma. "Gus," she said, "here is the phone number for Reginald Ashton. He is a member of the British club here in São Paulo. He does all the lighting for the many productions they stage at the club. He is a wizard who loves a challenge." Indeed, in two days Reginald Ashton nursed Stuart August's lighting ills back to health. In fact, he insisted on attending the dress rehearsal and three scheduled public performances in case he was needed.

Euphoria. Stuart August was ready to take on much more risk. If his young cast of males exposed weakness in his developing show, he needed something else for the audience to focus on. He had discovered a senior girl who had transferred in from the British school last year. The British school only went up to the tenth grade. Then the students had to transfer to boarding schools in England or to Escola Aparecida, the only American or international school in São Paulo to offer an International Baccalaureate diploma. Jenny Sparrow loved music; she was brilliant on the flute and was as accomplished on the piano. The Spoon River script provided background music pieces and a few folk songs that further illuminated the characters. August figured he would add some class to the drama.

Megan, his diva, brought back the pain. She was not familiar with the ensemble concept. She had wanted a leading part in his play. He tried convincing her that she was the star. She had more Spoon River characters than anyone. The characters were diverse, which enabled her to demonstrate a wide range of personalities. She was the star. Now he would add some of the songs for her to show off even more talent. She could add this to the tape she would use to support her entrance into a school of her choice. She still resisted.

When his mind drifted from the pain, he had another brainstorm. He learned that an American square dance club rented out the cafeteria once a week and do-si-doed the evening away. One of the Spoon River characters was Fiddler Jones, whose epitaph Rob delivered. Rob was accomplished on the violin and played during the delivery of the part. Yes, Rob could fiddle a hoedown, and the leader of the square dance club said he would love to teach eight Aparecida students how to do-si-do. Things were looking up. Now all he had to do was find four couples who would be willing to learn to square dance and would take the risk of performing on stage.

The diva, Megan, instead of adding more to the problem, solved this one. With the help of her mother she convinced her younger sister, Amber, to get seven of her friends to become students of square dance. Amber con-

66

vinced her boyfriend and six others to join in. Things were really looking up. Stuart August didn't even have to coach the dancing. The square dance club said all would be ready by the dress rehearsal date of December first.

Spoon River was flowing along ever so nicely. Jenny was at the rehearsals adding piano background and accompaniment to the singers. However, after a few weeks she complained to Mr. August that a piano was not enough. She wanted at least one more instrument to fill out the sound. If not, she was going to withdraw from the play.

When made aware of the problem, Ariane said that Adrien was the answer. He was an accomplished acoustic guitar player whom Jenny loved. His only love was the acoustic guitar. This unrequited love story stood little chance of success unless the two could be brought together. Mr. August found Adrien and asked him to join the cast. Adrien said he had no time. He was trying to find a cassette of the Spanish guitarist Segovia. August was in and out of luck at the same time. He had a Segovia tape with which he was reluctant to part. More pain. With a promise of the cassette, Adrien joined the cast. Jenny reconsidered. Harmony was restored.

Things were going so well. Stuart August began to relax. Even Megan had come around. Her mother informed Gus that she no longer thought her new play director was a fool. She could now see that all the parts had fallen into place, making this a unique production for Escola Apareci-da. She loved the singing opportunities, too. What theatre department wouldn't want her?

Not only was Megan happy, but her sister Amber enjoyed the square dance rehearsals with her friends so much that she convinced the square dance instructor to obtain new plaid cotton shirts to go with the boys' blue jeans and the girls' flared skirts. All the dancers were told to be sure and wash the new clothing before wearing any of it. It was all donated and came directly from the factory in the northeast. Amber convinced her mother to buy her cowboy boots. The rest of the guys and gals either had them or bought them.

Things looked as good as the future of a tragic hero in a Shakespeare play at the end of Act III, but as Shakespeare's heroes found out, Act IV brought storms and plagues foreshadowing the end.

The first tragic shroud fell on the Monday after Thanksgiving. Thanksgiving is not a Brazilian holiday, but the American Catholic parish affiliated with Aparecida was noted for its huge Thanksgiving dinner: turkey, cranberries, yams, and pumpkin pies. Most families of the parish attended. The dinner attracted a hundred other expats. As was custom at parish dinners, consumption of at least a little wine by all family members was an accepted behavior, accepted by almost all that is. Sister Aquilla, an elderly science teacher at Aparecida, noted that Megan and her family had consumed wine.

On Monday, Stuart August was informed by his principal, Dr. Franklin, that Megan's infraction of school rules concerning the consumption of alcohol was punishable by suspension from all extracurriculars for four weeks. As of that Monday she was banned from the school play. By the end of her suspension the semester would be over. Stuart August ranted, "That's a death sentence for Spoon River. Megan is about forty percent of all the scenes. She is the heart of the show." August pleaded his case. "How is this fair to the other cast members if the show is cancelled?"

"Can't you put the thing off until next semester?" asked the principal.

"That's two months away. Not only that," argued August, "I have been told that at parish functions such as the dinner most families and their kids have consumed wine. Nothing was ever made of it in the past. From what I hear Sister Aquilla never reported anyone before this. Her classroom battles with Megan are legend."

As word quickly spread, the school's director and the high school's principal were inundated with complaints and threats of moving their kids to the other major American school in São Paulo. On Wednesday morning Stuart August was called into the director's office. Also present were Dr. Franklin, Megan's parent, and the president of the PTA. The director, EJ Milton, addressed the group. "Megan's alcohol infraction violates school rules. She must accept the handbook-recommended reprimand. However, since twenty other students could also be subjected to punishment, we will do the following. Megan will sit out rehearsals the rest of the week. Next week's rehearsals and the production will go on with her. Megan will sit out her participation in student council and cheerleading for the first four weeks of next semester." Hardly anyone was happy with the decision, but all agreed to live with it.

Rehearsals Wednesday through Saturday went well. Stuart August was sure they had clear sailing the rest of the way. The plague visited on Monday. August learned that two of his male square dancers had broken out in skin rashes on Sunday. Evidently they had worn their new shirts without having had them pre-washed. Both were at the doctor's office on Monday morning where they were treated for an allergic reaction from the dyes and dust in their shirts. If the skin cream treatment worked as the doctors hoped, the boys would be able to come to school by Wednesday fully clothed. This presented a problem. August had scheduled a dress rehearsal for Tuesday evening. Spoon River was to open on Thursday. He had wanted a day between the dress and the show to fix any problems. The thorns in Mr. August's side were fully back in place and throbbing. The panacea for this was that the dress rehearsal on Tuesday went as scheduled. Six of the square dancers were in full costume; the other two were topless with much of their red rash in retreat.

August was saved until the second act of the rehearsal. Two of the Spoon River characters, a young couple, had resolved a lover's quarrel just before their death in a tornado. The script called for a kissing scene. This involved the tallest and the most mature looking of the freshman boys, Lars. He was supposed to kiss the Vogue cover girl, Ariane. At an early rehearsal Lars was too embarrassed to go through with the kiss. August asked Ariane to talk with Lars privately and be sure the kiss would not be a problem. She said she would handle it.

Days later she reported that all was fine, but they would not complete the scene until dress rehearsal. That was fine with August. With the skin problem solved, the kissing scene was the last hurdle. All seemed to be going smoothly. Lars, standing on a small platform, placed a tender kiss on the lips of Ariane. After the kiss she stepped back and said, "Very good, Lars, very good." As Lars ran off the stage in embarrassment, Ariane dropped down with head in hands mumbling, "I am sorry, oh, so sorry." It took twenty minutes to get a red-faced Lars back on stage.

Wednesday's fix rehearsal came off without a hitch. The cast, crew, director, parents, friends, staff, and classmates spent Thursday hyper. At 7:00 p.m., Spoon River was to open. At 6:15 with most of the cast in costume, Jenny and Adrien happily tuning up, Amber approached Mr. August with the saddest of looks. In rapid fire she reported, "Mr. August, we have a problem. Megan is in the girls' bathroom. She won't come out. She won't put on her black shirt and jeans. She's sitting in one of the stalls and won't talk. She has never been like this before a play. She has been in at least six before this. She says she has laryngitis. My parents aren't here yet. You have to do something." When finally finished, Amber gasped for breath.

"Lord," Stuart August said to himself. He knew he had to rescue this sick situation. He put his head down and marched to the girls' restroom. Outside the door he stopped and took a deep breath. "Megan, this is Mr. August. Get ready. I'm coming in there. Everyone else get out. You have two minutes."

A couple cast members came out shaking their heads. One blurted, "She said she lost her voice and can't go on." Two minutes later Stuart August walked in. Megan was in one of the stalls, wearing jeans and a flimsy t-shirt. He knelt down in front of her. "Megan," he sternly said with a hand on each of her knees, "you only have a case of nerves. We have all been through so much. We, you and I, are not going to be defeated by this. Show Sister Aquilla that she and laryngitis can't stop this show. I'm going to get you a remedy for your throat."

August went out and found Amber. "I want you to get Father Linny and have him open up the cafeteria. Find ten lemons and squeeze them. Don't add any sugar—absolutely no sugar. Put the juice in a tall glass. Explain all this to Father Linny and tell him we absolutely need this." Off Amber went.

August gathered the rest of the cast and crew backstage. "All will be well. We go on as scheduled. Get yourselves ready; go through your checklists, warm up your voices, and tune up your instruments."

Amber returned with a full glass of the sourest of lemon juices. August reentered the girls' restroom. Megan was standing in front of the sink with her black long-sleeved shirt on. He handed her the glass. She took a sniff and jerked her head back. He grabbed her by the shoulders and looked directly in her eyes "Megan, you are going to drink all that lemon juice no matter how it tastes. You are going to chug the whole thing. Don't stop. Then you are going out on that stage to give the performance of your life."

She did chug the juice. She gave the finest performance in the history of Brazilian bathroom escapees. Spoon River was a hit. Jenny and Adrien became an item, the dancers all joined the square dance club, one Japanese father was happy, and Rob was asked to play for the square dance club. On the first of May, El Blanco was off in search of the Spoon River cemetery.

Stuart August didn't break a leg, but it might have been easier.

August v. Richards

"Screw you, August. I'll talk to this dumbass anyway I want."

"Mr. Richards, you have been tossed from this class twice. The last time you got back in with your supposedly sincere apology. You just showed us the apology to the class and me was not sincere at all. Get yourself under control, or you will be gone with no return."

"Fuck you, you fag."

"Mr. Richards, you are out of here. Report to Mr. Kennedy's office." Rick Richards grabbed his books and kicked the door on his way out. Perhaps this was his end game, to get out of class. It was just another day in thirty-one-year-old Stuart August's English classroom. It was his tenth year of teaching, with the Vietnam War in full force and growing drug issues across the country. The Age of Aquarius had not yet reached Little Creek High School.

After school Stuart August entered Principal Kennedy's office. "Did Rick Richards get here during sixth hour? Here is my written account." Kennedy read it. "You know, this is the third time this quarter. He cannot insult students or me in that manner. He will not return to class. If you send him back, send a substitute teacher with him. If he returns, I am gone. Students and teachers of this school should not be subjected to abuse by a bully."

Mr. Kennedy took a deep breath and said, "You know, legally I can't do that."

"If I addressed you in front of the school board and its members or in front of the teaching staff using Richards's words, what would happen to me?"

"You would get a stern reprimand and a letter in your file."

"And if it happened again?"

"No doubt you would be terminated."

"Let me see if I have this right. You're telling me you wouldn't have to accept such behavior, but students and teachers have to."

"I'll talk to his dad and tell him the kid won't return to your class."

"Thank you." Mr. August left the office.

Two days later Mr. Kennedy walked into Mr. Stuart August's room. "Gus, Mr. Richards, the father, was just on the phone. He said he checked with the Department of Education and his lawyers. He says we have to allow his son to finish your English class. It is a required class, and he is a senior. If we don't, he says he will sue the school and you."

"Mr. Kennedy, tell him I know my rights. I have the right to a school board hearing on the matter."

"Okay. I'll do it, but, Gus, I don't think this is one you can win. However, I will support you."

"Thanks."

The next day the phone in Gus's room rang. "This is Bob Kennedy; Mr. Richards has requested a meeting with you Friday afternoon at four thirty. Will you meet with him?"

"I'll drive myself that day; my carpool will want to get out of here much earlier."

The next afternoon Mr. Richards entered Mr. August's room at 4:45 p.m. He was attired in a steel gray, three-piece suit with a crisp cranberry shirt and a striped cranberry and gray tie. He marched in front of the student desk Stuart August was seated in reading student essays.

"August, I cancelled an important meeting to have this chat with you. It might cost me money, but so be it. Just who the hell do you think you are? You're supposed to have some sense, so they tell me. Evidently you are a protected species around here. Let's be sensible; the Department of Education told me you have no leg to stand on. If my son is not back in your class on Monday, we go to court. I'll sue your ass off."

Now Stuart August understood a little better how Rick Richards acquired his vocabulary and where he learned his behavior. "You may be right, Mr. Richards. However, I have rights as well. First, I will demand an open hearing before the school board. Second, there I will describe to the public your son's behavior in my classes for the last two years. I have documented every indiscretion and have the school's records as well. I will provide examples of your son's vocabulary and suggest the board ask for corroborating witnesses. Thus, I will be able to tell the community and the local newspaper reporter exactly how your son bullies students and teachers in this school. He has been ejected from my classes eight times in two and a half years. Each time he has verbally assaulted students of color, those who belong to churches not usually represented in this community, those whose clothing is far less fashionable and far less expensive than his, and special education students. In addition, he has verbally assaulted me. I'll be able to present this at a school board meeting and if you insist, in open court. Sue to your heart's delight. I have Minnesota Education Association insurance for that. I do not own a house or other property. My car is an old Duster. My paltry income is public record. What you can collect from me won't pay your country club bill for six months. Good luck and goodnight, Mr. Richards." Stuart August picked up his papers, loaded his briefcase, and headed for his old Plymouth Duster.

The following Monday Rick Richards did not appear in Mr. August's class. On Tuesday Mr. Kennedy stopped Mr. August on the way to his classroom. "Gus, a minute in my office." Smiling, Mr. Kennedy asked, "Would you have any objection to Rick Richards finishing your class on independent study with another teacher?"

"Not at all, as long as my name is not listed as his teacher."

"Good. Will you give me a list of assignments he will need to complete his required class?"

"Not a problem."

Before Mr. August left his office, Mr. Kennedy stuck out his hand and shook that of Gus's. "Case closed—nice work."

Not Blocks, Not Stones, Not Senseless Things

"You blocks, you stones, you worse than senseless things
Oh you hard hearts, you cruel men of Rome."

So began Mr. August as he addressed his ninth grade English class, introducing them to the Julius Caesar unit. He hoped the lines would pique their interests.

Weeks earlier the principal of Escola Aparecida in São Paulo, Brazil, informed his English teacher, Stuart August, about an upcoming observation he was required to make. Stuart August, Gus, was teaching at the American school in the 1980s.

"Mr. August, you may pick the day and the class you want me to observe. I am required to make one class visit and write an evaluation. Just tell me which class and what day."

"Mr. Franklin, I'm afraid that would be hypocritical of me," replied Mr. August.

"I don't follow you, Gus," his principal came back. "How does my observation make you a hypocrite?"

"It's not the observation, it's the manner of it. As you are well aware, I do not announce to my classes when they will be quizzed or tested. Therefore, how can I be fairly tested by you when I know you are coming? I could pick my most responsive class and rehearse my favorite lesson. Your observation of such a class would be a pure sham, not a meaningful critique of my teaching."

"August, with you it's one damn thing after another; you are driving me nuts." After a full minute of silence Mr. Franklin said, "Okay, I see your point, but I must observe and write it up. How do you want to do this?"

Mr. August had been waiting for this. "Visit unannounced. Stay five minutes, ten minutes, the whole period. But don't come just once. Come often and don't always come to the same class. In this way you might get an idea of my teaching. Anything else is only a game. You could just as well write up a report without an observation."

"You can go, Mr. August."

Gus went.

Two weeks later Mr. Franklin showed up at the beginning of the hour for Gus's ninth grade English class. Gus's first thought was, Oh no. His second and third thoughts were, Franklin picked my worst class. He'll show me. As usual for this American college prep school, the class was small: only sixteen students, six boys and ten girls. Of all forty-eight ninth graders, Gus had inherited the lowest of the academic lot, including the four students with the most challenging discipline problems.

Matt, a six foot one Texan, was not a happy lad. This was his first year at Aparecida. His father worked for an international Texas food conglomerate. Matt wanted to be back in suburban Dallas playing football. Brazilian soccer was not to his taste. Furthermore, in Dallas his athletic prowess automatically assured him D grades or better in all classes. The academic rigor at Aparecida required far more work for such grades. So far Matt had managed a C minus in English by way of far more effort than he was used to.

Constanza was another ninth grade rebel. Bright, beautiful, and proud, she enjoyed butting heads with her teachers. She resisted Mr. August's methods. She resented being placed in a class with such misfits. She sulked; her work suffered. By far the best student in that group, she challenged Mr. August. "How can you give me a B minus? I have the best quiz and test scores in here. No one in this class writes as well as I. That means I should be receiving an A."

"Constanza, I don't grade on a curve. Your work compared to all ninth graders I have taught is only a shade above average, C plus."

At parent teacher conferences, Costanza's mother asked why her daughter had a B minus, far below her A average. Mr. August showed the

Argentine native her daughter's quiz, test, and essay grades. He handed her Connie's essay that he was about to hand back the next day. He also addressed Costanza's behavior and attitude in his class. "Mr. August, I will fix this."

The next day and every day following Constanza was attired in a dress or skirt, not her more stylish jeans. When Mr. August commented on her pretty dress, she just glared at him. Gus recognized how her mama was making her point.

Most of the rest of the class just didn't see the need to excel or didn't have the tools to compete with their highly motivated peers. Their classmates aspired to attend Brown, Cornell, Harvard, Stanford, or Vanderbilt. Danny just didn't fit in. He would rather work on model kits or build something. His personality was geared toward laughing and having a good time. Writing and studying literature did not fit into his game plan.

Nikki was as sweet a young lady as England could produce, but she was more interested in her family's dog breeding hobby than attacking the demands of an International Baccalaureate diploma. And so it was with the rest of Mr. August's ninth grade challenge.

When the next Monday morning arrived, along with it came Mr. Franklin. The class was studying William Shakespeare's Julius Caesar. After a two-day introduction to Shakespeare and the Elizabethan World Order, the class was into Act Three of the play. The last half of last Friday's class Mr. August staved off a revolt led by Constanza as to why his ninth graders had to read a four-hundred-year-old play. His contentions about appreciating language, understanding history and political manipulations, the art of literature, college preparation, and most of all, learning about ourselves and the people around us seemed to fall on deaf ears. They did concede that since is was part of a curriculum that they or Mr. August couldn't change, they would go on. But Constanza said the school needed to rethink the program.

As was his custom when teaching Shakespeare, Mr. August had his students sit in a circle and read most of the play in class. As they circled up, Mr. Franklin pulled a desk into the circle and sat opposite Mr. August. When Mr. August began assigning parts to his students, Mr. Franklin asked if he could read the part of Brutus.

The students looked at Mr. August with confused expressions. "Mr. Franklin will be with us for part of today's class." Mr. August explained.

"Oh, Mr. August, I just might stay the whole period," Mr. Franklin said, smiling at Gus.

As the students began reading their parts the principal took some notes. The students caught on. Today, instead of giving a test, the teacher was taking one. The class, as one integrated organism, seemed to tense up. How should they respond? Was this the time for revenge?

The class, with Mr. Franklin reading the part of Brutus, began with Act Three, Scene Two, in which Brutus and Marc Antony deliver speeches to the Roman crowd after the assassination of Caesar. Mr. August assigned the part of Marc Antony to Constanza. After all, she was the best reader and had the best mind to grasp the part. Luis, a macho lad from Mexico City, griped, "That's the biggest part in this scene, you told us last week. She's a girl; how can she play the part of a man?"

Nikki, the English girl, jumped in. "Didn't Mr. August tell us that in Shakespeare's time the female parts were all acted by boys and men? So why can't we do the opposite?" Several of her female cohorts joined in cheers to support her. The not-well-liked Luis turned red and snorted.

Evidently the majority of the class had resolved its dilemma about how to respond to the test of their teacher. Matt looked around the classroom and stepped in to end the potential ruckus. "Hey, Mr. August, it hit me last night. Last week we read the part where Caesar's wife warned him about the Ides of March, remember?"

"Yes," Mr. August responded, "let's go back and look. It was in Act Two, I think. Yes, here it is on page 234, 'Cowards die many times before their death / the valiant never taste of death but once.'"

Matt said, "Wasn't he saying that he was superior to everyone else?"

"Yes," Swedish Susanne joined in. "You said that his pride was showing through. You said that was the downfall of tragic heroes. See what happened to him? It got him killed."

Proud Luis saw his chance to regain face by shooting those uppity females out of the sky. "It wasn't his pride; it was Cassius, Brutus, and the others who were jealous that got him killed. Not his pride."

"Really, Luis," countered Constanza. "Remember his wife. I can't remember her first name, but she warned him about all the signs in nature that said something awful was about to happen. The horses were going wild, the lioness gave birth in the street, and graves opened up and spirits walked. It was all out of order. Mr. August, didn't you say that the Elizabethans believed that this was a bad sign, that nature was protesting a foul act?"

"Yes, Constanza. Nature demanded a well-ordered universe."

"So there, Señor Luis. Women can know things, too. His wife knew better than proud, macho Caesar. He ignored his wife, too proud. His pride killed him."

Things got quiet for a moment. "Let's go back to Brutus's speech," Mr. August suggested. "Mr. Franklin, you are on." He began Brutus's speech, which is often overlooked in favor of the one by Marc Antony. Mr. Franklin soon got to the heart of the speech where Brutus justifies his actions in being a part of the assassination; "Not that I loved Caesar less, but that I love Rome more."

At that point, Danny shouted out. "Matt, that's your line. 'Not that I loved Brazil less, but that I love Texas more.'" Everyone laughed, Matt included.

Quiet Yugoslavian Alemka turned to Mr. August. "I see what you meant when you said we could find ourselves in the play."

Finally, Constanza got to deliver the famous "Friends, Romans, countrymen, lend me your ears" speech. She did well, especially in the parts that stressed Caesar's ambition. She must have practiced the night before. If Mr. August hadn't assigned her the part, it was a good bet that she would have lobbied for it.

With the speech concluded, Matt raised his hand. "There is pride again. Mr. August, you said you like baseball? Do you think Reggie Jackson will end up like Caesar? You know, 'I am the straw that stirs the drink.'" Matt laughed.

81

"You know, that is one of the many reasons I like Shakespeare. As Alemka pointed out, he wrote about the people we read about, see, and know. He captured the essence of us."

Before anyone knew it, the class period was over.

The next day the class sat behind their big grins. "What did you think of yesterday? Are we a bunch of blocks, stones, and senseless things? Did we have hard hearts? Were we the cruel ninth graders of Aparecida?" asked Constanza.

"No, Constanza, I might say:
The elements are so mixed in you
that nature might stand up
and say to all the world,
'This is a class."

"What?" the confused class shouted.

"For that, you will have to wait until we get to the final scene in Act Five."

A few days later Mr. Franklin summoned Stuart August to his office for his review. "Gus, I have to hand it to you. That was the best Shakespeare lesson I have ever witnessed."

"Mr. Franklin, if you haven't already figured it out, I must tell you. That was not my ninth grade class. They put on a show for you. Sit in the hall and listen to them. You won't hear anything like the class you attended."

Mr. Franklin smiled. "You might be right, Mr. August. However, for that group to do what they did to shine a positive light on you says something. They might not like studying English, but they sure have great respect for their teacher. That tells me a great deal about your effectiveness in the classroom."

After the nine-week report cards came out, Constanza came to class wearing her faded tight blue jeans. Mr. August said, "Constanza, you are back to your old costume."

"Oh, you," she snarled. "I hope you and my mother both come down with the flu."

Mr. August smiled. The class snickered.

To or From?

"What are you running from? You have to be like all the rest, running from something, or you wouldn't be here," demanded Celeste. She said this while staring at a new stateside hire.

"Me?" The surprised special ed teacher gasped. Recovering from the onslaught, Shannon retorted, "I'm not running from anything. I just wanted to see the world, and didn't want to join the Navy to do it. It's the age of liberation, the 1980s are here, and so am I."

"No," Celeste challenged. "You are running like all the rest, like the ex-priest we had who was running from his church, his family and, I suppose, God. Now he has run somewhere else. We have had the divorced and the ex-everything. Right, Victoria? You're an ex-nun trying to hide your face in what you figured was sunny São Paulo. I suppose the smog here will hide you well enough."

Calm and cool, Victoria sipped her beer. "No, I walked out of a convent. I couldn't follow all the rules anymore. If anything, I walked out of the convent because I realized I had become a nun as a way of running away from a home life I couldn't stand. No, I didn't run here. I ventured to a place where the rules of poverty, chastity, and obedience didn't apply, or at least the last two." She then lit up a cigarette and blew the smoke toward Celeste.

Oscar dropped his face into his hands in despair. His and Celeste's idea of these TGIF get togethers was to idea bring the local and stateside hires together. At Escola Aparecida, like most American and International Schools outside of the US, fully accredited teachers from the States were a necessary part of getting and maintaining the accreditation that was necessary for diplomas that qualified students for admission to US colleges and universities. The carrot for US hires, besides the attraction of foreign living and travel, was a salary equal to or beyond what they could earn at home. These salaries were two to three times more than that of local hires. In addition, the stateside hires outside of Europe were often given a housing benefit. Thus, the strife between the two groups.

The TGIFs had been a limited success. That is, until an excess of wine loosened Celeste's tongue. She'd had a rough week. She and the other locals were told that their request for a raise for next year had been denied.

Stuart August, Gus, a stateside English teacher, was reluctant to get into the foray. It was the end of the semester; the school had a five-week Christmas break beginning the next week. He tried to avert the disaster. "Celeste, what are you and your boys going to do over the long break? I suppose your husband does not have time off now. Will you and the boys go to your parents in California?"

"Nice try, Gus, but it won't work. You are not changing the subject. You, too, are another runner. Right? You're running from a divorce. Your wife left you for England, so you had to save face and get out of town, or maybe it was to show her you could get a foreign job as well."

"Celeste, we've talked about this before. You know that when my wife was offered a job in London, I was prepared to go along. Since she said she would not be responsible for taking me out of the classroom, we separated and eventually divorced. We both wanted to travel and live abroad. So after the divorce I looked for a foreign teaching assignment. I am not running from. I am running to, to do what I wanted to do for a long time."

"No, Gus, you are a statey on the run."

Gus was reluctant to get further involved and closed his mouth. Another local hire, an ESL teacher, fired another broadside. "Didn't we have an ex-monk who ran away from his order because he was gay? Of all things, he ended up here teaching religion."

Stateside hire Angelo jumped in. "I agree with Gus. This was another case of not running from but to. The monk told me he wanted to get a job in Rio, which he called the gay capital of the Western Hemisphere. He had to settle for São Paulo, which, as he said, turned out to be just as heavenly.

Not all of us are on the run."

"Angelo, what puts you on the run? Why does a fifty-five-year-old science teacher who had never taught outside of the US suddenly come here?"

"I was tired of the US public school system and the private school pay scale forced me to become a truck driver. Science teachers are at a premium for international schools, a good deal for me. I like teaching."

Celeste was not to be outdone. "So, what about Jessica Jones, your assistant softball coach, Gus? She must have been on the run. Last year she jumped ship when she was on a so-called vacation with you and Oscar. She certainly was on the run."

Gus took a deep breath. He so wanted to get out of this staff-dividing confrontation. He hated misinformation even more. "Celeste, you lose that point on two counts. One, Jessica was kidnapped, and two, she was a local hire, not a stateside hire. The director let that slip at one of the men's league softball games. Her husband works for Pittsburgh Paints here in São Paulo."

In so deep already, Gus decided to dig in deeper. "Celeste, couldn't the same be said for some of the local hires? We have a Spanish teacher who is a political refugee from Chile. One of our math teachers is a double runner from the Iron and Bamboo Curtains, first the USSR and then Red China. Don't we have a few repatriated Brazilians who lived in the US for years and grew tired of the culture there? What about some of the spouses whose better halves work for multinational companies? Aren't many of them sent to densely populated and highly polluted São Paulo because they ruffled the wrong feathers in the US, England, the Netherlands, Sweden, or Italy? Need I go on? They were run out of country. What does it matter if we are running to or from? I think what matters is are we happy where we are. I know I am."

With that said, Gus decided it was better for all if everyone went home. He was the first to leave the Casa Borbagato. He hailed a taxi and headed for his apartment.

Once there he made a couple of chicken and cheese sandwiches. He ate those nestled in his beanbag chair with a new-to-Brazil soft drink, Diet Coke. After supper he nestled with a Hermann Hesse collection of short stories and several tape cassettes of Roger Williams, Oscar Peterson, George Shearing, and Earl Garner. Clean sweatpants and a sweatshirt helped his mood as he settled in for a Friday night, which had almost been ruined by a well-intentioned TGIF gathering.

Hesse was too heavy. Instead his mind, like a magnet, was drawn to the abandoned quarrel of a few hours ago. Yes, some of the stateside hires were in São Paulo looking for a Renaissance or even hiding out. Shannon, he knew, left upper New York state after having walked out on her fiancé two weeks before the exchange of vows. Angelo had indeed wanted to return to teaching, but he felt his health would be better served if he abandoned a young Muslim lady friend he had been living with and found a remote location. The woman's two brothers were on their way to the US to avenge the family honor. Hence, Angelo traveled to Iowa for a job fair and spent the remaining time in Miami before departing for São Paulo.

Gus shook his head as he mulled over the question of running to or from. He wondered why he was the father confessor that so many chose to unpack their conscience-laden stories to.

Jessica Jones had been one of those. Most everyone thought she was a stateside hire. She taught fifth grade and never seemed to click with the local elementary teachers who made up most of the first through sixth–grade staff. Most of the stateside hires on the staff were in the seventh through twelfth–grade high school, but she never made an effort to make friends there either.

When Gus's boys' softball team began practice, she hung around and then asked if she could help him as an unpaid assistant. She said she played some college softball in Pennsylvania. She showed skills when she did some hitting and took infield with the boys. Gus said, "Why not?"

So it was that she spent more time with Gus than anyone else at school. She dropped more and more personal information on him. She had a husband, but because flashing jewelry in São Paulo was an invitation to armed robbery, she wore no ring. She said her husband worked for Pittsburgh Paints; São Paulo was their second overseas post. They had three other postings in the US before that. She appeared to be in her mid-thirties.

After one softball victory the two of them celebrated at a Tex-Mex bar that served chili. It was the only place in São Paulo where Gus could find chili. On her third glass of beer Jessica let slip that her husband was with Pittsburgh Paints because he got the job through the government. Just before she got into a cab to go home, she mumbled something about US Marshals.

Gus nestled into his beanbag chair and said aloud for no one but Earl Garner to hear, "Why do people keep telling me their secrets?" Earl Garner, playing "Misty" on the piano, must have been too busy to respond.

To or from? Perhaps that was the path most people took searching for buried treasure or fleeing unearthed skeletons. Angelo had told him about his Islamic girlfriend and her brothers' quest to avenge the family. Shannon confessed that she had to seek a new haven after leaving the boyfriend two weeks shy of the altar. All of these tales emerged from the aftermath of too much to drink. Maybe Gus needed to give up the drinking habits of others. He himself rarely imbibed.

His second bottle of Diet Coke led him back to the Jessica Jones story. After a softball practice she told Gus that she knew that he and Oscar were planning to spend the Christmas break in Uruguay, Argentina, and Chile. Since her husband was scheduled to leave the day after Christmas for a four-week junket of sales meetings in the rest of Brazil, Venezuela, Ecuador, Bolivia, and Chile, could she join the two of them? She couldn't stand the thought of spending four weeks alone in São Paulo. She said it was too late to make realistic connections to go back to the States, what with the cost and overbooked flights. Holidays complicated everything.

Gus said he didn't mind, but she would have to get Oscar's okay. Jessica's approach to Oscar made it sound like it was a done deal with Gus, so Oscar reluctantly said yes. After spending Christmas in São Paulo, she joined the two in Montevideo on the twenty-sixth of December. The next day they left for Buenos Aires. Since they planned a circular trip back to Buenos Aires, they left for Mendoza, Argentina, on the morning of the thirtieth.

In Mendoza they hired a driver and toured the high plains and foothills of the Andes. They were amazed at how many shades of tan, brown, and red the arid terrain featured. On New Year's Eve Jessica and Oscar wanted to find a nice restaurant, have some Argentine beef, and ring in the New Year.

Gus had been in Argentina two New Year's Eves prior. He knew what they would find and told his companions. Despite his advice they hired a taxi to find a good restaurant that was not closed for prearranged private parties. An hour and a half of that confirmed Gus's information. The trio returned to their B&B. Thanks to the landlady and a generous tip, a hot, freshly baked loaf of bread, a brick of cheese, and six apples awaited them. Then Gus broke out two bottles of champagne which he had purchased in Buenos Aires that the landlady had on ice.

The party was a success. Just after midnight, Oscar said he was headed for bed. Jessica and Gus remained on the second-story veranda. She wanted to finish off the champagne. There it was again, overindulgence leading to confession. "I am sick and tired of being on the road. In the last seven years I have lived in three different cities in the States, one year in Panama, and now in São Paulo. Where will I, I mean we, be sent next? The boss at Pittsburgh Paints has been hinting that another move is coming. I am in the witness protection program. I mean, I feel like I am. I am forever imagining a command to relocate."

So it was that Gus recalled all of this from his beanbag nest. He remembered that before they left for Chile, Jessica said she needed to check in at the American Express office to see if her husband had left any messages. American Express card holders were granted that service: messages sent and received.

Not all of Gus's recollections of the trip were negative. He pictured their trip as they headed from Argentina to Chile into the heart of the Andes in a hired car. They admired an even more magnificent display of the desert mountain country. Now a variety of pinks and purples were added to the tans, browns, and reds of earlier. The sharp color stratification reminded Gus of a design of a child's fantasy; the color divides were so precise. In some places absolutely no blend appeared.

At the frontier the driver ignored the mile and a half–long line of cars. He entered the building and had all their exit and entrance visas stamped as he left a trail of ten-dollar bills scattered here and there. He had asked for them before he went inside.

As they left the border, the driver said that plans would have to be changed. He learned that the high pass to Valparaiso had been closed, landslide. They would have to go to Santiago instead. Jessica was furious. "I was to meet my husband there if he could make it." She vented for another fifteen minutes. For the rest of the ride to Santiago she sulked. She even ignored the scenic mountains.

Gus was convinced that the landslide story about not being able to get to Valparaiso was a ruse, as their driver from Mendoza was loading four people for the return trip to Mendoza. Instead of staying at the hotel their driver dropped them off at, they took another taxi to a hotel suggested in Gus's South America on $25 a Day.

The three planned on two or three days in Santiago. The next morning, when Oscar and Gus were about to knock on the door of Jessica's room, they found a note: "Sorry, see you tomorrow. -JJ"

Oscar and Gus shrugged, then booked a bus tour of the city. Gus was surprised that the hero of Chile was an Irishman, Bernardo O'Higgins. He was one of the leaders in Chile's fight for independence from Spain. Oscar, the history teacher, only smiled at Gus's surprise as they viewed the Irish-man's gigantic statue in the city's main park.

The next morning Jessica was at their door. "Sorry, guys, but I had to go to Valparaiso to see if my husband had left a message at American Express. He didn't. So what's up for today?"

said the smiling woman.

Santiago proved to be a pleasant city with little or no reference from anyone about politics, assassinations, or hostages. A few years back hostages had been held captive in the city's famous soccer stadium. The story was featured in a popular movie. Tourist trade was vital to the economy.

On the third night the three boarded a train for Puerto Montt. The train ran through Chile's farms, orchards, and vineyards before dark. After

89

sunrise the towering tips and occasional cones of the Andes appeared to the east. Further south they saw snow-frosted volcanic blown caps, beautiful. Gus had always loved train travel.

In Puerto Montt, more of the same. Jessica disappeared on her own to check out American Express. Oscar and Gus took a boat tour of the harbor and neighboring islands. They walked out of the city to visit craft fairs set up to catch the tourists. Gus found a beautifully woven Indian tapestry for a low price. He wanted to buy it. The cost of shipping and the riddle of where to ship it, São Paulo? the States? was prohibitive.

The three had reservations to travel through the Chilean and Argentine national parks via bus and boat. The two-day trek would land them in San Carlos de Bariloche. The tour was a journey through wonderland. Out of the bus window, snowcapped mountains drew ever closer as they traveled up the western side of the Andes. Much of the journey on the eastern descent was by boat, usually on dammed-up lakes that made for slow, smooth floating. Passengers gathered along the boat rail on deck were granted a majestic view of sheer granite and basalt cliffs looming hundreds of feet straight up. Once in a while a gliding giant condor would soar on the thermals, drifting left, right, up, and down, on a journey that no doubt ended in another world. Gus's musings about the Jessica Jones saga had temporarily been replaced by the scenic recollections of the Andes.

Gus remembered the rustic hut where he and Oscar spent the night. Again, without success, Jessica frantically badgered people to find some hint of an American Express office in that Andean hamlet. It was in that village that they crossed the border back into Argentina. From there they bussed to the western end of Lagos Gutiérrez, which left only a thirty-mile float that would land them near the jet set resort town of San Carlos de Bariloche. The lake was postcard perfect, with azure water, emerald shorelines, sapphire skies, and the ivory snowcapped crests of the Andes looming behind them.

About midway down the lake all hell broke loose. Three speeding cigarette-style boats emerged from the northern shore and assaulted them. The crew boarded the launch. Ski-masked commandos flashed rifles and shotguns. The comandante blasted through a bullhorn first in Spanish and then in English, "If all cooperate, no one will get hurt. If we don't get what we want, all will be shot." Words all too common in Latin America. They assembled all passengers on deck with shotguns holding them in place. Two of the commandos took control of the helm and disabled the radio. Two more captured the engine room and controlled the boat. The crew of the launch was then herded on deck as well. The raiders made passengers and crew empty their pockets, purses, and wallets into collection sacks that two of the raiding party happily made available. Four other marauders located the baggage rack and looted it for everything of value. As the buccaneers abandoned the launch the comandante grabbed Jessica and forced her to go with them as they returned to their watercraft. The passengers, including Gus and Oscar, were stunned. Again, in Spanish and English, "She will be let loose tomorrow after we are all safe."

Gus vividly viewed the replay from his own living room. First, it was the policia local, then the Policia Nacional. Since Jessica was a US citizen, on the second day the FBI arrived. "Who are you?" "Why were you on the lake?" "Where have you been?" "Where do you work?" "Why were you two with her if she is a married woman?" "Have you ever met her husband?" Those questions and dozens of variations of the same consumed two days.

On the third day all was repeated. This time it was a US Marshal asking the questions. Then in Argentina and now in his own beanbag hideout, Gus smiled to himself as he remembered New Year's Eve in Mendosa. He hadn't told anyone about that confession. He reconfirmed his many reasons for not drinking. He wasn't confessing anything to anyone.

As he replenished his Diet Coke mug, he drew up a new set of questions that begged answers:

Was Jessica's husband in the Witness Protection Program?

Was there even a Jessica's husband?

Was Jessica in the Witness Protection Program?

Was Jessica captured by those whom she or her husband might have testified against?

Was Jessica in on organizing her own kidnapping, the American Express stops?

Was the incident merely an armed robbery?

Was Jessica running to or from?

Stuart August smiled an even bigger smile as he went to his bedroom, sat on the edge of the bed, and removed a postcard from the drawer of the nightstand. The card featured a white, sandy beach, dozens of coconut palms, and one bikini-clad beauty. The card was postmarked Samoa. An elegantly handwritten message appeared:

HI! I HOPE YOU AND THE OTHER
GUY ARE DOING WELL. THANKS.

Gus fell asleep contemplating, "to or from?"

A Lying Dilemma

"Gus, you're not good for much of anything today. At the game this afternoon you often drifted to another world. Are you bored with my company?" asked Patsy.

Stuart August, Gus, often attended town baseball games on Sunday afternoons in Wilson County. The Wilson County League was a hotbed for amateur baseball in Minnesota. It had a long and continuous history. Gus had played and umpired amateur baseball. He had called games in the Wilson County League. He and Patsy Ross had often attended games together and usually went to Sully's Bar and Grill for hamburgers after. They'd been good friends who enjoyed baseball and a good hamburger. "Dammit, Patsy. It's not you. I can't get my mind off of the trial. Carolyn Bass was a student of mine and was on the speech team."

"You testified in that trial, didn't you?"

Gus seemed more somber than usual. "Yes, on Wednesday. I wasn't but a small part of the case. My testimony concerning Carolyn, I'm sure, had no part in the outcome except to reinforce who Carolyn was and what a creep Hamish Bass was. I guess I reinforced what had been said about Joe Baston, also."

Their hamburgers came and the two began their postgame feast and game analysis. "Gus, we wouldn't have lost that game if you had been the umpire. That jerk never gave Glatz the outside corner the whole game. I saw you call balls and strikes. You would have been fair, I know. I saw you call Legion games when Glatz pitched, and he was your student. You were great behind the plate."

Gus may have been a good plate umpire, but he was behind in cleaning his plate of two hamburgers, well done, pickles only. Patsy ribbed him, "I never knew that anything could spoil a good burger for you. Forget it. The verdict was quick, two hours, guilty. Everyone knew he did it. Good Lord, they found him outside the trailer with a shotgun in his hands. I don't know why his public defender didn't plead him out. I guess the lawyer was hoping for a miracle that would bounce him into his own profitable private practice. You know Hamish Bass, don't you?" asked Patsy.

Nodding his head, Gus answered, "I played in the same softball league with him. He was a foul-mouthed bully, a big ox, too. He stood at about six foot four and was more than 250 pounds. He had hands like a catcher's mitt. On the softball field he was known to have bowled over a catcher or a second baseman; he hurt more than a few. A softball game, recreational, and he plays for blood or just to hurt people. Sometimes after a game at the Legion Club, where most of the teams gathered, Hamish would get to drinking more than a lot. This led to his being tossed out and once led to an assault arrest."

Patsy quickly chimed in. "In high school I was in his oldest son's class. That was before you got here. They say Hamish beat his kids and his wife. His wife finally used her brains and left him. His three sons left just before or after graduation. For the last few years Carolyn must have been alone with him. I cringe to think about what her life must have been like."

Gus finally finished his two hamburgers and sat sipping his Diet Rite cola. His mind still seemed far off.

"Gus, tell me about Carolyn. You said she was on your speech team."

"Yeah, she was. I had her in English class as a junior, also. She was pretty bright but not much interested in school. When she put her mind to it, she wrote a good essay. In discussions of literature she said little. She must have done the reading because several times after the high achievers had dissected a character, she would throw in a short sentence that cut to the heart of the matter and ended the discussion. She liked to read.

"She wasn't part of the in crowd. Her clothes were usually out of style, well-worn, and didn't fit properly. They reminded me of garage sale wear from the last day of the sale. She was rather pretty and was physically mature beyond her just-turned seventeen years. She seemed sad and lonely."

"I'd say that made her ripe for picking by the likes of Joe Baston," added

94

Patsy. "I've heard stories about him for years. He must have been four or five years older than she was. I could just see him on recon looking for new young talent to defile. They say he deflowered more than a dozen roses. What the hell did she see in him?"

"Keep in mind, Patsy, she was lonely. She wanted to belong or be a part of something or somebody. I'm sure Baston must have recognized this and knew she would be easy."

"I bet that was why she joined your speech team, so she could belong, be part of a team. Did the speech kids take her in?"

"They tried, but she lived in an entirely different world. You could be right about her wanting to belong, but I think there was more to it than that. Patsy, when the team got off the bus after a contest, there was Joe waiting for her. I'm not so sure that one of the reasons she joined was to get away from the farm on Saturdays and meet Joe afterward. A couple of times she missed the bus or just didn't show. Now I'm pretty sure she spent that last Saturday with him while her dad thought she was at a speech contest.

"I guess that's why I am so bummed out about all of this." Gus took a big gulp of his cola and drifted off. He was reliving a phone conversation from the last time he'd ever talked to Carolyn. She had missed the bus. As Gus got back to his apartment that evening, his phone was ringing. "Mr. August, this is Carolyn," she gasped, all out of breath. Then in almost a whisper, "Mr. August, please tell my dad I was at the speech meet all day. If he finds out I wasn't, he will beat me. I can't take that anymore. He will beat me as soon as he comes in from the barn. I can see him coming now— please, please, please. Tell him I was there."

"Carolyn, I will do most anything to help you, but I can't lie for you. Let me talk to your dad. I'll see if I can help."

"NO, NO. He'll just beat me again. This time I think he'll kill me. I've got to get out of here." The line went dead.

He told Patsy about the phone call. She reached across the table and clasped his hands. "Gus, so that's what you've been stewing over. You think if you lied for her she'd still be here."

"I guess that is it. Why have I always said it is better to tell the truth? Maybe that is not so. If I lied, Hamish Bass wouldn't have acted the way he did that night."

"Gus, get a grip. You are not that stupid," Patsy said sharply as she grilled him with her eyes. "You just described Carolyn's dad as the devil himself. If not that night, then he would have done it on another night. It was bound to happen.

"And if you lied and saved her that night, what about Joe? He was using her. He would have continued to use her until she turned up pregnant, and then he would have abandoned her like a useless ride headed for the junkyard. Then Hamish Bass would have finished her off when he found his daughter was pregnant.

"Gus, you can't save them all."

Patsy got up and headed for the door.

Gus just sat there. The words in his mind were running a continuous loop. If I had lied, would she have lived? The continuous replay in his head pictured Hamish Bass pumping both barrels of his .12-gauge Remington into the naked bodies of Carolyn Bass and Joe Baston.

No Good Deed

With the wind whipping the falling snow at a forty-five degree angle, Stuart August risked descending a hill on the north side of Lake of the Isles in Minneapolis. At 8:30 a.m. it was still snowing. It had started around midnight, and since 4:00 a.m. Gus had been trying to book enough money to pay the cab lease, the gas, and show some profit for his upcoming quest. This January storm was an oddity even for Minnesota. The snow had turned to rain by dawn. That made the roads an even more hazardous skating rink. A rare snowstorm occurrence, thunder and lightning, contributed to the eeriness of the morning. As the snow returned, it picked up in density and with stronger winds. Perhaps this was an omen August should have paid more attention to.

As he descended the hill, he noted that cars trying to ascend had no luck at all. Two of them were stopped dead halfway up, wheels spinning. Another had skidded into the downhill lane. A driver who had tried the feat Gus was attempting had failed after swerving to avoid the stalled car in his lane. He was jammed sideways into a snowbank some twenty feet beyond an uphill car.

A quarter of the way down Gus knew his decision to risk the hill was foolish, but he wanted the fare from wealthy Kenwood to the airport. In spite of his stupidity, some of his brain and most of his reflexes still functioned. He negotiated the carnival zigzag, skidding down the course without incident except for near heart failure.

Perhaps his decision to drive that day reflected faulty thinking. Like most people, Gus thought poor driving conditions were a good way for a cabby to make money. Most people wanted to avoid driving; they would opt for a cab, grateful for not having to drive in such a mess. They would dig deep for tips.

The night lease driver, Zeke Zumwalt, had been honking the horn of cab #34 outside of Gus's one-room efficiency at 3:45 a.m. He and Zumwalt had been sharing #34 for the past month. Both had been driving seven days a week, twelve hours a shift. Both needed the cash. Zumwalt had a wife with two grade school–aged kids to support. Gus was earning money to pay rent, tuition, and fund an overseas job hunt in Europe. He had spent fifteen years teaching in Minnesota and had just returned from two years at Escola Aparecida in São Paulo, Brazil. He enjoyed his two years south of the equator but longed to teach in Europe. He returned to Minneapolis to work on master's degree in Speech Communication while shopping for a teaching position anywhere in Europe.

He planned his journey for winter quarter. Thirty-some letters of application and an overseas teaching fair in London, Gus thought, should satisfy his quest.

That morning Gus slogged through the snow and greeted Zeke, who drove them to the garage after filling the gas tank. Zeke checked out; Gus signed in. The two had become friendly. A few times Gus drove beyond his twelve-hour shift so Zeke could do things with his kids. Other times Zeke started early so Gus could tend to some tasks.

Now Gus was on his downhill carnival ride. He was learning that bad weather was not striking the mother lode for cab-driving hacks. Road congestion had slowed traffic to a crawl. People were in a bad mood because the weather made them late and cost them money. Sullen fares do not tip well.

Despite the conditions Gus made his airport pickup and listened to a harping businessman while they made snail-paced progress to the airport. There Gus had hoped for a fare back into downtown Minneapolis. During his thirty-five minute wait, he reflected on his two years at Escola Aparecida. He truly enjoyed the motivated college prep students. The K-12 school had kids from thirty-four different countries who contributed to his education. He made new and fascinating friends. Then there was the travel: Rio, Montevideo, Buenos Aires, Tierra del Fuego, Machu Picchu, and more. He salivated as he remembered dining on lombo de porco. He couldn't afford food like that in Minnesota.

He projected the same and more for the next two years in Europe. The first step was his European junket. He would stay with friends and families of friends he had met at Aparecida and before that, foreign exchange students back in Minnesota. In spite of the bad weather omen he was determined to find better luck in Europe.

On his last day before leaving he picked up Zeke at his rented old home in North Minneapolis. "Zeke, this has worked out great for me. I will miss your ugly face at four in the morning. I look forward to seeing it when I get back. Is there anything I can get you while I'm in Europe?"

"You know, Gus, I always wanted some of that expensive French brandy."

"Consider it done, Zeke. Take care. I'll see you in three weeks."

Stuart August landed in Oslo and was greeted by a family he had met in São Paulo. The daughter, Bente, had been in his eighth grade class. She was a wonderful writer who spoke and wrote in four languages. Of course, he was also greeted by a snowstorm. The family's house was five stories on a steep mountainside. The view amid the falling snow was postcard perfect. The five floors were stacked like a slanted ladder reaching toward the top of the hill.

A few days of visiting and touring Oslo were wonderful. Attractions included the Kon-Tiki Museum, Frogner Park, and Oslo's famous Folk Museum. Then August boarded an electric train for Stavanger on the North Sea. The ride through snowy southern Norway was picturesque, like a dream, no sound and the sight of red geraniums inside the windows of the farm houses. Stavanger was the hub of the North Sea oil industry. The oil business made the demand for the international school August desired. The location, Norway, and the pay, perhaps the best in Europe, appealed to him. He was one of five to be granted interviews for the English position. The interview gave a positive vibe to Gus. As he expected, the next step was waiting. He hoped good omens were back.

From there he ventured to Denmark by ferry. He spent time with a former foreign exchange student and her family. Gitte was twenty years old and attending college. Copenhagen was his next stop. Gus arrived on a late

Sunday afternoon. The winter snow had returned. With nothing to do and few places open on a dark late afternoon, he walked the streets of central Copenhagen. The snow, this time gentle, was pretty. Huge flakes like gently falling Christmas ornaments drifted to the pavement. He passed cafés, all closed.

His wandering must have been noticed. Soon a young woman approached him and spoke to him in English. "You must be a tourist. There is little to do on a Sunday evening here. If you would like a coffee or a Coca Cola, I know a place just down the way." Gus accompanied her to a storefront that contained a few tables, bookshelves, and people sitting on couches and chairs talking or reading.

It didn't take long for Gus to realize he was the project of a Church of Scientology conversion blitz. He said to the woman, "Oh, yes, I know of the Scientologists. I even know where they are headquartered in Minneapolis." Gus had often driven by the place on East Lake Street in his cab. He enjoyed the attempt the woman was making trying to land a new convert. Gus played along, asking questions. However, this didn't seem to produce the results the woman hoped for. She asked him to wait a few minutes. She then disappeared into a back room. Ten minutes later, instead of her returning, a much prettier woman sat next to him and said, "Inga had to leave, but that is okay. Let me tell you more about us and L. Ron Hubbard." After an hour of being flirted with with the intent to convert, Gus left the cozy storefront and ambled back to his hostel. A nice evening in Denmark became a pleasant memory. Perhaps the omens were getting better.

By train from Denmark and through the Netherlands, Gus made his scheduled interview at the International School of the Hauge. The Hauge is a truly international city. Since the first International Conference in 1899, it became the home for settling world disputes. It has housed the Permanent Court of International Justice, the Hauge Tribunal, and the World Court.

The interview seemed to go well. Gus really couldn't be sure. Perhaps the principal who interviewed him was just bored. He said he liked Gus's letters of reference, experience in Brazil, and his résumé. However, most of the two hours were spent discussing Gus's listed hobbies on his résumé.

The American principal was fascinated by his listing of fantasy baseball, poker, and cab driving. The man wanted to know how fantasy baseball worked. He asked for more and more cab driving stories. The end result would become the all too familiar theme, "I wish I had an opening for next year. I'd hire you in a minute, but my possible English position disappeared as the potential resigning teacher just signed a new contract. People are reluctant to leave here. The pay is very good and we provide housing, which many European schools don't. Then there is the culture, the World Court, art museums, and the location in reference to the rest of Europe."

Brussels produced more visiting with a former foreign exchange student now working for an international bank. Visiting again was a treat, but another interview produced the usual, "We don't have an opening at present."

Dusseldorf provided the next super interview. Gus really liked the principal. The man said he lived to do all he could for his students. The tone of the school supported this, as students and teachers seemed to generally like him. Gus wanted to work for the man, a real principal for kids rather than a politician. The city on the Rhine River was shining and new after having suffered extensive bombing in WWII. All in all, a good place to be, but again no immediate position open. Ironically, four years later back in Minneapolis, Gus met a family that had lived in Dusseldorf. The kids had attended the school and sang the praises of the principal.

Gus moved onto London by train to Calais, France, and then boarded a ferry for the White Cliffs of Dover. The duty-free shop enabled him to purchase a bottle of cognac. Perhaps some good luck for Zumwalt.

A fancy hotel in Kingston held an overseas teaching fair. Gus landed six interviews that netted two offers. The most interesting of the two was in Geneva, Switzerland. Living there would have many upsides: the scenery, the food, the variety of cultures, and the central location. The other offer came from the outskirts of suburban London. The sticking point for both positions was pay. Both schools made it clear that the salary would only go far enough to cover rent and basic living needs. Housing was not provided. There would not be enough money to travel and act the tourist.

In Europe there were not many American or international schools that included housing as part of a salary package. Unlike schools in Asia, Africa, and South America, American-certified teachers already living there were plentiful. The vast number of Americans working for multinational companies and filling scores of US diplomatic posts provided many certified spouse applicants already there. Gus said no to both offers.

With five days left on his junket he visited with a family he had known in São Paulo. Then he played the tourist and took a leisurely train ride into Devon absorbing the pastoral scenes of stone fences, sheep, and rolling, green hills. He stayed in quaint pubs. The best part of the amble was visiting Jenny, who was his student musical director of Spoon River at Escola Aparecida. She was the daughter of the people he dined with days before.

He returned to Minneapolis without a job and resumed driving cab. He sought out Zeke Zumwalt and gave him the fancy French brandy. "Thanks, Gus. I'll save this for a special day," he said. August went back to driving three twelve-hour shifts a week and taking spring quarter classes. He no longer needed to wait for answers from Stavanger or any other school. All answers were no.

He had hoped his luck would change, and it did. He received a phone call from his friend Oscar in São Paulo. The teacher who had replaced him there was just fired. His old position was now open. Since the school had been unprepared for the firing, they had no applicants in mind, and it was already the first of May. Gus made phone calls to a few people at Aparecida and applied for the job. He said he would gladly return.

All seemed green-lighted. His old principal, colleagues, parents, and students wanted him back. There were only bureaucratic hurdles to overcome. Bureaucracy moved slowly.

While the wait dragged on Gus received a phone call from an international boarding school in Cyprus. An employment agency headhunter had obtained his résumé and letters of recommendation. The school was unexpectedly in need of an English teacher, one who would also be a dorm supervisor. Gus agreed to a phone interview with the director of the school. It lasted two hours. All went well; he was told the job was his, but again he had to wait, slow-moving bureaucracy. Gus pictured the deep blue Mediterranean. He looked forward to the Greek island of Corfu, which he read about in the works of Gerald Durrell. He looked forward to Athens, the Nile, and the pyramids. That dream was interrupted by a phone call that said, "Sorry, we have filled the position with a husband and wife team. This will meet our need to fill a female dorm supervisor position."

São Paulo still had not gotten back to him. He made calls and waited for confirmation. Meanwhile another call provided another phone interview. It was now near the end of May. A long phone call ended with Gus being offered an English teaching position in Ankara, Turkey, at an all-girls school. Did he want to live in Ankara? How would he adjust to Turkey? He thought that Cyprus would've been more appealing to him. Gus gambled on São Paulo and said no the girls in Ankara. Was he pushing his luck? São Paulo was no guarantee. After all, it had been four weeks since the original offer.

Finally, the call came on Memorial Day. He would move back across the equator. Gus loved being back with his friends, old and new students, and the lombo de porco. After a good year, he returned to Minneapolis for a Minnesota summer. He decided to go over to the cab garage and see his old buddy, Zeke. He got to the drivers' room just before shift change. He said hello to a few of the people he knew but couldn't find Zeke. Most of the room had cleared. The people he asked about Zeke didn't know him at all. Finally, one guy said, "Oh, I think I know who you mean. Yeah, he was the guy who had a drinking problem. They said he was sober for over three years. He died after he rammed his car into a tree after he drank half a bottle of cognac some fool had given him. It happened on his birthday. Dead on impact, the papers said."

"I didn't know; I didn't know," mumbled Gus as he walked back to his car. His mind kept asking if maybe all the bad luck omens he thought were his last year were actually Zeke's. Then he wondered about karma and how his attempt at a good deed had turned out so badly.

Other
Stories

Cornucopia
Get Thee to a Nunery
The Road Warrior Bride
Kamikaze

Cornucopia

One at a time, they kept coming. By the end of the day as many as fifty cars and pickup trucks joined the three Wilson County Sheriff's Department cruisers. "Tammy, what in the world is going on?" asked Milly Dance, one of Tammy's neighbors.

"They are looking for bones on the edge of Jacoby's Swamp, the part that extends a few acres onto our land. Two weeks ago Tommy's hound, Digger, dragged a bone into the yard. Tommy thought it looked human and called Wilson County. They sent the bone to the University of Minnesota for identification. Sure enough, it was a human femur. That dog brings us more trouble than he prevents. He's supposed to be a watchdog."

"Oh my Lord, Tammy, who could the bone have belonged to?"

"They don't know. They said it appears to have been a bone that was out there for years, maybe as many as twenty, long before we bought this place," Tammy replied.

"Why do they think it came from the swamp, Tammy?"

"Since Digger was stinking of swamp and covered in mud, he had to have found it there," said Tammy.

As she looked around, Milly asked, "What happened to all the cats that used to run wild around here? I don't see any."

"Just part of the unexpected cost of winning the lottery on this place. The exterminator from Middleton said it was the only time he ever had to round up the rat, mouse, and squirrel control unit. He removed twenty cats. He advised us to acquire a few neutered barn cats to keep the vermin out. They're around here someplace. Like the dog, they are not pets but farm hands."

Later a tall, attractive blonde woman carrying a notebook and pen entered the antique shop that was part of Tammy and Tommy Longmier's homestead. She introduced herself as Julia Stark, a reporter from the Middleton Times. "Since the county won't talk to me, maybe you will. I assume you are Tammy Longmier and this place belongs to you and your husband, Tom. Would you mind telling me what is going on?"

Tammy repeated the dog story once again. Julia Stark looked around the shop and noted several people milling about. Many purchased soda pop, chips, or candy from the pretty girl behind the counter. "Your shop doesn't seem to be doing much antique business, but the confections are hot stuff. Tell me how you came to have such a shop out here off the beaten track. If I find it interesting, maybe I can do a feature for the paper on Tammy's Tatters."

"It's a long story," replied Tammy. "The name was a product of my youngest daughter, Tara, whom you see over there behind the counter. The story began with a dream turned nightmare. Then the nightmare turned back into a dream, and now this, the bone. It might well be back to the nightmare. It's a long story. Do you have time?" Julia Stark said that until the deputies came back to their cars, she had time for a good yarn.

The story spun out. The Longmiers, originally from Middleton, were standing in that very yard on a cold, rainy day in April 1984, eight years ago. They were then living in the Twin Cities. Tommy was a CPA working for Target, making a good salary. Tammy was a home ec teacher. After the birth of their three girls, Kena, Lara, and Tara, she went part time. She also did consulting for a few interior design shops.

Both were becoming more and more disenchanted with big city life. Tammy was frustrated with public schools deemphasizing her field, home economics. Not only had the name changed to FACS (family and consumer science), but there were fewer classes being offered. After all, the program didn't fit state testing requirements that gained the attention of legislators and school boards. Tommy was disenchanted with the coming reorganization at Target. He had liked his department and most of the people he worked with. Now all was changing. The competition for newer and more lucrative positions was turning nasty.

After discussing their bucolic dream of having an orchard and truck garden in the green fields of home, Wilson County, on a whim the two found themselves at a farm auction on that cold, rainy day. They arrived late with no time to look around. They really had no intention of bidding on anything. Oh, they had the money to do it: savings, wise investments, and a great deal of equity in their suburban home. Their credit line was good. They had not intended to bid, however, Tommy thought it would be fun to make a low bid, much lower than the appraised value suggested. To start off the bidding he tossed out a low number and laughed as he began to talk to Tammy about the dream that had no chance of becoming a reality. Their ruminating was interrupted by a, "Sold to number thirty-six." Tommy looked at his paddle, number thirty-six. He almost passed out. Tammy's rosy cheeks turned white. She hoped that her rusty red hair had not turned gray the moment she realized the paddle Tommy dropped was number thirty-six.

Later they found out that almost all of the auction crowd had come out of curiosity. Area farmers were not interested in buying because the Hauptmann place had a tainted history. It had been abandoned for years. Back taxes were due. Then, too, those who checked out the house and barn knew what shape they were in. Local common knowledge fostered tales of the place being haunted. No one seemed to want anything on the place.

After closing on the property and paying the back taxes, the Longmiers reexamined their dream. The dream twisted into a nightmare. The house had no electricity or indoor plumbing. The water in the kitchen came from a driven well, pipe and handled pump. The privy was about sixty paces out the back door.

When Tammy got to that point in her tale, they were interrupted by a couple who asked about the price of an old butter churn. "Is this a churn that was owned by the Hauptmann brothers?" the elderly lady asked. Tammy told her it was and sold it for the asking price, a rarity in the antique business.

"Who are the Hauptmanns?" asked Julia Stark.

"You must not be from around here," stated Tammy.

"No, I'm from New Ulm. I majored in journalism at the U of M. The Times is my first full-time job."

"Maybe you should talk to my daughter, Tara. Since the sixth grade she has become the historian when it comes to the Hauptmanns." Tammy led the reporter to her daughter. "Tara, this is Julia Stark from the Middleton Times. She wants to know about the Hauptmanns. Why don't you go outside and put your research to use?" Tara and Julia strolled in the farmyard, which was now a parking lot. The two sat on an old glider with a price tag on it.

"So you are the expert." Tara was the youngest of the Longmier sisters. She was in her sophomore year at Middleton State College, an English major looking to pursue a PhD in folklore at the University of Indiana.

Eagerly, Tara replied, "Yes, I was infatuated with the Hauptmanns, those German bachelor farmers. It started as soon as we bought this place. I couldn't believe those two old geezers lived out here. They used candles and kerosene lamps for light. They made do with chamber pots and an outhouse. My mom had us clean up the chamber pots, yuck. We sold them in the store. She called the two nicest ones chamber pots and the older, less fancy two thunder buckets. She got more for the thunder buckets," laughed Tara.

"When we moved here, I was in the sixth grade. We had to write a paper about the history of the house we lived in. So I asked everybody I could find about Roman, Adler, and their place. They died about four years before we bought the place. They were both in their eighties. Roman died six months before Adler. Adler was eighty-three. He had been dead for a week before anybody found him. One of his neighbors found him on the path to the outhouse. The neighbor came to complain about the pigs that had broken out of their pen and were ripping up his field.

"I got Dad to take me to the courthouse in Middleton. There I found that in 1866, Fritz Hauptmann homesteaded 160 acres in Sperel Township. The record showed he had a wife, Homalita, and a son, Hans. Hans and his wife, Gertrude, had one son, Benedict. Benedict married Uness Obermier, and they bore two sons, Roman in 1893 and Adler in 1897."

"I grew up in a German community in New Ulm," stated Julia Stark. "The Germans there all had large families."

"Yes, I know. When we moved here the county agent, Mr. Zimbal, told my dad that the Hauptmanns were known for four things. One: they couldn't produce bountiful crops, and that included children. Two: they were misers, never spent a pfennig if they could help it. Three: they were scrapers. They were paid to tear down anything and everything. Then they charged to haul it away. The misers they were, they kept almost all of what they hauled. I know they kept it because we are still finding stuff. Some of it was even buried. Oh, and they were noted for charging a high price to do the junk jobs. Four: they were confirmed bachelors. No one ever saw them with a woman. The brothers did attend church most Sundays and always on Christmas, but they never socialized at all. Kids at school said they must have been gay. I won't touch that rumor mill."

"They sound like a pretty interesting couple," said the reporter.

"Yes, I guess they were. I will get into some of the stories the kids at school told. They said that the old house was haunted; maybe that was because both of them were dead and still here on the farm before anyone else knew. The kids said Roman was buried somewhere on the farm. So the ghost stories were abundant. In the four years before we bought the place kids used to come out here for ghost hunts. Before the brothers died, kids said it was a tradition for the high schoolers to storm the farm on Halloween and TP the trees, tip the outhouse, and smash pumpkins. They also told stories about a lot of bodies being buried on the farm."

"I guess that part may be proven true," said Julia as she pointed to the sheriff's cars. Tara said she had best go help her mom around the shop.

The rumor of the bones on the old Hauptmann place spread like a winter flu. More and more people came to check out the antique shop. "Here comes my sister, Kena," Tara said to Julia before heading back inside. "She is the most responsible of us all. She lives in Middleton. She's an elementary school teacher. Why don't you talk to her? I'll introduce you." After catching Kena up on the day's events, Tara introduced her to Julia Stark.

Julia was more than happy to visit with Kena. "What can you tell me,

111

Kena, about the fieldstone barn and house?"

"The neighbors filled us in on that," replied Kena. "This farm, even more than the surrounding acres, was famous for producing a yearly harvest of rock. We were told by folks around here that the Hauptmanns made and wore out more stoneboats than anybody. Folklore has the first Hauptmanns piling up heaps of stone on the corners of the fields. They also cleared acres of oak. After twenty years on the place, old man Hauptmann and his son, with the help of some neighbors, sawed the oak into lumber. They erected an oak frame for the barn and built the walls out of the stones they had stacked over the years. These barn walls are at least two feet thick. Come, I'll show you."

"You mean they built the barn first?"

"Yes," replied Kena. "I was told they lived in it along with the cattle for four years before they completed the new house. The old house, legend has it, was just a shack. The new house was built in the same manner as the barn. The thick stone walls made the place cooler in summer and easier to keep warm in winter. Come, I'll show you the house."

Julia Stark was awed by what she saw. The outside of the house displayed alternating wall sections of stone with sections of oak wood. The wooden sections contained the doors and windows. These were ribbed between the beautiful fieldstone masonry. From the outside the rich reds, tans, and blacks looked like a mosaic. The wooded sections had windows sided in green. Several chimneys suggested woodstoves and fireplaces.

The inside was brighter than Julia had expected. The interior displayed the artistic touches of a designer: cupboards, curtains, valances, and light fixtures all were rustic, yet elaborately fashioned. The kitchen was old farmstyle roomy, up to date with a long table that could easily seat twelve, no need for a dining room. The electric stove, with two ovens, invited an ambitious chef. The old pump with handle still attached and working was integrated into a modern sink. The dishwasher and refrigerator both had a woodgrain finish. The kitchen looked like a page torn out of Home Beautiful's rustic edition.

Upstairs, a tour of the bedrooms and bathrooms made Julia want to move in. "Wow, this is a big place, yet so homey. It's absolutely beautiful."

"Dad wants us to sell the quilts, old beds, and chests in the shop. We won't let him," said Kena. "My dad took out an extra loan before we moved in. He got part-time work as a CPA with two area businesses. My mom started substitute teaching that fall. My dad is handy as a carpenter. He hired a plumber and electrician and worked with them so he could eventually learn to do without them. Between him, my mom, and us kids, we got this place in order in two years. My sister Lara is the artist of the family; most of this is her doing. She works for a decorator in Middleton. I think she'll have her own shop in a few years. She is what I think my mom always wanted to be before we got this place.

"Let's go back to the store. I should be helping there." When they entered the shop, a new face was behind the counter. "Come, I'll introduce you to Lara. She's the middle child who never was overlooked; she made sure everyone noticed her. She is a fashion plate, but her face and physique were enough for everyone to notice anyhow," said Kena.

The shop had acquired several new faces in the last hour. Kena called Lara over and introduced her to the reporter. "Lara, this is Julia Stark, a reporter for the Middleton Times. She is thinking about doing a story on Mom's shop."

Two young women were looking at a shelf containing bluish-green Mason jars. Lara quickly sold five of them. Young homeowners loved them. They were not too expensive, and they gave kitchens a rustic look when filled with pasta, beans, dried peas, or nuts. Tara smiled as she recalled how Digger, the hound, had unearthed the door to an old outside root cellar. The Longmiers found a few hundred Mason jars filled with canned beans, tomatoes, pickles, and even some beef and pork.

Digger continued his work in the sandy cellar and uprooted five two-quart Mason jars filled with cash. "The jars," said Lara, "must have smelled like money to have had Digger go after them. Mom said it wasn't the smell of money, but dill from the pickles that must have inhabited the jars before the cash. Roman and Adler didn't trust banks." More mortgage payments for the Longmiers.

"Lara," the reporter stated, "I hear you are the one who gave this place its name and created the sign for it."

"It was natural. The barn was in shambles. We discovered so much stuff: old chairs, tables, desks, dressers, shelving. We found a few cream separators, horse harnesses, cow stanchions, pitchforks, small motors, belts from threshing machines, and even old winter clothes. Roman and Adler kept everything they ever found. They had given up on cattle years before and used the barn to store their treasures. Some of it had to be tossed, but some of it was in pretty good shape. Mom put on an old coat. It was tattered but not too bad. I hollered at my sisters and said, 'Look, Tammy in tatters.' Mom shuddered at the use of her first name, then she smiled.

"Kena suggested we sell all the junk, start our own antique shop. Mom got all excited and said maybe we could make enough to cover a mortgage payment. Kena asked what we should call it. Mom said, 'Lara already named it: Tammy's Tatters.' I designed, constructed, and painted what you see on the outside of the building."

Then Tammy walked over. She sold a couple of horse collars that she had repurposed as picture frames. Lara told Julia, "Mom put some old tintypes we found in the attic in the horse collars."

Julia asked Tammy how she advertised her shop. Tammy told her that she visited a dozen antique and secondhand stores around Wilson and neighboring counties. She got a feel for prices and what stock they had. She picked up copies of several shopping newspapers. The newspapers were free and existed off of business and personal ads. Anything anybody wanted to buy or sell could be found in them. Tammy let people know what gems Tatter's featured.

Tammy opened the shop the third summer they were on the farm. The supply of items seemed endless. The family emptied four farm buildings and cleaned up more than a dozen areas around the farmyard.

After a month of cleaning, the Longmiers fixed up the front end of the barn for the shop itself. Tommy fixed up the old shelving and built new ones. The girls decorated, painted, and laid down flooring. Like seeds, it all took root, budded out, and blossomed. The results produced the best harvest the farm ever had.

They used the rest of the barn and loft for storage and workspace. That way they were always moving new stock onto the sales floor a little at a time. This kept people coming back to see what old stuff was new.

Julia had gathered all of this information when Tommy came into the shop. He told Tammy that the deputies had found several more bones. Maybe there were a dozen bodies mired in the swamp. "Tammy, there will be people from the U of M out here to recover as many bones as possible. I suggest we set up some kind of food stand with hotdogs, Polish sausages, and brats. That will be easier than hamburgers. I'll see if I can get Tara to run it. She's here for the summer anyhow. She can hire some high school kids to make it work.

"And you know what? Tammy, with those people here and I see what looks like a reporter talking to one of the deputies, the Times story on the bodies will bring all types out to rubberneck. I think I'll move a couple of the old cars, a truck or two, and maybe a tractor out from the shed. Maybe we can make a sale or two."

As Tommy said this, Julia Stark wandered over to interview him. "Did I hear you say old cars?" asked Julia as she introduced herself. Just then Jake Pitzer, the deputy in charge, waved Tommy outside.

Julia Stark followed and got as close as she could to eavesdrop. "Mr. Longmier, I just confirmed that we will be back out here all next week to recover as many bones as we can. The theory right now is that this end of your swamp was used as a dumping ground for bodies the St. Paul mobsters needed to get rid of. During Prohibition Harvey Koop, who was said to be the biggest bootlegger in this area, was friendly with St. Paul mobsters. He probably sold most of his hooch to them. His property was on the other side of the swamp. He is rumored to have had several stills within the swamp itself. We have notified the FBI about the bones, and they think Koop was paid by others to dispose of bodies. He must have dumped them on this side of the swamp in case they were ever discovered. He would have known that the Hauptmanns owned the fringe on this side and rarely paid any attention to the field abutting it. In short, you are going to have much company the next few weeks. I hope that doesn't give you too much trouble." Tommy smiled in return.

Julia Stark mirrored that smile from her post just around the corner of the shed Tommy and the deputy had been standing behind. When the deputy left, Julia emerged and cornered Tommy. "Tommy, I want to do a feature on your place out here. Did I hear you say you had vintage cars?"

"You did. Come inside the shed here. I'll show you. We found cars and trucks and a few tractors in some of the buildings. Several were buried under bales of hay and straw. A few were in that last shed over there."

"What did you find?" The reporter in Julia took over. "These cars look in pretty good shape. Did you find them this way?"

"No. Altogether we found over fourteen cars, trucks, and tractors. I wanted to know what they might be worth. I was able to find an area classic car club, the Wilson Cruisers. A couple of the members came out and told me what I had. In all we discovered, let me see, I think it was fourteen or fifteen vehicles, some cars, a few trucks, and four tractors. They told me what they figured they were worth as they stood. Then one guy said that if I cleaned them up, got them running, and made a few other repairs, I could get twenty or thirty percent more. I figured I could make a few years' payments on my mortgages with that."

"What cars did you find?"

"Let me see, there was a 1936 Lincoln Zephyr V-12."

"V-12? Wow."

"Ya, they made them big in the '30s. We also found three Studebakers, a 1947 Champion, a 1957 Starlight Coop, and a 1962 Avanti. The Avanti clocked the fastest speed of any car at that time. They raced them on the

116

Bonneville Salt Flats. The Bonneville cars had a medallion mounted on the dash. That made the one we found worth a whole lot more."

"Tommy, why all the Studebakers? I never saw any around New Ulm."

"There was a Studebaker dealer in Middleton, Haney Motors. I don't know how the Avanti got to Wilson County or how the Hauptmanns found it. For that matter, we have no idea how they came by most of these cars and trucks.

"As to the other cars, there were several Fords—both Model Ts and As—and a 1926 Chevrolet. Oh, yes, there was this Auburn here, also. I'll move that one out front for sure. I won't part with it until I get my price."

"Tommy, you said you had some trucks, too."

"Yes, I had a 1931 Ford Deluxe that was made in St. Paul. That sold quickly. I think I sold it too cheaply. We found two Divcos. You can stand up while you drive those. They were used as delivery trucks. They also sold quickly. By then I was wising up. That's why I have the 1928 Hupmobile over there. If you find some old ten-dollar bills, you can see on the back of them a Hupmobile on the road in front of a Treasury Building. At least that is what some people say. It's hard to tell. That doesn't move until I get my price either."

"And the tractors, Tommy?"

"We found four: a 1936 John Deere, a 1951 John Deere B, a 1951 Farmall, and a Minneapolis Moline. The Moline is the only one of those I have left except for the 1951 Farmall, which I still use."

"What is that other big old car over there?" asked Julia.

"That's a 1924 Packard. The car club guys figured it was used to transport Minnesota Thirteen in the '20s. There are extra tanks built into it under the back seat and in the trunk. Most likely, so the story goes, Koop owned it. It, too, goes outside but stays here until I get my price."

Julia browsed over her notes for a minute. "Mr. CPA, you need to work on your math. My notes suggest about twenty vehicles." Tommy just smiled.

"So, you fixed all these yourself, Tommy?"

"No, Julia. The car club guys were so excited about some of this they came out to help; actually, they taught me. I joined the club. We often hold meetings out here. Once in a while I find an old car, or I should say Tammy does when she is out picking for the shop. Then we buy it, fix it up a little, and sell it, all part of Tammy's Tatters."

Julia Stark drifted over to the glider she had sat on earlier. Tommy followed. Julia shook her head. "All of this, an antique shop, vintage vehicles, and a truck farm? You people are one family commercial empire." She sat there stunned.

"Oh, I forgot the Duesenberg."

"The Duesenberg?"

"Yes, Julia, the Duesenberg gave birth to the truck garden. After we remodeled the house and got Tammy's Tatters up and running and sold a few of the vehicles left by the Easter Bunny, we found the biggest hidden egg of all, a 1923 Duesenberg. It was in an old corncrib we were tearing down to salvage the old lumber to sell to a remodeling shop in Middleton. We found it under a ton of old shelled cobs. The Duesy was well-protected by old tarps and saved from rodents by the feral cats. No doubt you heard about them. The car club went crazy on fixing it up. That's when I learned just how much these could be worth. I sold the Duesenberg to a collector in Wayzata. That gave us enough money to start on our original dream, a truck garden."

"How did the Hauptmanns get their hands on a Duesenberg?" asked the reporter.

"The Wilson Cruisers figured it was among the booty the Hauptmanns collected off the old Koop place after the great tornado in the spring of 1941. Local history said the storm ended Koop's run as a bootlegger, an occupation he continued well after the repeal of Prohibition. After the tornado, no one ever saw Koop again. Maybe he got blown into the swamp. The Hauptmanns were reported to have salvaged all they could find at the Koop place and from all the nearby fields after the tornado. They probably never got paid for any of the work, but they hoarded all they found.

"In addition to the Duesenberg, the corncrib also gave up a Massey Ferguson tractor. I guess that made five tractors we found. A collector from Fargo bought it before we got it running. I bought ads for all vehicles in area shopping newspapers, and I placed flyers at all the car club swap meets. I know you overheard Pitzer say we would have plenty of traffic here for the next few weeks."

"Yes, Tommy, looks like I'll be out here with a photographer to cover that story and continue to work on a feature about this place."

The Longmiers' farm and Tammy's Tatters continued to do well in the next several weeks. The State Crime Lab van and cars, rumors of the FBI, and the ever-present Wilson County cars attracted more nosey sightseers. Many of the new faces picked up some farm-fresh produce. They said that's what brought them to the farm. The Longmiers' truck garden offered the crowds tomatoes, sweet corn, potatoes, carrots, cucumbers, an assortment of berries, and more.

Tommy remembered that third spring. He had fixed up the old Farmall, a plow, and a drag. The Duesenberg provided seed money to make the truck garden a reality. He got twenty acres ready for planting in late April. Tammy and the girls pitched in. They planted sweet corn, potatoes, carrots, squash, pumpkins, and strawberries by the end of May.

The county agent, Frank Zimbel, advised them on what and where to plant. He got Tommy to spread all the fields with pig manure that had accumulated over the years. Mr. Zimbel said that he was told that the Hauptmanns' farm, with its rich harvest of rock, had gradually become better farmland. Zimbel was told by the former agent that the tornado of 1941 also helped. The twister lifted tons of richer soil from miles away onto the Hauptmanns' fields. The cyclone also sucked up most of the water from Browny Lake a mile away and dumped it on Roman and Adler's fields. Along with the water came a ton of fish that dropped out of the sky. Zimbel said that the Middleton Times reported that passersby who went sightseeing after the tornado said, "The Hauptmanns' field was jumping like it was alive." A few days later the stench of dead fish brought confirmation to the jumping fish story. Fish make good fertilizer.

Tommy had also plowed up another sixty acres and with the help of his crew of family females, planted more than 100 apple trees, different varieties that would produce in early September and provide a continuous harvest with a new variety every few weeks. Plum trees and some grape vines were added to the mix.

The Longmeiers, with help of local high school kids, were harvesting vegetables and fruits and selling them to local grocers and markets. They had a stand in their own yard by the fourth summer.

Their homestead was doing well during the weeks of the swamp bones investigation. The food stand, with Polish sausage being the biggest seller, did well, too. On one of the days of the investigation, Julia returned for the fifth time. This time she had a photographer with her who was taking shots of everything. Julia, however, was not taking notes. She was moseying through Tammy's Tatters; she was shopping. She noticed some beautifully crocheted pieces. Perhaps they were doilies. Whatever they were, they were works of art. "Oh my, so much money I can't believe it."

Tara, who worked in the shop all summer, heard her and came over. "I see you found one of our best pieces. Mom won't break up the set, and she won't come down on the price."

"Why is that?" inquired Julia.

"I found these in the attic. The lacework was in an old steamer trunk with all manner of shipping tags on it in German. Mom figured that the original Hauptmanns brought them from Prussia. She had them appraised by an expert in the Twin Cities. The lady told her to sell them for no less than the price you see and not to sell the pieces separately. So Mom had them mounted in this frame."

"You found them in the attic?"

"Yes, I found a whole bunch of stuff: a feather tick, a coffee grinder, a portrait, probably a representation of the Black Madonna of Poland, a loom, some gold earrings, and more. Mom called Dad to come and see what we found. He looked at it and then at Mom and said, 'Tara's treasure chest will help Tammy's Tatters make more mortgage payments.' Most of what I found has already been sold. Look over there, those quilts, all hand-made. They were in the cedar chest that was up there. We already sold the cedar chest. Mom hasn't moved on any of the prices from anything in the attic."

Julia Stark decided she couldn't afford the lacework. She settled for a hand-stitched German quilt. "Julia," said Tara, "if you want to make your own quilt, there is a quilting frame in the corner."

"Since I already have an expensive quilt, why would I need to make my own?"

A week later the collection of legal agencies called a press conference at the Longmier farm. By then the story had taken root in the Twin Cities. TV crews and newspaper reporters, among them Julia Stark and a photographer, converged on the farm. The Minnesota Crime Bureau's Captain Samuel Drucker spoke: "With the help of the University of Minnesota and the FBI, we have ascertained that thirteen bodies have been recovered, or rather pieces of thirteen bodies, eleven male and two female. All met with foul play. We believe the ages range from eighteen to fifty. The bodies were dumped prior to 1941. It is our conclusion that the bodies were disposed of by the Koop family in exchange for payment. Identifying the bodies may never be conclusive; we can only speculate. Since all members of the Koop family are now deceased, or whereabouts unknown, the case is closed."

The Longmier family did record business on the day of the press conference; they ran out of all hot sandwiches, bags of chips, candy bars, and soda pop. The cash register in Tammy's Tatters exceeded a two-week summer's take. Most of the ready pieces from the back room eventually made it to the sales floor by the end of the day. Digger's swamp find was as good as finding Rumpelstiltskin in the hay loft spinning straw into gold.

That fall, as the family peddled the last of the orchard and truck garden, Tommy went to the field to dig the last of the Russet potatoes. As he returned to the farmyard, he heard Digger barking his head off. Tommy found the dog a few feet from a pine tree near the old pigsty. When Tommy went to look at what the old hound found this time, he spotted some uprooted goat horns and a skull. Digger kept up his excavating and uncovered what appeared to be a square piece of steel, about eighteen inches by eighteen inches. Tommy grabbed the old silage fork he had been using in the potato field and helped the dog. It wasn't a slab. Rather, it was the top of a steel box. By the time both had dug completely around it, Tommy determined it was a safe. The word "Koop" was stenciled on it.

Tommy went back to the house where his four women waited with supper for him. The girls had come home for the weekend to help with the harvest and to work in Tammy's Tatters. Tommy asked if they had time to look at Digger's new find.

After they got the safe out of its grave, they began to speculate on its contents. Tammy smiled and sang out, "Maybe this will give us the funds to turn this place into a bed and breakfast. This place just seems to keep on giving."

Tara blurted, "We'll call it the Cornucopia B&B."

Kena sang out, "Lara, are you ready for one more signature sign?"

Get Thee to a Nunnery

"Raise your right hand. Do you swear to tell the truth, the whole truth, and nothing but the truth, so help you God?"

"I do."

"State your full name on this day of October 23, 1962."

"Phyllis Virginia Malaski."

When Phyllis Malaski had taken the witness stand, her lawyer, Whitley J. Bahr, began. "Miss Malaski, it is highly unusual for a defense attorney in a murder case to put the defendant on the stand. Have I told you this?"

"Yes, you told me and advised me against it; however, I did and still am insisting on it."

"Miss Malaski, you have heard the Wilson County attorney present his case that clearly indicates a county deputy sheriff's officer found you sitting on a stump next to the body of Cletis Malaski, your father, with a .22-caliber pistol in your hand?"

"Yes."

"You have also heard the ballistics expert testify that the bullet that killed Mr. Malaski came from the gun you were holding?"

"Yes."

"You know, Phyllis, that I have no defense to put before this court and have advised you to plead guilty and ask the court for mercy."

"Yes."

"Then why have you insisted that you plead not guilty? Did you not murder your father?"

"No, I did not murder him. By definition, murder is the unlawful killing of another. There is no law that I am aware of that states I must submit to the behavior that led me to that orchard where they found the corpse of the man who was supposed to be my father."

"Please tell the court why we are here today."

"I want to tell the entire story of how and why the man who called himself my father died in that orchard."

"Why, then, do you insist on a trial by jury if you do not deny shooting Mr. Malaski?"

"One, I may have shot him, but I did not murder him, and two, if I plead guilty, I would not get this chance to tell the entire story."

"Surely, newspapers and other media would want to hear the story. You could've told it to them."

"No, I want to tell the story under oath; I want the story to be on record in this state. I want no one to doubt what the entire story is."

"Okay, Phyllis, let us start with your second reason for wanting this trial. Tell the story."

Phyllis Malaski took a deep breath and looked to the jury. The jury sat back and seemed to relax as they began to listen to the stunningly beautiful defendant relate her saga. Her lawyer asked Phyllis to begin with some background for the jury. He wanted information concerning school and family life.

"Okay, Mr. Bahr. I am the youngest of five children, the only girl. Two of my brothers still live at home. We lived on a dairy farm. We milked about thirty cows twice a day. That was a good-sized dairy farm in the '50s. We had some hogs and chickens on our 160 acres, too. We planted corn, oats, and alfalfa. Along with my brothers I always did farm work, but mostly I had to do the housework."

"Phyllis, what about your mother? Did you help her?"

"No, she died when I was six. At first we had a hired housekeeper, but by the time I was eleven the man who says he was my father got rid of her. He said that I could do what she did, do it better, and for free. So I cooked and cleaned. In the summer I planted a garden. I did the canning of foods we didn't store in the root cellar or eat right away."

"Phyllis, what about school?"

"I went to a one-room schoolhouse for seven years. It was about three quarters of a mile away. I walked. In winter on the coldest, snowiest days one of my brothers would take me by sled or in a car. My next brother is five years older than me."

"What about high school, Phyllis?"

"When I was twelve, I had learned all our one-room school could offer, so they sent me to high school. I took the bus ten miles to Crossing."

"What was high school like for you?"

"You see, I was a year or more younger than the others. I looked like a kid and didn't really fit in. I didn't have much fun in school except for the schoolwork. I liked school. It was better than house and farmwork, which I still had to do after school and on weekends. I excelled. Most of the teachers liked me because I liked the learning.

"My schoolmates basically ignored me until, well, until I began to fill out and look more like a young woman, not a skinny kid. The transition came quickly and was hard on me. I had no mother or sisters to talk to, and I didn't know what it was all about. Oh, I knew the biology of the farm and what that was all about, but I didn't know about me. I was lucky though. I liked my gym teacher in ninth grade and went to her for help. I guess she did for me in some of the ways a mother would have. She had me ask my oldest brother's wife to take me into town and get some proper clothes and other things I needed."

"Now, Phyllis, you said your body changed. Did this present issues for you in school?"

"Oh boy, did it ever. Instead of being ignored, the boys who had told me I was a child now wanted to talk to me, touch me. They asked me to go on dates. They said I was pretty and that I had the body of a knockout."

"How did that play out at home?"

"It didn't. I was not allowed to date. Sometimes a girl and two guys would show up at the farm and ask me to come with them to a dance or go to Middleton for a movie. The first two cars came and were told to get out. The next one that followed was chased away with a shotgun blast. There were no more attempts to pry me away from the farm.

"At school I was constantly pestered by the boys. As a result the girls avoided me. They didn't like that all the attention that used to be directed at them was coming my way. Even a few of the girls who had been my friends began to drift away."

The judge interrupted and asked Mr. Bahr how much longer this was going to take. He told the judge they would be at it several more hours at a minimum. Judge Bailey then said, "In that case, we are adjourned until 9:00 a.m. tomorrow."

The next morning Phyllis retook the stand. Whitley J. Bahr paraphrased the latter part of yesterday's testimony and said, "Since you didn't have a social life in school, tell us about your social life on the farm. Tell us about the summers and Sundays."

"During the summer and on Sundays when the weather permitted, I did what I always did. I walked the farm's nearby woods. We had an orchard, and I spent time there sitting and reading, but I couldn't always do that."

"Why?" interrupted Mr. Bahr.

"My dad liked the orchard, too. He often came out there and read."

"What did he read?"

"Mostly the Bible, I guess. I didn't stay there when he came."

"How did you and your father get along?"

"I didn't like him. He didn't say much to me when I was growing up. He just yelled at me to do the housework better and tend to the chickens and the garden."

"Was he mean to you, Phyllis?"

"Not until I began to change physically. As I got to be what the boys at school called a 'wowzer,' he would often stare at me and sometimes called me Lot's oldest daughter. A few times he took his belt to me."

"When did he do this?"

"Well, I watched the other girls at school and learned a little about how to make myself look prettier. I got my hands on some lipstick and blush. When I did that, he took me to the barn and used his belt on me, so when he was around the house, I made myself scarce and walked the farm."

"That must have made a lonely life for you, Phyllis."

"It did, but the summers in high school weren't so lonely."

"What happened in the summers?"

"A boy from the city about my age spent weeks on his uncle's nearby farm. He was a nice kid, quiet, shy, and real awkward around me at first. I think we were both lonely. We talked a little about the deer, the badger, and the birds. We walked the woods; that's where I met him. I showed him the badger hole and the pond where we watched birds. He and I both liked the red-winged blackbirds and the mallards. He told me about the city and how he was harassed by his classmates because he was, as he said, 'a bookish runt.' We were two misfits who enjoyed being with each other.

"This wasn't always so easy. I couldn't let my father know about Paul; that was his name. Paul wasn't always at his uncle's, but when he was, he had farm chores to do there as well."

"How long did this relationship last?"

"I guess it lasted too long, Mr. Bahr. You see, Paul liked me and was aware of my looks. He was a young boy. We were both lonely and, well, we both witnessed sex on the farm. You know, the animals. Well, we both knew what we wanted, and we both knew how to do it, but we were naïve in the ways to avoid the likely outcome. At age sixteen, I became pregnant.

"By the time I realized this, school had started again. I tried to hide it with loose-fitting clothes. The phy ed teacher who helped me before took me aside and said it was time to face facts. I could hide it no longer."

"What happened next?"

"My father exploded like the dynamite my brothers used to blow out tree stumps."

"Did he beat you?"

"No, he yelled at me and called me a harlot. He said I defiled him, and then he locked himself in his bedroom for a full day. When he emerged, he grabbed me and pushed me into the car and drove forty miles to St. Cecelia's. It was the mother house for that order in Minnesota. He told me to get out of the car and never come home again."

"What did you do?"

"What could I do? I found a nun and asked for help."

Phyllis went on to tell the court how they took her in. She had the baby, which she never saw. She didn't know whether it was a boy or a girl. The baby, she was told, was healthy and adopted out. Paul was never made aware of the circumstances or of what became of Phyllis. For the next two and a half years she studied to become a nun. She got her high school diploma and took preliminary vows. She felt guilty about the adopted baby. She was not at all happy about becoming a nun. However, she took the name Sister Paula. Now that she thought about it, maybe that was a subconscious effort to remember Paul.

However, wearing a habit and a veil and living with other nuns was not what Phyllis wanted in life. On her third anniversary of having given birth, and before she took final vows, Phyllis fled the convent.

All of this she told the jury before noon recess. When court resumed, Phyllis was asked by her attorney to tell the jury about fleeing the convent.

"I knew I couldn't stay there. I packed a bag with what civilian clothes I could find. We weren't supposed to have any money, but I knew some of the nuns, usually the younger ones, had some stashed away. I left them IOUs as I collected their nest eggs. I repaid it all within two years. I sent each one the money with no letter of explanation.

"I walked ten miles to Middleton and caught a bus for Minneapolis. I had no idea what I would do there. I had never been there before. The only town I had been to of any size was Middleton, and that was small by comparison. At the bus station I went to the lunch counter to get something to eat and drink. Money was in short supply. A young girl started to talk to me. She asked a lot of questions. It didn't take her long to figure out that I was helpless, homeless, and unwise to the wicked ways of the world. She was nice; she befriended me and offered me a couch in her apartment to sleep on until I could find work and a place of my own.

"After two hopeless weeks of searching for work, my new friend Roxy told me it was time to meet her boyfriend, Dr. Jay. You can deduce what this led to. I was soon put on Washington Avenue to earn my keep. I learned more in six months about sex than I ever did on the farm or with Paul. Because of my looks, Dr. Jay saw that I was paid good money for my services. He knew about my escape from the convent. Sometimes he pulled me off the street and sent me to a hotel. There he charged twice as much for my services as he did for Roxy and the other girls.

"Because of my flight from the convent he fretted about my running away and threatened me. If I tried, he said he would find more ways to punish me than he already had. He had slapped me around and threatened to scar my face. I knew I would not stay with him. This was far worse than the convent."

"Phyllis, did you manage to escape?" asked her lawyer.

"Not then, but my street life ended. Dr. Jay knew that I was a hot commodity, and he was worried that I would run. He found another way to make money off of me. He sold me for over twenty thousand dollars to a high-end escort service. Even though the work was about the same, occasionally worse, my living conditions improved. I was placed in a beautiful apartment, which was home and sometimes my workplace. I was schooled on buying the finest clothes and cosmetics. I was sent to classes on etiquette and conversation. I was encouraged to read and to study art and music. I became an escort in demand. I earned much more money than before and was told to save for the day when my body could not earn enough to support my luxurious lifestyle. I met CEOs of multinational companies, star athletes, politicians, movie stars and other celebrities, even a bishop. I traveled all over the country."

"Did you manage to save any money, Phyllis?"

"Three years of that life enabled me to squirrel away over twenty-five thousand in various accounts. I became the favorite escort of a suburban entrepreneur. I sincerely believe he had fallen in love with me. One evening in a five-star hotel suite, he cried. He told me that he wished the two of us could run away together, but he could not do that to his wife and children. He was a nice guy, but I could never have gone with him. I saw my chance. 'Dicky,' I said to him—he liked it when I called him Dicky instead of Richard. 'Dicky, I think I understand, but if we can't run off together, I need to leave here and this life. Would you help me?' He said he would."

"What did you ask him to do, Phyllis?"

"I told him I needed $5,000 and a .22-caliber pistol and shells for it. He said he would do

that. Three days later he called the agency for me again. We met at the same hotel. He gave me the money and the gun. I asked him to meet me in two days outside of my apartment and drive me to Wilson County. He agreed."

"So that is how you got to the orchard and the farm?"

"Yes, Mr. Bahr."

"Your honor, I am requesting an adjournment at this time until tomorrow. Tomorrow morning we will wrap up Miss Malaski's testimony and the defense will be ready for the jury. I will have no closing statement."

"Court adjourned until 9:00 a.m. tomorrow," replied Judge Bailey.

The next morning the courtroom was filled to capacity. Local reporters as well as those from Minneapolis, St. Paul, Duluth, and Fargo, North Dakota, were present. The rest of the courtroom was packed with people from small towns near the Malaski farm. Phyllis Malaski was not dressed in the expensive blouses, jackets, and skirts of the previous days. Instead she wore a bulky white sweatshirt and a black skirt that dropped almost to her ankles.

After the call to order, Attorney Bahr resumed questioning. "Miss Malaski, earlier you said that on occasion Cletis Malaski took his belt to you."

"Yes."

"Did Dr. Jay or any other man or women ever do anything like that to you?"

"No, they beat on me, but they knew that leaving scars and bruises cost them money."

"Phyllis, why are you wearing a sweatshirt today?"

"So I can show the judge and the jury this."

Phyllis then rose from her witness chair, turned her back to the judge and jury, and raised the back of her shirt, revealing several long welts that looked like raised red stripes running diagonally across her back. Then she turned to the courtroom audience. Amid the loud gasps from the jury and the courtroom visitors, Mr. Bahr asked, "Phyllis, are those the result of your father's lashings?"

"Yes."

Judge Bailey pounded his gavel for silence and said, "Mr. Bahr, there will be no further displays such as we have just seen." Phyllis let go of her shirt and it dropped over her scarred, bare back.

The county attorney called for a mistrial. After a thirty-minute recess, the judge stated that the motion for a mistrial was denied. He strongly suggested that Mr. Bahr bring the case to a quick conclusion.

Bahr asked Phyllis what happened on that fall day when Dicky drove her to the farm in his Bentley. "I asked Dicky to drop me on Township Road 36 nearest the orchard. It was late Sunday morning, and I expected he would be at the orchard reading his Bible."

"What part of the Bible did your father read?"

"I guess he probably read all of it, but once in a while he would leave it on the kitchen table or a counter. I looked at it. The book of Genesis seemed to be the most worn. Sometimes in the living room he would sit and read. I looked over his shoulder several times. He was so rapt in it he never noticed me. I know he had underlined the passages about Abraham and other Old Testament people who had several wives and many children by them. I noticed when I picked up the book once, it fell open to the part of Genesis about Sodom and Gomorrah. He had underlined the parts about Lot's wife turning to salt and Lot and his daughters, who had wandered off to live in a cave by themselves. All others of the nearby town shunned them. Lot's daughters didn't want to be childless, so the oldest got him drunk and lay with him. The next night the daughters got Lot drunk again, and the youngest lay with him. Both gave birth to Lot's children. The son of the eldest daughter was called Moab, the father of the Moabites. The son of the youngest daughter was called Ammon, the father of the Ammonites.

"When I was in the convent, I looked up the story. I wondered why my father never used the name of either daughter when he called me names. I found the answer. Their names were never given. I guess the behavior of women was more important than who they were.

"It was on a Sunday afternoon, before I went to the convent, when I saw him reading this part when he noticed me looking over his shoulder. He called me a daughter of Lot, the mother of the Moabites. Then he marched me out to the barn and made me take off my clothes and lean over a straw bale. Then he lashed me. I hid my back from everyone. I would not shower at school after phy ed. I used a wooden spoon to apply carbolic salve. He lashed me a total of four times while calling me names from the Bible."

"Phyllis, did he touch you or molest you in any other way?"

"No, he did not, but, Mr. Bahr, how can a man do what he did to me several times if he was my father? That's why I say he is not my father. No father would do what he did. If I did not do what I did, he might have lived forty more years without paying. That is why I say I did not murder him. A man has no right to do to his daughter what he did to me.

"That day I told Dicky to wait two hours for me to return. If I didn't, he should leave, find a telephone, and call the Wilson County Sheriff's Office and send them to the Malaski farm. If he heard gunshots, he should do the same.

"I had walked to the orchard and saw him sitting in his Adirondack chair reading his Bible. I quietly walked up behind him. He never heard me. I looked over his shoulder and saw he had the book open to the passage on Lot's daughters. I put the pistol just behind his ear and pointed it toward his brain. As I fired, I said, 'I hope the devil gives you worse than I am giving you now.'"

Silence filled the courtroom. After a full minute, Mr. Bahr asked, "What did you do then?"

"I sat down on a stump. I listened to the birds and took a bite out of the crab apple I had picked in the orchard. I thought of the times Paul and I had spent in that orchard not being lonely. I wondered where he was and where our baby was."

"Phyllis, if the jury does its duty and finds you not guilty, what will you do?"

"Mr. Bahr, I have had considerable time sitting in jail since my arrest. You know I have the funds to arrange bail, but chose not to. I have given this much thought. If I am allowed to go free, I will seek acceptance in a cloistered convent taking vows of chastity, poverty, obedience, and silence. My bank account, including the $5,000 from Dicky, will be given to the convent."

"Your honor, the defense rests. I have no closing statement."

The county attorney then gave a short closing statement. "Ladies and gentlemen of the jury, you have heard the testimony of the sheriff's department, the ballistics expert, and Miss Malaski's own words. I ask for the only verdict possible: guilty."

The jury deliberated for three days. They then reported that they were hopelessly deadlocked. Judge Bailey declared a hung jury and directed the county attorney to seek a new trial if he so wished.

Rumors about the hung jury had both guilty and innocent counts covering the entire gamut of possibilities. The relentless press badgered and badgered the jurors for the truth of the tally, but not one of the twelve would divulge any information. After six months, Wilson County announced it would not seek a retrial of Phyllis Virginia Malaski.

Phyllis Virginia Malaski requested acceptance into the convent of the Poor Sisters of Hope. She took her final vows three years later and to this day is known as Sister Paula.

The Road Warrior Bride

As weddings go, it was nothing short of bizarre. Robert Wren, Bob, was on his way north to attend it. To add to the weirdness of the day, Bob was on his way to collect his guest, a woman fifty years his junior, a woman he had known for only a few months. The 11:00 a.m. wedding was to take place at a drive-in movie theater. That was only part of the bizarre.

Bob had been invited to Carlee Hudson's wedding. He hadn't even known her last name until he was handed the wedding invitation. He had gotten to know Carlee, a card dealer at a Twin Cities suburban racetrack and casino, over the last eight years. Much to his surprise, he learned that she drove eighty-five miles to work four days a week. The total weekly mileage was over 650 miles, or about 34,000 miles a year. When Bob asked her why she drove so far, she replied, "It's too far to walk. I looked into it, but no trains or planes were available." This deadpanned, straight-faced response was a prelude to her uniqueness.

Her personality was enigmatic. She was stern, dry-witted, a woman of few words. Yet she had an acerbic sense of humor that held the audience of her blackjack table. She could banter with the smartasses and the flirts. For the poorer players, when they were verbally assaulted, she showed a sense of caring and kindness. She rarely smiled but could make others do so. She could be moody, saying little. Other days she engaged in dialogue, terse but friendly.

Some days her card table had few players if the cards were unfavorable and her mood was dour. Other days her table was crowded, players waiting to get a seat. Even on some days when she was having a don't-bother-me day, she still drew a good-sized crowd.

Perhaps that could be attributed to her attractiveness. That, too, was a puzzle. She had a narrow chin, pretty face, long blonde hair, and deep-set dark blue eyes that seemed to possess Medusa power. Her stern, compelling look seldom produced a smile. She was thin, but not anorexic. With seemingly no bustline yet a shapely backside featured by her tight black dealer's uniform, she held many a long stare. She was an enigma. Beyond all odds of being a beauty, she was a modern Mona Lisa.

Players, both male and female, were drawn to her table like bees to nectar. The nectar was often sweet but sometimes acrid. Rumor had it she was the biggest tip magnet at the casino. This puzzled many on her dark, morose days. Some dealers were jealous. How could such a stoic, flat-chested woman outdo them at the tip box?

Another bit of the bizarre adding to the wedding day was Bob even being invited. White-haired, like so many others of his age, he was drawn to her table. Over eight years Carlee and Bob talked often, especially on her cheerful days, when smiles would escape her pretty face and light up the table.

Shelby, Bob's guest, wanted to know how he got invited to the wedding. She was a twenty-year-old college student in a nursing program. She worked part-time as a dealer. Starting only a few months ago, she quickly became fascinated with Carlee. Apparently, Shelby wished to be like Carlee. On a practical side Shelby wanted to draw the sizeable tips Carlee attracted. Dealers' wages were nothing outside of the tips they received. They earned way more money at a casino than they could at other jobs that didn't require a degree or special skill. Shelby learned about the wedding and yearned to attend. She just had to be there when her mentor married. Bob had received the invitation while playing at Carlee's table. Since dealers couldn't hand anything directly to the players, her pit boss handed Bob the invitation. Shelby, at a nearby table, had seen this and knew what it was.

When Bob played at Shelby's table when Carlee was on break, Shelby asked him if she could have a little chat with him when she went on her break. The chat had much sincerity and even some flirting. There was enough of both to grant pretty Shelby her wish; she would be Bob's wedding guest.

As they headed north, Bob told her he called Carlee the Road Warrior.

Over the years, he learned about the adventures of the Warrior. There were three separate meetings with deer. The first two resulted in dents only. The third totaled Carlee's car. She had the good fortune to escape unhurt. Bob made a comment that it must have been a terrifying incident. "Not really," Carlee replied. "I needed a new car anyway, too many miles." More evidence of bizarre Carlee.

The guest pumped Bob further. "You know, she only invited a few people from the casino. I think you were the only player. Why did she invite you?"

Over the years, Bob Wren had gotten to know Carlee a little outside of the casino. One of her many car adventures involved a red dashboard engine light a few miles from the casino. There was a Mazda dealer in the town. She pulled in. They told her they would check it out. Then they shuttled her over to work. That afternoon as she was dealing blackjack to Bob, he said, "You look like you're having a tough day."

"Yeah, I had car trouble on the way in. I just called the garage on my break. They can fix the car, but it won't be ready until seven o'clock. What am I going to do for three hours after work?"

Bob was ready to rescue her. "I'll treat you to an Italian dinner after work and then take you over to the garage."

"Let me think about it."

Her thought process deduced that white-haired old Wren was harmless, she would be hungry, she liked Italian, and what would she do instead?

Later she saw Wren and said, "I'll take a hit on the marinara sauce. See you at the door at four o." Bob told Shelby that the dinner led to several more over the years. That is how he learned so much more about this haunting nymph.

"Tell me more, Bob. What the hell is this about a carbuncle?"

"The carbuncle—later, but as for the rest, I don't know if I should be divulging more of what she told me. Carlee is a pretty closed person."

"Bob, I so admire her. I wish I was more like her."

"Shelby, did you ever think that maybe people like and respect her because she is real, genuine; she is herself. She's happy to be who she is. People trying to create their own image doesn't seem to work. Be you, Shelby. You have a lot going for you. Be you."

Shelby sat quietly for a while. Bob wondered if he should tell her that Carlee was born in the backseat of an Olds Eighty-Eight. Her dad dallied too long getting her mom to the hospital. Dad paced the roadside as two officers delivered a baby girl. Bob had asked Carlee if that is where the 'car' came from in her name. "No, Wren, I don't think so. I have four older sisters: Connee, Cathee, Cammee, and Carree." Then Carlee rattled off the names again and again. Each time faster and faster, all delivered with a wide grin and loud giggles. She repeated the litany faster and faster until it was all just gibberish. Then she quickly returned to her stoic demeanor.

This, Bob told Shelby. Shelby laughed and said, "I heard her do that, too, when she was asked about her sisters. She sounded like a maniacal witch, but she seemed to be having so much fun."

Bob then told Shelby about the day Carlee seemed so jumpy when dealing cards. When asked what the trouble was, she only responded, "Spiders, spiders."

Later, Carlee explained. That morning she had almost ran off the road when she discovered a spider crawling up her arm, headed for the sleeve of her t-shirt. She spied two more on the dashboard. Quickly jamming on the breaks, she pulled off on the shoulder, jumped out of her Mazda, and hopped up and down, screaming. One car, then another, and finally a county patrol car all clustered around Carlee. When anyone asked her what the problem was, she screamed, "Spiders, spiders, I think they want to kill me." The disbelieving deputy investigated and found a spider's nest underneath the passenger's seat. He cleaned it out and sprayed underneath the seat and the rest of the car with some Deet. An embarrassed Carlee thanked all, drove on, and was late for work. She made her son clean her car inside and out the next weekend, three times.

During one of their dinners Carlee told Bob she had a son, Cooper. When asked how she decided upon Cooper for a name, Carlee perked up, smiled, and gushed, "Long story. As you know, I love to drive. I guess it all goes back to my grandpa, my mom's dad. I spent a great deal of time with him and Grandma. He was much older than most of the grandpas of kids my age. He farmed until he retired. I spent summers on the farm. He taught me how to drive a stick shift when I was eleven. I could hardly reach the pedals or see over the steering wheel. I drove only on the farm. I loved it. I have loved driving ever since.

"When I was twelve, Grandpa and I watched a lot of movies he rented, anything that had old cars in it. In the movies I saw those California carhops. They had short skirts and flitted about on roller skates. I made Grandpa buy me roller skates, not too practical on a farm. The county deputies would catch me on the nearby tar road and bring me home and tell Grandma to keep me there.

"In junior high I wanted to be a mechanic. Grandpa helped me con the shop teacher into letting me join the boys' car mechanics club after school. That lasted four weeks. Even though I was flat chested, a few of the boys kept grabbing at my shirt in search of the little buds that were really there. They grabbed my butt, too. I never said a word. I waited. After a few weeks, two of them were holding some bolts in place. Somehow their grubby little fingers met with a heavy wrench, two whacks each. The shop teacher asked me what happened. I said he should ask the boys how and why it happened. The next day the boys, fingers in splints, said they didn't know anything as they glared at me. I didn't say a word.

"I told Grandpa about it that night. He gave me a pat on the back and said I should retire from the club while I was ahead."

Carlee told Wren that at thirteen, Grandpa let her drive him into town to go to the bank, the hardware store, and a few times to the liquor store for a case of Miller High Life.

Carlee went on to say that while she was in high school, Grandpa had some health setbacks after Grandma died of a stroke. Grandpa moved off the farm, which was taken over by one of Carlee's uncles. Grandpa moved into a retirement center. "I still visited with him and his friends there. I spent more time with those guys than the few high school friends I had. Those guys used to have a weekly poker game, nickels and dimes. Grandpa staked me to two dollars and asked me to sit in. Two hours later I had all the money in the game. Grandpa told me the next week there would be no more poker.

"His buddies made him invite that pretty little girl back. Over the next three years I must have made three hundred dollars. More than a few times I also managed to lift a bottle of beer or two from their stock. I think they knew but they just smiled.

"During my high school years, I was Grandpa's driver when he needed to go somewhere. Sometimes we just went for a drive. Sometimes I drove one or two of his buddies. Those guys enjoyed having me around, I guess." Bob reminded Carlee that they were having a nice ride down memory lane with Grandpa, but could she please get back to the name, "Cooper."

Bob added, "Carlee, you're usually short on words and closed about your past, but today you're a faucet of information on full open."

"You're the wordsmith, Wren. You must be contagious. Okay, the name. Grandpa said he had two regrets. One was he never rented a metal detector to find and dig up the old Packard-Capone car his dad, my great-grandpa, was said to have buried somewhere on the farm. He said Great-Grandpa made the mortgage payments during Prohibition by delivering moonshine. Toward the end of that era, Great-Grandpa heard that the T-men were coming. He buried the car somewhere in the pasture. The feds never found it. Grandpa said he was always going to find it and dig it up. Maybe someday I'll do it." Then Carlee went quiet. "You know, if I ever get money, I'll do it. Grandpa died; he can't. I will.

"The other thing Grandpa said he wanted to do was own the fanciest, most expensive Mini Cooper in the world. He was going to drive like James Bond in a souped-up Mini."

"Now I see," said Bob Wren, "Mini Cooper—Cooper."

Carlee smiled and said, "I couldn't name a kid Packard or Capone."

Bob didn't tell Shelby all of this, but he did tell her about Cooper's name. "Bob, what about Cooper's father?" Shelby queried.

"I asked her about that once. She said she was seventeen and a few months before graduation. Cooper arrived in November of that year. She said to this day she has told no one who the father is."

Later, at the wedding reception, Bob overheard a conversation among the locals who were still speculating about Cooper's paternity. He heard that she never seemed to have a boyfriend that lasted more than one or two dates, and those were few and far between. All denied having any knowledge about who Daddy might have been.

What Bob didn't tell Shelby was that during one dinner when Carlee was more loquacious than usual, she said, "Cooper's real beginning was in the backseat of a Cadillac Eldorado." She offered no further information when questioned.

Bob did tell Shelby that one of the road adventures Carlee had was with a semitruck. The driver cornered too sharply at a stoplight and clipped the front end of her Mazda, dents, no injuries. After that encounter the semi driver became a regular at Carlee's tables. He was a heavy tipper.

Bob then told Shelby about the chainsaw. Carlee had been driving along the highway—too fast—when she ran over a shiny flat object connected to a bigger piece of metal. She pulled over and checked her car for damage. None, apparently. She then walked back up the road to remove the junk from the highway. The piece of junk turned out to be a chainsaw. Carlee picked it up and tossed it in her trunk. The next week she sold it for thirty-five dollars at a pawn shop. In Carlee's own words, "A road warrior never knows when she will be attacked by huge semis or angry chainsaws."

Of course, there were other adventures. Of course, there had to be flat tires. Twice teenage boys stopped for the rescue. Once she ran over a skunk. Her Mazda reeked for weeks, even after a dozen washings that featured several cans of tomato juice and dozens of squeezed lemons.

"Are we near the church?" asked Shelby. "I need a pit stop."

"Not a church, remember, a drive-in movie theater," Bob reminded her.

After a stop at the Big Woods Diner, both noticed that the beautiful red late-September maples were disappearing. They were gradually replaced with tall green pines.

"How about more Carlee Road Warrior stories?" prompted the wedding guest.

Bob went on to tell the story that led to the wedding. "Of course, Car-

141

lee's lead foot invited intervention. In the first few years she had several warnings and two tickets. That got expensive. She must have behaved, got lucky, or had St. Christopher on her side. For the next four years, no stops."

Then Carlee told Wren she had some bad and good luck at the same time. Twice the same Minnesota Highway Patrolman stopped her for speeding, bad luck. She told him she searched for all the sad face she could muster and told the trooper how she was running late for work and that she would be docked points. Then she said she managed a tear or two and got off with a warning each time, good luck.

She promised the nice, good-looking trooper that she could and would slow down. Slowing down was apparently not in Carlee's genes. On her way home one evening the patrolman stopped her for a third time. "Miss," he said, "you have got yourself a ticket this time." He paused for what seemed like a full minute to Carlee. "Of course, instead of a ticket, we could discuss the issue over coffee at the Big Woods Diner up the road. I could educate you on the values of safe driving."

"You mean the place we just stopped at?" Shelby asked.

"Yes," Bob replied.

When the trooper mentioned stopping at the Big Woods Diner, Carlee responded, "Coffee? Don't drink it. My mother said it would stunt my growth. She must have been right. By the ninth grade I still had no need for a bra."

"Well, how about a glass of chocolate milk and a hamburger?"

"Calcium and protein—good. Let's talk."

That led to more safe driving instructions over the next few months. By the time he asked her to the '50s Classic Car Show at the State Fairgrounds, they were officially dating. This eventually led to the wedding. It also began Carlee's love of '50s rock and roll and a new music playlist for the ride to work.

After Bob related all of this, Shelby asked, "But I heard Carlee was engaged for a while. What happened there?" Bob told Shelby he had noticed what looked like a diamond engagement ring on Carlee's finger a few years back. He asked her about it. "Oh, that," she chirped. "Yeah, I guess so, maybe someday, maybe not. I'm not good at adult things, especially decisions. Then again, I'm not sure there is anything to decide."

A year or so later, over one of their Italian dinners, Carlee told Wren that the guy was okay and Cooper could use a father figure in his life other than her dad, since Grandpa wasn't around any longer. She told Wren that her dad intended insisted she give up driving and find a job closer to home.

Carlee had been there before, concerning Cooper. When she had Cooper and had just finished high school, her parents told her she could live in the basement of the family home. There were already two bedrooms and a bath down there plus a rec room that had a sink and refrigerator. Her parents bought her a kitchen range. They also agreed to provide daycare for her if she got a job.

Jobs in the area for unskilled labor, especially for women, were few and didn't pay well. After a year of waitressing Carlee's folks paid for a training course that enabled her to become a card dealer at the nearby Native American casino. Carlee's income did increase, but she was frustrated by the casino policy of sharing tips. She knew she took in more money than the other dealers.

Carlee was not one to sit back and let the world dictate to her. When the racetrack casino opened, despite the eighty-five-mile drive, Carlee applied for a job. It was a no-brainer for the casino. Carlee had experience and was good. It was a no-brainer for Carlee also; she could keep all of her tips. The road became a way of life that she was now reluctant to give up.

Carlee's vastly increased income afforded her a place of her own. She still wanted and needed her parents' support with Cooper; hence, she rented close to home and continued to drive. She enjoyed the driving, the self-time it gave her, and the music in her ears while on the road.

Bob and Shelby finally arrived at the Timberline Drive-in. The setting merited the name. Tall Norway pines provided the background. The huge movie screen blanketed the green sloping hill that stood behind. The warm, sunny day enhanced the scene. At the entrance gate, ushers dressed as traffic cops greeted each car. Wren's invitation labeled him VIP, and he was issued a ticket that read: Row A. Slot 32. It turned out to be front row almost center. The ushers told them to use the speaker on the post and let it hang from the car window.

When Shelby and Bob found the spot and activated the speaker, they heard '50s music. On the screen in front of them a live band played. The band's bass drum proudly displayed "The Jailhouse Rocks." They were the top throwback group in the five-state area. "I've heard of those guys. They must command more than a few bucks," commented Shelby.

Non-alcoholic beverages were served up by carhops. Carlee didn't get her roller skate girls because of the uneven parking lot that was necessary to have cars park at a twelve-degree angle rising toward the big screen. The carhops settled for cowgirl boots and hats to go with their short skirts, western shirts, and vests.

An emcee encouraged guests to partake of the beverages but discouraged the use of any alcohol they may have brought with them. "Remember, we will parade to the Lake County Fairgrounds for a reception after the ceremony. The parade will be escorted by the Minnesota State Highway Patrol."

Getting all the cars in place took some time. The guests listened to the band while they waited. Then the movie screen visual switched from the band to the arrival of a white Cadillac Coupe DeVille. The convertible took a position facing the rows of cars. Then a procession of four bridesmaids entered the picture. According to the program issued by the ushers, they were Carlee's sisters: Connee, Cathee, Cammee and Carree. They wore maroon and beige A-line dresses and held similarly colored bouquets of asters and mums with a ribbon of pansies in their hair. The bridesmaids seated themselves on the back and sides of the rear seat with their feet resting on it.

Following the procession of sisters, four male friends of the groom, dressed in Minnesota Highway Patrol uniforms, rode in on two golf carts. Two of them knelt on the Caddy's trunk behind two of the sisters; the other two stood on wooden boxes outside of the Cadillac adjacent to the other sisters. The governor was said to have signed off on permission for the use of uniforms and patrol cars for the wedding.

The media were out in full force. Newspaper, radio, and TV were represented. Dozens of guests abandoned their cars and moved up close, hoisting cell phones to record the scene. The videos ended up on every means of social media in existence.

The arrival of the minister followed. He walked onto the scene under a canopy supported by long poles held aloft by two boys and two girls dressed in choir gowns. The minister was a fully ordained vicar of the Church of the Road. The Church of the Road billed itself as a traveling ministry that was available at campsites, racetracks, car rallies, county fairs, parade grounds, and any other group who paid its price. The minister always drove to the affair in an auburn 1930s Roadster.

Next to arrive was the groom. Lights and siren and a Minnesota Highway Patrol car delivered him. He exited the car and entered the Caddy, standing on the back seat floor facing the rows of guests.

Then a convertible Mini Cooper arrived with Carlee seated above the back seat. Her dad was at the wheel. When they stopped next to the Caddy, Dad escorted daughter out of the Cooper and into the Coupe DeVille next to the groom.

The minister stood in front of the Caddy on a garage ramp. Microphone in hand, he performed the ceremony. As soon as the bride and groom jointly shouted, "We do," a three-wheeled traffic cop motorcycle invaded the scene with lights and siren. Cooper dismounted and dashed into the Caddy. He then joined the hands of the newlyweds in handcuffs. The minister rang out, "Let no man put asunder." Instead of being a ring bearer, Cooper was a cuff bearer.

As horns honked and people cheered, the bride and groom raised their cuffed hands, forming an arch, and exchanged kisses. The knot had been tied.

The minister asked the drivers to orderly exit the grounds and follow in parade behind the wedding coach under the escort of the Highway Patrol. With lights and no siren, Bob and Shelby followed to the fairgrounds. As their car paraded, Shelby sternly intoned, "I haven't forgotten about the carbuncle."

Bob began the story as he had learned the bits and pieces from news reports, including an article in The New York Times and some from Carlee herself. A red, good-sized gemstone, often a ruby, was referred to as a carbuncle. One of the biggest and most infamous was the ruby known as the Mandalay Sunrise. The stone had been valued several times in the 1930s from one to fifteen million dollars. From time to time it was supposed to have been stolen from various private collectors who never publicly commented. Few facts were ever confirmed. Occasionally, the Mandalay stone popped up in the news and was said to be on the move. Nothing was ever substantiated. Reports of theft and secret ownership occasionally made the newspapers.

Nothing about the gem was heard from the 1980s until a few years previously. The new tale sprouted in Asia. The Mandalay Sunrise was on the move. After having been insured by an Indian entrepreneur from Mumbai for twenty million dollars by Lloyd's of London, the underground scuttlebutt screamed "heist." It was said to be moving from India to Marseilles, France; then it was rumored to be in London. A year ago, the tale resurrected itself in Toronto and was supposedly headed to a Midwest US billionaire. After that, all was silent.

Bob went on to tell Shelby that this next part he got mostly from Carlee. Carlee's love affair with driving always demanded a well-cared for car. Since money almost always exceeded the demand, she sought bargain help. Always a magnet for attracting males, she had offers. She said she was careful about whom she trusted. A guy she went to high school with offered to fix and fine-tune her Mazda. He charged her way below a reasonable price but asked if she'd go to dinner or at least for an occasional beer with him. The guy evidently hoped a few friendly visits might lead to his dream come true, winning Carlee's hand. Carlee's Mazda benefited from his care. The guy called himself Porsche. Besides working part time at a local garage, he hung out at the Native American casino in the area. He did odd jobs there as well.

Porsche thought of himself as a player and planned to score big one day. Maybe he thought money would win faint heart. This thought led him to toadying up to a money-flashing slick who seemed to have popped out of nowhere. Some said he came from Canada. At the casino, the big spender let it be known to Porsche that he needed to transfer a small package to the Twin Cities without a soul knowing about it. Porsche offered to drive it. Slick said no, people would know he drove there. It had to be done without anybody knowing what was going on.

Porsche told him about Carlee's drive to work at the harness track. He told the guy about his fixing Carlee's car and how he had a key to the Mazda. He could put the package in her trunk without her knowing about it. He also said he could provide a key to the slick so he could retrieve the package at the other end. Porsche wanted five hundred dollars to do the deed. He settled for two hundred and fifty.

On the day of the transport, the box was to be removed from Carlee's trunk before 5:00 p.m. in the racetrack parking lot. It was December, and it would be dark by then. That day was slow at the casino, and Carlee asked for and received an early out. She was supposed to work until 6:00 p.m., but at 4:30 she arrived at her car only to find the trunk lid up. She rounded the car and spotted a guy looking for something in her trunk. She yelled, "What the hell are you doing?"

The surprised guy backed his head out of the trunk, straightened, and smacked Carlee across the face. While blood ran from her nose, the culprit picked her up and tossed her in the trunk and closed the lid. He then got into her Mazda and drove off. The thug was supposed to have removed the package and transported it to Rochester, where he would turn it over to someone else.

Carlee said she had lost consciousness only for a few minutes, maybe more. All she knew was she was in a small, enclosed space. She fumbled around searching for her phone, her purse, anything that might be used to get her out of wherever she was.

She heard traffic sounds and then music. Her mind cleared. She started to remember: her open trunk, the guy, pain in her head, blood from her nose. Yes, her car. She must be locked in the trunk.

As she fumbled around in the trunk all she found was a small package, which she stuffed inside her bloody coat. Miles later heavy metal radiated

147

from the car radio. She yelled, screamed, and cursed. The louder and more she yelled the louder the banging of the bass guitars and drums got.

Twenty minutes or more passed when things got worse for Carlee. Something was crawling up the inside arm of her coat. She stiffened. Then something dropped on her face and headed for her neck. "Spiders, oh God, spiders." She slapped, clawed, screamed, kicked, and kicked some more trying to roll over. She kicked in every direction she could.

In the process she must have kicked out a taillight. Her louder screams had gotten the attention of her kidnapper. He turned his head to yell at the trunk for the little bitch to shut her effing mouth. His carelessness caused the Mazda to swerve on the highway. The swerving car, sans right taillight, caught the attention of a highway patrolman sitting in a speed trap. Lights and siren produced a high-speed chase. The heavily patrolled area contributed to a three-patrol car Mazda hunt. In a matter of minutes with one patrol car in front, one beside, and one behind, the kidnapper gave up. All he said at the time was, "Lawyer." After securing the driver, the officers popped the trunk to rescue a screaming, hoarse, terrified blonde. The screaming stopped.

Apparently in shock, the bloody-faced Carlee just sat there staring, clutching her arms over her bloody coat. The officers tried to help her out of the trunk. She wouldn't budge. The statue wouldn't speak. Paramedics tried to coax her out of the car. Finally, they physically removed her and put her in an emergency vehicle. She didn't seem to be injured, no blood except for the nosebleed, which had long stopped. They could find no broken bones. Her vitals were sound. After twenty minutes of silence and still clutching her chest, she blurted out, "I am not saying a word until my boyfriend is here."

One of the highway cops moved closer for a better look. He said, "I think I know who she is and who she means. I saw her with him at a classic car show."

An hour later Carlee's highwayman arrived at the Stockholm County Sheriff's Office. When her hero arrived, Carlee told how she discovered the guy digging in her trunk and how she ended up there. Then she unclasped her arms from her chest, opened her jacket, and produced a little box. "I think he was looking for this. I never saw it until now. It was dark in the trunk."

By then the FBI had been called in because of the kidnapping. They arrived quickly from their new Brooklyn Center fortressed offices. The agent opened the box. "My God, I think this might be the Mandalay carbuncle we have been told to be on the lookout for."

The kidnapper, evidently realizing he was involved in much more than the transfer of a package, talked. "Hey, I was only told to unlock the trunk, find the box, take it to Rochester, and leave it with a guy at a Kwik Trip there."

Carlee's hero, a quick thinker, made some calculations: ruby—stolen—reward. He walked away, discreetly got out his cell phone, and called a noted Twin Cities lawyer and told the story. Carlee's hero told her not to say more until the lawyer arrived. The lawyer was at the sheriff's office in forty-five minutes.

And so the story went. Porsche, Dennis Plate, was arrested. He said he would testify against the fancy dude from the casino if they could find him. They never did. Porsche pleaded guilty and was given a suspended sentence, community service and parole. Worst of all for him, he realized he had no chance with Carlee.

Carlee's new lawyer arranged a reward settlement with Lloyd's of London for her, a healthy percentage of twenty million. Of course, that took almost a year.

When Gus finished telling all this to Shelby, she said, "So that's how they could afford this wedding."

"Yes," replied Bob. "Carlee's lawyer got a juicy cut. Then he set up a trust fund for Cooper that ensured a college education and a large sum that would be turned over to him at the age of thirty. A financial agent from a major investment firm was to handle Cooper's trust. Carlee also had the same agent manage her funds."

At the fairgrounds the Jailhouse Rocks played on. Grills, aglow with charcoal embers, were sizzling with hamburgers, hot dogs, sausages, and skewers of vegetables. Bowls of chips, dips, and fruit salad were heaped on a picnic table. Joining them were trays of vegetables displaying a Minnesota garden harvest. A mound of tinfoiled baked potatoes begged to be popped open. A variety of condiments, butter, oils, and sauces were at hand. Urns of ice water, coffee, tea, and lemonade were available. This last added more to the bizarreness of the day, a dry Minnesota wedding.

On a separate table was a cake that resembled Carlee's Mazda, with a frosted bride in white sitting in the trunk. Next to the car trunk was a tan and brown–frosted highway patrolman.

The food caterers in attendance were the same carhops from the drive-in. Under their guard was another table piled high with wedding gifts and what looked like a glove compartment from a car containing wedding cards. Among the cards was a generous gift of a lifetime AAA membership for Carlee, compliments of Bob Wren and guest.

After the consumption of too much of the picnic, cake, and a mingling with the guests, Bob and Shelby were ready for a return road trip. They kissed the bride, hugged the groom, and said goodbye, wishing them both happiness.

On the drive back, Shelby said, "I heard Carlee quit the casino."

"Yes, they bought a house in Middleton, Minnesota. Carlee's patrolman arranged an interview for her with medical dispatch. She got the job and now delivers medicine and medical supplies on an emergency basis. She is on call five days a week, twenty-four hours each day. She covers the northern two-thirds of Minnesota and the northern third of Wisconsin. It pays well. She will drive a company car, a Mini Cooper. They told her some days she wouldn't drive at all; other days she might do four hundred miles or more. She will be paid for her time behind the wheel and won't have to cover car expenses. That alone should reduce her car insurance by two-thirds. She will have more time with Cooper and her own road warrior."

"Where do you suppose they will drive to on their honeymoon? The North Shore?" asked Shelby.

Bob laughed, "Oh, no road trip. They are flying to Hawaii. Carlee has never flown or seen the ocean."

Indeed, a most bizarre bride, courtship, and wedding.

Kamikaze

Two women who appeared to be in their mid-forties made their way to a shaded spot with fewer monuments in the area. The maple trees lined out a cove that housed great stones for an entire family. They spread a blanket under a shady maple. They tossed two pillows atop the blanket, and they placed the picnic hampers they brought with them next to the pillows. Then they moved in front of a black granite stone with an angel carved on its face, perhaps a guardian angel. They knelt down, bowing their heads and making the sign of the cross. After a few minutes of silence they returned to the blanket and unpacked the hampers, taking out carrots, celery, dip, two peanut butter and jelly sandwiches, Tupperware containers filled with fruit, two Rice Krispies bars and two wine glasses. Then out of one hamper came a corkscrew and a bottle of white wine, Sancerre Sauvignon Blanc, expensive. They settled the wine into an ice bucket and left it to chill.

The two were attractive. The blonde wore sandals. Above them extended model-length legs and a pricey-looking outfit that featured bridal white shorts and a baby blue top. Her blonde hair flowed over her shoulders. She carried herself with a slow confidence that suggested authority.

The redhead was shorter by a few inches. She was no less attractive. She, too, wore sandals and similar attire, all black. Her rich auburn hair flowed down over her back. She also carried herself with confidence but moved with much more command, a woman in control.

This was the fourth consecutive year they had met at the cemetery to exchange news, enjoy a picnic, and pay homage. They looked to be two old friends not intimidated by each other's beauty and presence. They appeared to be catching up with the past. The conversation seemed to have a sense of solemnity about it; smiles, yes, but not much laughter. Sunshine with low humidity and cool shade presented a day worthy of celebration and a day to pay homage. Yet here they were in a cemetery, the home of the dead.

"I never knew his name until we started coming here," said the green-eyed redhead. Her name was Catherine Boone. Her married name was Erickson, but after she divorced, she reclaimed her maiden name. She was never called Catherine or even Cathy; from the age of two it was always Rusty.

"We only knew him as Kamikaze when we were growing up," added Honey Holms, the blue-eyed blonde. When she married in 1969, she had retained her maiden name, unusual at that time. Her birth certificate listed her as Kristina, but her hair had rechristened her Honey from a young age. "I only learned his name about eight years ago when visiting my folks. As kids, all anyone ever called him was Kamikaze."

Both had grown up in Middleton, Minnesota. Honey, after high school, did two years of junior college before becoming a TWA stewardess, as they were called then. She was intelligent and charismatic besides having stunning pinup features. She allowed her fine figure to do most of her talking. She didn't say much. Most took her for a dumb blonde, but she was sharp. Quietly, she let others believe she couldn't think for herself; however, she was far ahead of them. She used her mind to work her way up into a management position at TWA. She left the airline to start her own company offering instruction to women who were interested in modeling and fashion. Her company offered the skills she had used to work her way through the glass ceiling. She offered young women a way to be far more than attractive mannequins. She grew up around money. Her father owned a highly successful manufacturing company. She knew money, how to handle it and how to make it.

Rusty, too, grew up moneyed. Her family owned an independent department store in Middleton. She worked in the store, women's clothing, before she was of legal age to do so. First, it was the stockroom, and then the sales floor. She was a natural. Each day on the sales floor she wore a different outfit from off the rack. She sold many of that same style each day. Her hair, pretty face, green eyes, and dynamite body made a success-ful sales pitch. After majoring in fashion design in college she moved to LA and, like a sponge, absorbed more about the fashion world. Within a matter of years she developed her own line: chic leisure clothing based on attractive sportswear for women. Intelligence that exceeded her looks led to success.

"Do you remember when we first saw him?" asked Rusty as she sipped her Sancerre Sauvignon Blanc.

"It was at the Municipal Swimming Pool, wasn't it? What were we, thir-teen or fourteen? Remember how he would cannonball off the high board in our direction? He always tried to splash us. All afternoon he would jump and make weird noises as he used his hands to splash more water our way," reminisced Honey.

"He did that day after day, most of the summer. He splashed water on the towels we laid on. He wanted to get our suits wet. He knew we rarely got into the water. The next summer he got even more aggressive. I remember he got you totally wet in your white one piece."

"Was it because he yelled those weird noises when he jumped that ev-eryone called him Kamikaze?" asked Honey.

Rusty shrugged. "I don't know why he was called that. Remember, he wasn't around just at the pool. He rode his bicycle everywhere. Like a dive bomber, he would speed up and almost hit people, especially young girls, before he would veer off and make that weird-sounding noise. I don't think I ever heard him speak."

"He wasn't only around in summer. In winter he terrorized all of us, especially you, Rusty, at the skating rink in our neighborhood. Then there was the night he chased you on skates way out on Lake Germain yelling those weird noises and pointing to your hair. When he caught you, he dumped you in a snowbank and rubbed snow in your hair like he was put-ting out a fire. He really liked your hair, which you were always showing off," Honey teased.

Rusty sharply retorted, "He liked my hair, but he couldn't keep his eyes off of your chest at the pool. You fully earned the chant directed at you around the town that summer, 'Honey bunny, with the awful brafull.' You made sure everybody could see how well you were endowed."

"My chest wasn't the only source of local poetry, Rusty, dear; don't forget those super tight jeans and short shorts, 'Who likes short shorts?' I think you worked at earning the catcalls that followed your tail, 'Hey, full-moon Boone.'" Honey smiled as she said this.

"We were little hellians then. Do you think we were asking for what happened?" Honey asked.

"Honey, we were just kids, having fun, not sure what our young blossoming bodies were all about. The music on the radio encouraged us, "Short Shorts," the movies aimed at a teen audiences, Bikini Beach, Beach Blanket Bingo. No one talked to us about any of this. Our mothers never warned us."

"But we must have been aware of something. Why else did we sneak our secret bikinis and halter tops out of the house so our parents wouldn't know, Rusty?"

"I think it was our dads that we didn't want to know about those forbidden fruits," chuckled Rusty.

"Rusty, we were pretty naïve, but I don't think the behavior of teenage girls has changed much today. Oh, I know they know a hell of a lot more about stuff we weren't aware of, but are they more endangered today? I have often been told we had it easier and safer growing up than kids today."

They both sat in silence for awhile. Then Rusty poured more wine as Honey held the glasses. The two clinked glasses and nodded toward the nearby granite angel. They sipped the wine, then munched on the fruit and veggies. They devoured the peanut butter sandwiches. The sandwiches were Honey's idea. "Reminds me of those days that brought us to this place. We were just kids," she said.

"Honey, I don't think teen girls are more at risk today then we were, but I think they are more aware of the risks and what the risks are. Just more pressure for them, I guess. Since I never had any kids, I don't know about parenting today. You have two daughters. What did you tell them?"

"Whenever I told them anything, I would get, 'Okay, Mom,' and rolling eyes, but I was scared to death. I did tell them about us. They were shocked. At least the eye rolling stopped whenever I gave them a lecture."

Rusty stood up. "Enough of this negative stuff. We are here to toast Kamikaze." She lifted a refilled glass of Sauvignon Blanc toward the granite monument. Honey did the same. "To our guardian angel." They both drank and sat back down and nibbled on carrots and fruit. Honey broke out the Rice Krispies bars, another reminder of those days gone by.

"Rusty, do you remember all the different bicycles he had? I remember. It seemed like he had a new one every four or five months. They were always the latest, most advanced, and expensive ones on the market."

"Yes," Rusty chimed in. "He had English bikes, fast, lightweight. He dressed like a European bicycle racer."

Honey added, "He wheeled on those things like a maniac, even in winter. I can still see him scaring kids, leaving them in his wake on a snowy day. He must have been some athlete. I never saw or heard of him losing control, crashing on the ice and snow of the poorly plowed streets of Middleton."

"His parents had money; those bikes were expensive. He must've been close to forty years old when we knew him. Remember his hair was starting to gray? We were about fifteen when it happened. The stories around town said he was a slow-developing kid who never learned to talk. Some said he understood people talking, but he never spoke."

"Yeah, I heard my parents say he was brain damaged. It had something to do with his birth. I don't think he was crazy like so many kids said. He never hurt anyone, but he sure as hell liked to scare people. He was always fixing up one bicycle or another."

Rusty jumped up on his gravestone. Sitting atop it, her legs dangled over the etched angel. "It was a good thing for us that he wasn't crazy. I guess it was also a good thing that he was fixated on your chest."

"Rusty, are you still jealous?" teased Honey. "Don't forget he liked your hair and your butt, too. You know, that summer I often felt weird walking home from the pool. Remember, I kept saying that someone was watching us? You said if anyone was watching, it was Kamikaze trying to get a last look at us. You pointed out that he wasn't always on his bike. Sometimes we saw him walking near our houses. It shouldn't have been Kamikaze we were worried about. I never even knew that groundskeeper. I didn't even know he existed. If he had showed up in church, I wouldn't have known him. I guess he was one of many people we failed to see, to know they existed. He didn't play a part in what we thought of as our world."

Rusty lamented, "We were so into ourselves, all worried about cute guys that we tried to impress. We were so critical of other girls who we thought tried to challenge us on our looks. We were mean to those who offered us competition, but, boys and girls, people in general who fell into that no account category, we didn't see. They didn't exist."

"Rusty, we might have been better off if we had seen him, said hello, or just acknowledged his existence. We might have been more aware of his whereabouts."

Now back on the blanket, Rusty reached into her hamper and produced a small bouquet of short-stemmed roses. As she pulled off a petal and sniffed it, she said, "You know, I was somewhat aware of him. I did see him at the pool ogling us through the bushes near the fence where we laid out every day on our towels. I remember thinking, 'What a loser. Can't he find some women to ogle instead of us kids?' However, when I felt someone was following us that summer, he never entered my mind. He had returned to invisible."

"But, Rusty, no one on foot was following us that day. Remember when we got close to our neighborhood, we often ducked into the thicket of bushes in Landy Park? We would check to make sure our skirts and shorts weren't too short; we would unroll the tops of them on the way home. We would button up our blouses, and oh, my God, I can't believe we actually did this. We would shed our fabulous halter tops and put on bras and t-shirts. We had a lot of changes of emergency clothing in those bulky pool bags."

"I don't think those things triggered it. Since that day I have read about people like him. He would have done what he did sooner or later. But that day as we got close to the thicket of bushes to shed our halter tops, we saw

156

that puppy on the sidewalk. It was hurt. You said, 'Oh, poor doggy,' and bent over to see what was wrong. I did the same."

Just then a van had pulled up to the curb and the side door flew open. A man stepped out and slapped rags over the faces of the two girls as they were bent over the puppy. The girls passed out. The man quickly dragged them into the van, motor still running, and slowly drove away. There were no apparent witnesses on the street or in the park.

"Rusty, you made it all come back. I woke up in that van, my hands and feet were tied, and my mouth gagged. I wet my shorts."

When the girls failed to come home that evening the authorities were notified. By the next day every radio station within a hundred miles had broadcast alerts about the missing teenage girls. The Middleton Times ran a full story. Twin Cities TV stations flooded Middleton. The city police, the Wilson County Sheriff's Office, the Minnesota Bureau of Criminal Apprehension, and the FBI became involved. For three full days there was no sign of the teens. Panic among teenagers and parents alike ran rampant.

"Remember when we got back home our families told us how scared they were for us and how much they prayed for our safety and return?" said Honey as she sipped more wine.

Rusty laughed. "My mom had stopped going to Mass on Sunday some years before that. She hasn't missed a single Sunday since."

Honey glanced toward the road where their cars were parked. "I suppose people wonder what we are doing here having a picnic in a cemetery. I don't care to explain. I almost never talk about what happened, except to my daughters. I'm glad we decided to meet here every year on this date. I guess I needed to face the issues more than I had. This is so much better than phone calls."

"I know, Honey. Since we started this I rarely have had the nightmares I had before." Rusty slid over and gave Honey a hug.

"God, I'm having a flashback," said a terrified Honey. "I can see it happening. I looked over at you, Rusty Boone, and you were naked. Your hands and feet were tied. Then I looked down and discovered that Honey Holmes was also naked and as encumbered as you.

"Can you imagine that? Before he left us each evening he gave us our clothes back. He always left us food and emptied the chamber pot. When he left, he made sure we were tied up with washline rope. Our hands were tied in front of us. Our feet were hobbled. But we could move around some. We were tethered to the pole in the middle of the shack. That pole looked like it held up the shabby ceiling. When he was there, we had to take turns being naked," said Honey.

"Yes, he told us if the untied naked one ran away, he would kill the other. I believed him," said Rusty.

Honey broke in, "And then he would tell us what he planned to do to us. He would start groping whichever one of us had no clothes on at the time. Remember, as soon as his hands came alive your tongue started wagging. You yelled, swore, and threatened. We both told him if he did anything more, we would haunt his soul for the rest of his life. He would never shut his eyes without seeing us coming for him in his sleep with knives bigger and sharper than the one he threatened us with. You screamed that every member of our families would do the same. Your voice sounded like a devil possessed. I even got scared."

"Boy, do I remember," said Rusty, now getting worked up. "I'm sure I actually scared him. I screamed so loud. I swore using every word I ever heard. I'm sure I made up a few more. I told him that if he did any more of the things he promised us he would do to make us happy, I would kill him. I would cut his guts out inch by inch, slowly, piece by piece with my cuticle scissors. And if he killed us we would haunt his soul, if he had one."

"I think you really did scare him, Rusty. I don't think he knew what to do with us except look at us naked. His big plans were going up in the flames of your voice from hell, the redheaded devil."

"You know, Honey, I often wondered why each night he tossed us our clothes. We got pretty adept at dressing each other despite being tied up. Do you think he was worried we would be cold at night? Or do you think my threats made him be a little bit kinder to us?"

The wine was gone and the two women began to gather the remains of the picnic. "On that third—or was it the fourth night?—I figured he would

158

either kill us or finally carry out his erotic dream. He had both of us naked. I was so scared. Rusty, I was sure it was over. I didn't even see or hear Kamikaze kick in the door and bash him over the head with that tree branch. That groundskeeper never saw what hit him."

"I know, Honey. I, too, was sure we were goners. I watched in amazement as Kamikaze used the washline rope to tie him up. Then he ripped off the guy's shirt and used it as a blindfold. He found our clothes and tossed them to us. He untied us. Remember all the miming he did?"

"Yeah, it was so bizarre. Rusty, I thought of it like a game of charades in that shack. He couldn't or wouldn't talk. His finger went to his lips like he didn't want us to tell anyone. He pointed to himself. Then he did it again and again until we told him we wouldn't tell anyone about what he did."

"Right then he started to make noises. Honey, I thought they resembled the sound of a siren. Then he spun his hands around his head, flashing lights? And then the finger in front of his mouth again."

"He was saying, 'don't tell anyone it was me.' He wasn't stupid like most of us believed. Rusty, I really think he knew his life would change if he became a hero."

"Boy, it all comes back again. He found some more rope and walked over to us. We had our clothes on by then. He showed us the rope and made gestures like he would tie us up again. He then mimed dialing a phone and made his siren noises and spun his hand over his head like the flashing lights of a cop car. We nodded our heads yes. He tied us up and left."

"Rusty, how in the hell did he ever make it known to the Wilson County Sheriff's Office to look for us there? He must have erased all traces of his footprints, and bicycles tracks as well. The cops never reported finding any. The cops never mentioned him at all."

"Honey, I know how he did it. He took our pool bags and everything else with him. I read the newspaper accounts of how they found us. There were rocks thrown through a few windows a mile away. Deputies then found bits and pieces of our pool bag items that led them to the shack near the creek."

"Breadcrumbs, Rusty, like Hansel and Gretel."

"Honey, he was not a kook or a terrorist like we all thought. He was just a kind man who liked to have fun. He was a guardian sngel who saved two brassy teenage girls who thought they were hot stuff, two sexy fifteen-year-olds who wanted the world to know who had the best bodies. We just thought about ourselves. If the town knew what a hero he was, his peaceful, simple life would have been changed forever."

The two women walked around and looked at all the other stones in the tree-lined alcove. It was really a private family plot within the cemetery. Honey traced the angel on the beautiful granite stone with her finger. She said, "He must have been following us home often that summer. He must have been watching and following the groundskeeper following us. He had to have seen that dirtbag grab us and drive away. I'll bet he followed on his bike as fast as he could. The newspaper said the shack was five miles out of town near Spring Brook in a wooded area."

"Honey, it must've taken Kamikaze three days to track him all the way to that shack. If he knew where we were being held, he would have rescued us sooner."

"Rusty, the rest of that summer he still splashed us at the pool and smiled. I know I always smiled back and waved, but not in a flirting way. I think he knew we were thankful and would keep his secret."

"I recognized his smile, too. After we got kidnapped, we didn't get to go to the pool often. Our parents wouldn't let us. We only got there when an adult drove us and picked us up."

"I know. Kamikaze was always on his bike ready to follow us. He watched until we safely got in a car."

Middleton and the rest of the world would never know who the guardian angel was. The Wilson County Sheriff's Office, the FBI, and everyone else believed the girls' story about the rescue. They told the truth about everything right up to the point when the door blasted open. The Guardian Angel, as he was described in the press, was said to have had on a ski mask and gloves. He was said to have rushed in and clubbed the kidnapper, tied him up and left, a true guardian angel. "One of the FBI agents asked me if the angel had wings," Rusty said. "I looked at him and said 'Yes,' as I

160

winked. That last part never got reported to the newspaper."

"Just a dumb blonde and a loud-mouthed redhead," laughed Honey.

"But it changed our lives. Although we were assaulted, we didn't get raped, but we were never the same. We weren't even allowed to go to the pool or anyplace else that summer unless an adult was with us," Rusty said. "Our parents changed phone numbers; the press never let up. At school that fall kids basically shunned us or hounded us for details. We both had nightmares for years and years. What a mess."

After Christmas that year both girls were sent to separate boarding schools outside of Middleton. "At least you applied yourself, Rusty, and boosted your grades and test scores. You didn't let the crap we went through keep you from getting into a good college in California. You thrived in fashion design. Today you must be worth almost as much as your father."

"Honey, you didn't get derailed either. After two years of junior college you snagged a stewardess gig with TWA. You moved up the ladder, and look at you now. You run a profitable consulting firm in Minneapolis. You teach women how to smash the glass ceiling. You have a beautiful home on the lake in Wayzata and two wonderful daughters. We owe a lot to him," she said as she pointed to the black granite stone, now with a vase of red roses next to it.

"I know whenever I would get back to Middleton in the years shortly after, I would still see Kamikaze zipping up and down the streets blitzing people as he rode on a newly updated, imported bike. His family saw to it that he was king of wheels."

"Honey, do you remember that after he saved us, he always held his hand over his heart whenever he saw us?"

"I remember." The two packed up their picnic gear and made sure no litter was left behind. They knelt in front of the tombstone with the boldly sketched guardian angel on it.

Robert K. Ulmer
April 3, 1930 - August 27, 1981

Picnic hampers in hand and moving toward their cars, the two met up with a well-dressed woman, perhaps twenty years older than they. The woman said, "Please excuse my interruption, but I have to confirm my deduction. I presume you are Kristina Holmes and Catherine Boone. My name is Julie Ulmer Lind, Bob's sister." She pointed to the stone the two women had just left. "Two years ago, the groundskeeper here, such a wonderful man, called me and told me that he had observed two women who came to Bob's grave on this date two years running. I missed you last year, but I got here in time this year."

"Oh, Ms. Lind, I suppose you want to know why we do this?" asked Rusty.

"No, and please call me Julie; I know why you're here. On behalf of Bob and our entire family, I want to thank you. Thanks to you two, Bob was able to continue his happy life in Middleton in a manner of his own choosing. Notoriety would have changed his life.

"Complications at birth affected his brain, making it impossible for him to live as most of us do. You respected Bob. We suspected his part in your getting free from that awful man. Bob had his way of communicating with us. He didn't speak, but he understood most of what was said. He made us take him to the trial when you two testified. You are two gutsy women. I saw Bob exchange smiles with you two while he held his hand over his heart. Those were the only smiles I saw on your faces that day.

"After Bob died, peacefully of natural causes, I found his treasure trove in the garage where he kept and worked on his bicycles. He had clipped all the newspaper stories with pictures of you two. I saved them, but I didn't bring them. But, here. Bob had these with the newspaper stories. I am pretty sure they are yours. Take them if you want. Bob surely felt you two were special."

Julie handed over one green and one blue halter top. Honey took the blue, and Rusty took the green. After a moment or two of shock the two looked up to see that Julie was already at her car. Both yelled to her, "Thanks."

"You know," said Rusty, "I had forgotten that the cops never found these in the shack or along with the pool bag items strewn on the path that day."

"Rusty, I'm ashamed to admit I often wondered what happened to my favorite show-off piece and wondered, too, if we had not worn those that day, maybe we wouldn't have been attacked."

Rusty took Honey by the shoulders and looked straight into her eyes. "Honey, how we looked, what we wore that day didn't cause our abduction. What girls and women wear never has been and never will be an invitation to anything. The blame is on him, not you or me. People are responsible for their own actions. No excuses."

Honey broke into tears and clasped Rusty tightly. Finally, she said, "Thanks, Rusty, I am working on it." The two women promised to keep in touch and return next year, same time, same place to honor Bob Kamikaze.

Stories from

The
Old
Man

The Saving Grace of Road Apples

The Old Man had just gotten off the phone. He felt bad. He had been talking to a good friend. He met Oscar thirty-eight years before while teaching in South America. Oscar was back in the States for a visit. Like The Old Man, he, too, was now retired. Retirement for him was drastically different from The Old Man's. Oscar was living with his wife in Southeast Asia. He met her there while honoring one of his many overseas teaching contracts. The sadness came not from retirement for either or from the many health issues old age brings on, but because Oscar was denied a retired life in the US.

"Old Man," Oscar said over the phone, "I really enjoy being back in the US, but my visits here have to be short and few in number. We can't afford to live here. We are fine where we are and can last until I'm eighty-eight if we don't have any major financially draining issues. At least, that is what my investment people tell me. But in the US we wouldn't last ten years."

The Old Man was just sick as he empathized with his friend. Like The Old Man, Oscar loved baseball. The two had seen at least a dozen major league games together over the years. Many of the games were in Minnesota when Oscar came to visit. The other games were across the US before Oscar married. He had called to say they could not afford a stop in Minnesota this trip. The Old Man reflected even more on the phone call. Oscar was one of the best people he knew, certainly the best history teacher he had ever witnessed in action. Oscar's one major imperfection: he was a Yankee fan. Now living in Asia, Oscar couldn't even follow his Yankees on TV. Being a Yankees fan was a fault The Old Man forgave. After all, Oscar grew up in the state of New York. The Old Man could forgive the errors of a misguided youth, but really, hadn't he ever heard of the Mets, or the Giants, or even the Dodgers?

As The Old Man sat in his recliner after the call, he thought about his years teaching with Oscar. When The Old Man first went below the equator, he envisioned a life of continuous overseas teaching. He loved the students, the travel, the new friends. His second two-year contract was even better; the pay had improved by leaps and bounds. That was the life: motivated students, inexpensive travel, outstanding cuisine, and new friends.

The Old Man thought awhile and concluded he was lucky to have done it the way he did. He was lucky to be where he was now. As he listened to his favorite easy listening music channel, he thought about how he abandoned the itinerant overseas teaching life. The decision to return to his old school in Minnesota when his five-year leave was up had been the best choice.

The process started during his second two-year contract. He met his new principal, a great guy. Sean had been all over the world teaching English and being a principal. He had stories from six continents. "When I was in Kenya," he would say, and then go on and tell one great humorous story after another. "One time I was working in Barcelona," he'd start, and more stories would pour out. There were stories from the Philippines, Japan, and from Ireland. He even did two years in a remote region of Alaska. He spoke highly of friends he worked with, one now in Athens, another in Libya, then there was a gal in Japan he longed to see again. The locations and the stories appeared endless.

That's what got The Old Man thinking. Here was Sean some thirty years overseas. He spoke of carpets, paintings, and pieces of furniture he fell in love with, some of which he purchased. When he left that particular location, he had it shipped to one of his retired friends in places like Malaysia, Costa Rica, Portugal, any place with a cost of living that could be supported by US dollars they managed to save.

Saving for itinerant sophists was not easy. International teachers were in grave danger of addiction, not of booze or drugs, but travel. Some of the travel was inexpensive, depending on the economy of the country visited. Some places were much more expensive, such as Australia, East Asia, and northern Europe. Travel eats money like a grizzly eats before winter.

The Old Man remembered. He remembered a lot. That's what old men do, and then they tell you about it, two, three, or ten more times if you don't watch out. He remembered looking at Sean, who was his senior by about fifteen years. He wondered if that's what he would become, a traveling minstrel with a thousand and one stories and no home.

The Old Man had studied his overseas colleagues. Many of them had three or more different overseas postings, two years here, two years there, sometimes even four, rarely more than that in any one place, nomads.

The Old Man knew that in the last year of his contract he had decisions to make. Sean said he would have to retire to a country where his dollars would stretch. The Old Man heard a fifty-five-year-old elementary teacher say he had purchased his retirement place in Malaysia because he could afford to live there. The Old Man recalled that for the first time in his life, he had to do better planning for retirement. He had a few dollars in an insurance investment. He had a few bucks in stock. The father of one of his former students was his broker. "I owe you," he had said, "for what you did for my kids in school." Then The Old Man had considered his Minnesota Teacher Retirement plan. He had fifteen years in already, but unless he did at least another fifteen, that would not carry him very far. Then The Old Man remembered that his thoughts back then turned to health insurance. He would never be able to retire in an industrial country that had socialized medicine. They wouldn't let him stay. Medical costs in the US were prohibitive without insurance and Medicare. Could he continue his joyous journey in overseas teaching?

In October of that last year The Old Man took a four-day weekend trip to Blumenau in southern Brazil. The area was settled by a large number of German immigrants. The place was known for its Oktoberfest and its many fondue restaurants; there were many German Swiss there as well.

On Friday evening he visited the beer garden and the wurst tent, where he consumed more sausage than he should have. He felt like he was back home in Wilson County. The Old Man wondered if that was the last time he drank a glass of beer. He sat all evening and listened to several polka bands and watched men and women glide across the floor to a schottische or polka wearing traditional German dresses and lederhosen. He went in search of German chocolate cake, which he never found.

Now he sat back in his recliner and closed his eyes. He could just about smell it. That next morning in Blumenau he got up early to find a good spot on the street for the parade. He had borrowed a chair from the hotel. The German-themed floats, the polka bands atop a hayrack, he was back home. He never realized before, but he did enjoy the sound of a glockenspiel. And then the smell wafted his way. He loved it. It took him back to the farms of his youth in Wilson County. He had inhaled deeply as a few of the horses pulling the wagons dropped road apples. Horse shit. He was going home. He knew he would return to the fields of central Minnesota.

Now as he thought again of his friend Oscar, the sadness returned. The Old Man was retired, living comfortably, and just waiting for the Twins-Yankee game to begin on TV. He knew this invited more sadness. Perhaps not because of Oscar's retirement plight, but because the Twins couldn't beat the damn Yankees.

Useful, Still

The Old Man answered his phone. "Hi, it's Maia. I hate to ask a favor, but I just received word that an evening class I was waitlisted on just opened a spot. The class starts at six, and I can't take Roddy with me. Could you . . ."

"Problem solved, Maia. Drop him off. I have just cooked up my childhood favorite goulash. Roddy and I can eat, and then I can teach him about baseball as we watch the Twins game. Bring a few toys in case he doesn't like baseball."

"Thank you so much, Old Man; I owe you."

The Old Man met Maia while he was serving his three-week sentence in sub-acute care. He was sentenced for the felony of having knee replacement. Maia was the night duty nurse's aide. The Old Man had always been an early riser. Sometime between four and five he would awaken for the rest of that night. This prompted a trip to the bathroom. He needed help getting out of bed on the first days there. Maia was the one who answered his SOS. She was cheerful and friendly.

After The Old Man didn't need help getting out of bed to go to the bathroom, Maia still stopped in to see how he was doing. She would arrive at 5:00 a.m. and stay twenty to forty minutes visiting with The Old Man. The first day that she had answered his call for help, the on-duty RN made a face and said, "Damn, that old man again." All of the night staff referred to him as 'that old man.' Usually a few swear words accompanied the moniker.

So Maia asked The Old Man what he wanted to be called. Did he want a formal "mister," the name on his chart, or did he go by a nickname? She told him she resented her coworkers calling him "that old man."

"Maia," The Old Man replied, "tell you what. You just call me Old Man. Coming from you, I like it. But give the rest hell when that's how they refer to me. You're the only one I want to use that nice name."

Over the three weeks, or at least the five nights of those weeks that she worked, The Old Man got to know Maia. She would stop in his room at 5:00 a.m. She said she was efficient and got things done. She couldn't do things in the pokey way the other aides worked. She said, "I get my work done. Then I have time to visit with you. I like your style; you don't take crap from that bitchy night nurse. You seem like a nice guy."

Over the weeks The Old Man learned much more about Maia than she learned about him. Boy, did he learn. Her life was material for a soap opera. The first disaster of her life was revealed when he asked her how such a young girl got stuck working nights in his jail.

"A night shift is the only way I can make my life work. I'm a single mother with a three-year-old son. I can't afford regular day care, but I have a neighbor, Mrs. Berg, who likes Roddy. She takes him at night. She has an extra bedroom set up for him. I take him to her place at eight in the evening and pick him up at eight in the morning. She knows I don't have much money, so she doesn't charge much. Then I have Roddy the rest of the day."

"When do you sleep, Maia?"

"When I can, Old Man, when I can. I usually get an hour and a half between eight and ten before I have to be at work. Then when I get off at six, I drive close to Mrs. Berg's and grab an hour or more in the car before I pick up Roddy."

"Maia," said The Old Man, "you can't live on that little sleep."

"Oh, I make Roddy take a nap twice a day. I sleep some then, too. He sleeps with me. I always have an alarm handy so I don't oversleep. I catch up on sleep on my days off. I get to sleep the whole night. I have learned how to do that, sleep the nights I don't work. I guess I am so exhausted by then it makes it easy."

The Old Man squirmed in the chair that she had helped him into. "Lord, Maia, you can't survive that way."

"Old Man, what choice do I have? If I ever want to get anywhere and give Roddy a better life, I have to do this. Look at the time. I have to go. See you tomorrow. Don't let your prison guards get to you."

That was how The Old Man got to know Maia. Now Roddy was asking for more goulash. The little guy loved the elbow macaroni and tomato sauce with basil, oregano, and garlic. Of course, the hamburger led to his asking for more. A Rice Krispies bar, a regular donation from The Old Man's sister, topped off the meal.

Roddy seemed to enjoy the baseball game, too, at least for a while. Then he found his Legos to be of more interest. The Old Man had a good evening with Roddy. He thought the kid did, too.

During the weeks of confinement The Old Man learned more about Maia. She was the oldest of three. She and each of her siblings had different fathers. Her mom was not an easy woman to live with. Each daddy lasted at most three years. Her mom liked to party and couldn't hold on to the few jobs she was able to get. "I guess I was a young mother at the age of seven. For the next four years, basically, I was the mother to my brother, Earl, and my sister, Joleen. I changed diapers and fed them when we had the food. I begged food off the neighbors when we didn't. I did laundry and found a few places to get clothes for the growing Earl and Joleen. Then my mom overdosed and the court sent each of us kids to live with our fathers. None of them were fathers, really, just studs who liked to get women pregnant and move on. I ended up with my dad's sister in Reno, Nevada. That is where I spent my middle school years. They didn't know me and didn't want me. My cousins ignored me and my aunt called me a little bitch who would end up like her mama. I was older than my cousins and got three times as much housework as anybody else. I didn't mind that so much. I was used to it and was pretty good at it.

"Finally, my aunt got a lawyer who was able to get me shipped back to Minnesota to live with my grandmother on my dad's side. I started high school back in Minnesota, but I wasn't wanted there either. I got to be good friends with a girl, Sara, in my class. I spent more time at her house than at my grandma's. Then my usual luck, all bad, dropped in on me again. My friend's family moved to Wisconsin just beyond the St. Croix. For the next six months I was miserable.

"Old Man, I have to go," Maia said as 6:00 a.m. neared. "I will be back next week with another day in 'As the World Bashes Me.'"

The last week in subacute, a new episode in Maia's soap opera aired. "I hope you didn't feel too bad when I left last week. I should have told you that my friend Sara's move to the cheesehead state was actually a good break for me. We talked often on the phone, and I told her how bad things were with my grandma in St. Paul. Sara's folks had moved onto a five-acre lot in the country. After I spent a weekend with her there, her parents invited me to move in with them and finish high school there. My grandma was more than happy to let me go. I wonder if she still continued to get money from the county for me after I left. For me, it was Christmas in November."

"What happened next, Maia?" asked The Old Man.

"Nothing bad right then. I got a boyfriend, got better grades, and got accepted into a community college. All this happened even though I was diagnosed with ADHD. I never could sit still. I always have to be doing something. I can't seem to concentrate for very long. I got some help with all of that at school. I guess that's why I get my work done so fast. I'm like the Energizer Bunny, I can't stop. If I do, I drift and have a hard time getting back. They got me headphones, and I listen to classical music to block out interferences as I work and study."

"Maia, that sounds great. So how did all of this turn bad? It seems like you had a couple good years."

"I did. Do you think that poor choices and lack of common sense can be inherited, Old Man? I mean, I must have gotten these traits from my mom. Neither of us were any good when it came to picking males off the vine. The boyfriend I mentioned liked me well enough. I guess it wasn't me that he really liked. It was my body, sex, sex, and more sex. I think that is why he followed me to college. I got pregnant, and he got gone. He wanted me to get help and get an abortion. I told him I couldn't do that. That's when he left. But I did see to it that his name appeared on Roddy's birth certificate. I suppose I should get a lawyer and try to get child support, but I can't afford a lawyer."

Those a.m. sessions with Maia grew on The Old Man. He liked her, and she was good at her job. She helped him and made him comfortable. He enjoyed talking to her even though her biography was depressing. He felt her sadness. That she was a pretty twenty-two-year-old who helped start his day with some sunshine didn't hurt.

Before he was granted parole from his subacute care, he made sure Maia had his address and phone number. It was then they discovered that they were neighbors. Maia lived in a subsidized housing apartment just six blocks from The Old Man. He told her to stop and visit, bring the kid. "Maia, don't be afraid to call anytime you need anything."

After The Old Man got back home and Maia stopped in a few times with Roddy, The Old Man figured it was finally time to collect on his reputation. He taught high school English and speech for thirty years. Many students had thanked him for being such a strict and demanding teacher. They said they were well-prepared, and because of him, college was a breeze. More than a few of these students turned out to be lawyers.

The Old Man got on the phone one evening. When the ring was answered, he asked, "Do you know who this is?"

"Yes, I do. I have caller ID, but I would recognize your voice anywhere," answered Tom Ramler. "I bet you were browsing through your old grade books and discovered there was a paper I had not turned in. Now you want it, or you'll have all my diplomas revoked because I have an incomplete on my record."

"Tom, that sounds like you have a guilty conscience. I need to check my records. Actually, I called for two reasons. One was to ask how you and Alex are doing. And, two, to ask if you meant it when you said 'I owe you. If you ever need anything, just call.'"

"The answer to your first question is that we are doing fine, better than we deserve. The boys are grown, have moved out, and have jobs. Secondly, yes. What do you need? Do you need defense in a paternity suit?" laughed Tom Ramler.

"Tom, it's not me, but a young friend of mine. She does not need defense but rather she needs an offence in a paternity suit, more of a child support issue."

"Okay, tell me the story."

The Old Man did. He emphasized that the girl could not afford lawyer fees and mentioned the phrase pro bono.

"Great, Mr. Speech Coach, I have one of your other products of high school speech who can help your friend. My son David is a lawyer with our firm. I can have him get the details from Maia and go to work on your case. Our firm will give him the hours pro bono."

Two days later The Old Man had Maia and Roddy over for dinner. He served his chili, which took two days to properly prepare. He told her about Dave Ramler and told her to call him for an appointment. She should also gather any and all paperwork connected with Roddy and his father. He suggested any information on locating the father would be of help to Dave.

The Old Man convinced her that Ramler and Son would come to her rescue. He knew from his chats with her that she wanted to become a registered nurse. She needed money for tuition and help with Roddy to make it. As it was now, he sat with Roddy some evenings and afternoons so Maia could get things done, go out with friends, or just catch up on her sleep.

During his last week before escaping subacute, Maia told him of another chapter in her soap operatic life. Her other grandmother, her mother's mother, was a fairly wealthy woman. She outlived a financially successful husband. The woman had two daughters. Both were rebels who defied their mother. Maia's mother ran away from home while the younger sister stayed on with their mother. "I had to get away from home," her mother told Maia.

Maia told The Old Man, "When she told me that, I wondered if Gran hadn't wanted her to run away. Mom said they hated each other. After my mom ran away, Gran moved with her other daughter to northern Minnesota into a fancy lake home. The other daughter, my aunt, married someone from the Grand Rapids area and had a couple of kids, my cousins, I guess. Gran always told everyone, I learned from my mother before she died, about how she had disowned my mother and left her out of her will.

"After my mom overdosed, I never heard anything about them. My mom and her sister had had some communication. That's how I learned some of the things about my gran. I read in the paper last year of an accident on Highway 10 near Motley. I think one of those who died was my aunt. I must be jinxed. Anybody who had any connection with me comes to a sad end. Be careful, Old Man. I fear for Roddy, too."

As the weeks went by Maia kept The Old Man informed as to the status of the child support lawsuit. David Ramler had been able to locate Roddy's father, who was living in Jordan, Minnesota, and was making a good living as a card dealer in one of the casinos. The guy drove a Corvette. The Old Man wondered if perhaps he was dealing more than cards. He claimed he won the car in a private poker game. David was sure that Maia would be coming into child support money with back payment. If not, the daddy would do jail time. For the next month The Old Man babysat for Maia. A few times he took both of them out for supper at the only place The Old Man ever found that had a good sloppy joe on the menu.

One evening Maia stopped in with Roddy. She was as excited as The Old Man had ever seen her. She gave him a crushing hug and a kiss on the cheek. "Old Man, David Ramler called today and asked if I could come to his office and sign some papers. Can you believe it? Roddy and I are going to get a monthly check that will be big enough to increase my monthly income by forty percent, and I will get back pay for the last three years. I'm going to buy Roddy all new clothes. Now I will be able to continue classes to become an RN."

She grabbed Roddy and danced around The Old Man's living room. She spun round and round with Roddy, both laughing. Finally, she plopped down on the couch. "And you know what, Old Man? Mr. Ramler said that he took the information I gave him on my gran. His investigation showed that my Gran died eight months ago. Then he confirmed that my mom's sister was the one killed in the car accident near Motley. According to Mr. Ramler, my gran's will left her entire estate to my mom's sister. A stipulation in the will stated that if Gran's daughter preceded her in death the estate would be divided among Gran's grandchildren. Mr. Ramler said that legally entitles me to an equal share of the grandchildren's inheritance. The lawyer for my gran never sought to find me or my brother or sister, or perhaps he didn't know of our existence.

177

"Mr. Kramer says he will take my claim to court to recover my share. Then he asked if I would agree, since he did my child support pro bono, to him receiving thirty percent of whatever I get as an inheritance. If we lose the case, I owe nothing. He is sure we can win. It may take six months or more.

"Just think, Old Man, I may get to go to school on campus during the day. Mr. Ramler said Gran had a bundle. Roddy will get the better life I want for him. Old Man, you are my lucky charm."

The next day The Old Man sat in his recliner thinking, It's good to be useful to somebody, even at my age.

The Old Man Tells It Like It Was

Frustrated, The Old Man hit the power off button on his TV remote. He was watching an NFL game. His frustration came from a player on a team losing 27–10 doing an insane dance and pointing his finger at the quarterback he had just sacked. Losing by seventeen points and celebrating a tackle, The Old Man fumed. The tackler should be humbled by the score rather than being proud of making one play. This happened dozens of times in the games he watched. His stream of consciousness navigated to the overall behavior of so many of the players: trash talking, intimidating tactics such as standing over a player after a tackle and then deliberately, slowly stepping across the player while dragging his foot rather than stepping back and away. No, rub it in; make a show for the cameras.

What happened to humility, being a good sport? Trash talking NBA players were as bad. Even in his favorite sport, baseball, players were all out of whack. The peacock-strutting home run trots, pitchers shooting arrows at batters after striking them out, what was the game coming to? Why wasn't anyone putting a halt to all of this? Where were the coaches and managers? Why weren't the players displaying such antics benched? Who was in control of the asylum these days?

In the NBA, players dictated all. Just look at his Timberwolves. A player didn't like the Minnesota cold and the lack of national press coverage, so the star demanded a trade. He reinforced his demand by playing only when he wanted to. The guy didn't even suit up at all for some games.

The more he thought about it the sadder he became. He couldn't remember his heroes, Harmon Killebrew, Tony Oliva, Rod Carew, Jim Kaat, and Kirby Puckett doing this. He scoured his memory and couldn't recall any of their behavior reflecting what he was seeing today. He remembered the words of an old athlete turned sportscaster, Dick Nesbitt: "When you lose, say little. When you win, say less." Ownership and humility.

They said that it was the money. It was the money talking. The stars had it by the boatload and dictated to management. It was no longer "he who pays the piper who calls the tune," it was, "the piper who calls his own song." Why, he thought, if he were a parent today, he couldn't even take his kids to a professional football or basketball game. Not only would he not want his kids to witness the actions of the players, but he thought he would be lacking as a parent if he exposed a child to the vulgar language and bullying player behavior. Recently someone told him about the behavior of fans at a Vikings game. The vulgar, abusive fans shouting at their own quarterback, not to mention their treatment of nearby fans wearing jerseys of the opposing team, sickened him. Had most of the sports world gone to the devil's school of intimidation and abrasive behavior? Was sportsmanship and humility no longer being taught? From t-ball to the pros, it seemed as if sportsmanship was no longer part of the game.

As he sat in his recliner and seethed, he supposed that today's sports crowd would shout, "Yeah, Old Man, tell us how it used to be. Tell us about the good old days, you old goat."

He turned the TV set back on, found his favorite music station, and listened to the instrumental versions from Out of the Song Book of America. He mused on. Those were the good old days. Oh, even then there were the seeds of what was growing wild in the sports world. The problem was that those who used to uproot the weeds of unsportsmanship and vulgarity had given up or, more likely, had been run out of today's sports picture by agents and obscene salaries.

"Sure, Old Man, get real. Tell us like it used to be."

The Old Man shouted back to his imaginary critics, "I know how it was. I was there. I did it." His long-delayed instant replay drifted back to 1971. He had wanted to coach in a small town summer recreation program. He could have had the job, but his National Guard two-week summer camp posed a problem. He would have to miss the beginning of the season. The job was given to a first-year teacher from the same school at which the man taught. The young buck was quite a star himself. He didn't really want to coach a bunch of unskilled kids from the ages of six to fifteen, however, he could use the money and could find nothing else that allowed him so much time to play golf. He took the job. The Old Man was off to Camp Ripley for two weeks trying to avoid poison ivy while dodging the Vietnam War. When he completed summer camp without getting the itch despite living in a tent in the woods, he began a search for a job. He needed the money. After all, he was getting married in August. He had only a few weeks to earn enough for a honeymoon.

The job he really wanted was the one he got. The stud that was hired for the summer program was told his services were no longer required. Numerous parents as well as opposing coaches had complained, forcing the organizers of the program to make a change. The use of vulgar language and unsportsmanlike behavior was visible to anyone who paid attention.

The then-younger Old Man was hired to put out the flames, clean out the brush. His first step was to organize practices stressing fundamentals. During his seven hours with the kids each day he hit grounders and fly balls, teaching the basics. Over and over boys and girls were taught fielding and throwing basics. Infield and outfield practices were a repetition of catching and throwing to the correct base. Hitting, bunting, and base running were part of a repetitious routine. The fired coach had put in two or three hours a day and then went to play golf. The kids complained about the new routine, said they weren't having any fun. When he asked them how many games they had won that year, they said none. He asked them how much fun that was. They replied that they hated it. The boys' team of twelve to fifteen–year-olds was 0–5. They lost to every team in the league. The last game was 39–0, called after four innings.

The first game The Old Man coached was against the second-worst team in the league. That team was 1–4, having beaten his team by six runs. During their second meeting with that team, The Old Man's star player was pitching. The kid was far superior to any player on the field for either team. His natural ability destined him for stardom; his behavior in the eyes of The Old Man destined him for the bench. In the third inning the phenom, Dennis, struck out the first two batters. The next batter he faced was the

181

only kid who had gotten a hit off of him. Dennis's first pitch, a fastball, hit the kid square in the back. As the kid dropped to the ground moaning and about to cry, Dennis laughed out loud and said, "What a fucking baby." The Old Man called time out, walked to the mound, and told Dennis to take a seat on the bench. "You can't do that. Who ya got to pitch?" Dennis didn't move.

The Old Man latched onto Dennis's shirt by the collar, goose-stepped him to the bench, and told him to sit down and stay there. "If you want to play high school sports, you better stay on the bench." In shock, Dennis just looked at him. The Old Man then trotted back to the mound and gathered the entire team around him. He handed the ball to the second baseman and said, "Timmy, you pitch."

"I've never pitched before, Coach," said Timmy.

"Today you will," replied The Old Man as he patted Timmy on the back. The Old Man then pulled the best kid he had left off the bench to play second base.

Still gathered on the mound, the team complained. Danny, the first baseman, said "Coach, we have a lead, the first time all year. We can't win without Dennis."

"Boys, we've worked hard for a week and a half. You have done what I have asked. You can win, Dennis or no Dennis. Show me you believe in yourselves. Just like in practice, do it."

They did. Timmy got the next batter to pop up. The Old Man's boys scored two more runs and won 5–2. For these boys that was the start of better things. With Dennis back in the line-up with a cleaner mouth and little better attitude, The Old Man's scrappers won the next three ball games.

The younger boys' team won two games, and the two girls' teams won four games between them. Hard work, fundamentals, and a good attitude were paying off. The games were more fun, even those they lost.

On the Monday morning of the final week of the season, The Old Man had a phone call from the coach of the team that had whipped his ragtag outfit 39–0 in four innings. The coach told The Old Man he would not play the final game. "I won't let my kids be exposed to your team's terrible sportsmanship, vulgarity, and dirty play, all of which we saw in that first game."

"Billy," said the then-younger Old Man, "You have known me for eight years. You know that is not how I ever played or coached the game. I wasn't there during that first go-around with your team. I guarantee that what we bring to your town on Friday will be close-mouthed, well-behaved gentlemen and -women. We may not be very talented, but we will give you a good, clean game. Billy, give us a chance, please."

Billy did. The Old Man told his team about the phone call. On the day of the game the younger boys' and the two girls' teams both lost but were competitive, displaying a stellar attitude. The twelve to fifteen–year-old boys' game was totally different than the first game. The Old Man's team, with Dennis pitching, trailed Billy's team 2–0 in the third. Timmy, the scrappy second baseman, coaxed a base on balls. Dennis lined a single to center. The Old Man had Timmy running on the pitch, runners on first and third. The inning was going just as The Old Man envisioned it. He had the next batter, Arnie, second to Dennis on the team as an athlete, bunt. Arnie laid a beauty down the third baseline. The third baseman raced in, fielded the bunt, and threw to first. The Old Man, coaching third base, had Timmy moving slowly down the baseline. As the throw was made to first, he sent Timmy to the plate, scoring. The third baseman stood there halfway down the line proud of his throw to first, which had nipped Arnie by half a step. This left third base open. The Old Man yelled as loud as he could with his right arm windmilling as Dennis glided into third base. Billy's pitcher must have been a bit rattled. His next pitch dug into the dirt near home plate and scooted past the catcher to the backstop. With The Old Man screaming, Dennis broke for home. The inning ended with the score 2–2.

Now Dennis had his adrenaline flowing. He shut down Billy's team completely. In the top of the sixth, the last inning, Arnie led off with a walk. A sacrifice bunt got Arnie to second. With Billy's left-handed ace on the mound, The Old Man gave Arnie the steal sign. Arnie got a good jump and slid safely into third. With first baseman Danny at the plate, The Old Man called time and motioned for Danny to come halfway up the line. "Danny, concentrate. Watch the ball out of the pitcher's hand and just hit it. Make sure you make contact. I know you can do it."

The Old Man returned to the coaching box and told Arnie to be ready and listen. Billy's lefty, who had regained his composure after the fourth inning, fired a fastball over the plate. Danny had not laid wood on the ball the entire game. With his eyes following the ball, Danny swung. His awkward swing, a bit late, connected and sent a high fly ball to right field. The Old Man yelled for Arnie to tag up. "Arnie, when I say go, run like the devil is on your tail. Do it just like we practiced it a dozen times." Arnie slid across home plate safely. Dennis struck out the side in the bottom of the inning. The Old Man's ragtag team won 3–2.

"I never would have believed that your gang of misfits could have done this," Billy said as he slapped the younger Old Man on the back. The Old Man then thanked Billy for giving his kids a chance.

When the bus reached home, The Old Man said he would go to the bakery, get doughnuts, and pick up some pop if the kids wanted to stay and celebrate. The Old Man's winners all stayed. As they ate and drank, Timmy said, "Coach, we all thought you were nuts when you came here and made us do all that boring stuff. But you know, that boring stuff made us a winner in a game we should not have been able to win. You also taught us how to act. Thanks." Everybody cheered.

The Old Man, almost in tears, said, "I am so proud of all of you."

Sitting up in his recliner, The Old Man shouted at the TV to his imaginary critics. "You see, that was the way it was. It worked. It can still work. You can learn something from an old goat."

Vlad the Impaler

The Old Man lay back in his recliner after another coughing jag. He could go years without getting a cold. Now the second one of the winter was kicking in his chest. The worst part of it was he felt even more rotten because he was missing his weekly poker game at the card club. He could find nothing on TV to hold his interest. Fifty-some regular and cable channels had nothing new except reality shows designed to capture the mindless. He could no longer watch reruns of Gunsmoke or Law & Order, which he had almost memorized. The same for M*A*S*H. He was sick of that arrogant Alan Alda anyway. That left American Pickers with only about twenty new shows a year. He had seen all the others three or four times at least. He rued missing poker. "Damn," he cursed as he turned to a smooth easy listening music channel. He wondered if Vlad, the pesky little impaler, was able to get into a hold 'em game.

Vlad had the characteristics of a gnat, flitting about and taking unexpected nips out of unskilled or timid poker players. He was a smooth talker who tried to lull a player into a comfort zone before taking a bite. At other times he was in attack mode, trying to intimidate newcomers.

The Old Man vividly recalled the first time he played at the same table with him. Vlad was on one side and, it seemed, a tag team partner was on the other side of The Old Man. They chatted back and forth over The Old Man's head about how much money one could amass and leave in a will without their heirs having to pay taxes on it. After some discussion they decided six million was the limit. That would make each of them safe, if only for a while. Millions of dollars in their estates and they were playing the cheapest-limit poker game at the club. The Old Man wondered if they really had that much, and if they did, why they were playing for these low stakes. Most of the other players were retirees on a fixed income or young

185

folks who had little expendable cash. In June, it was the newly graduated eighteen-year-olds who were spending graduation gifts. By the smirk on the faces of the two, especially Vlad's, The Old Man was sure the conversation was meant to intimidate.

Months and several poker games later, The Old Man determined that Vlad's style of play depended on intimidation. His aggressiveness soon lost its intimidation factor on The Old Man. Before he caught on, The Old Man dropped intermediate hands when Vlad bet into him. As he watched, The Old Man learned that those not intimidated by Vlad often called him and won hands that Vlad played as if he had a top hand. The Old Man even learned to like playing against him. It was fun to beat him.

Meanwhile, The Old Man grew more disgusted with Vlad's behavior. When he could intimidate, embarrass, or push a player around, he did. One afternoon Dominic, a regular retiree, was having a horrible card day. He just moved from another table where he had lost all but $19.50 of his $100 buy in. Dominic, as he often did, looked like he had just crawled out of bed. His stringy, gray hair begged for a comb. His wrinkled pants needed an iron and his shirt wore the evidence of at least two lunches. Since he had just come from a broken table, he didn't have to post a bet until he was in the big blind. The first three hands he tossed in. On the fourth hand he put his two dollars in the pot. He had good starting cards. As soon as Dominic did this, Vlad jumped up and said, "He can't play. He doesn't have the required twenty-dollar minimum to join the game." The entire table groaned and stared at Vlad. The dealer said that technically Vlad was correct, but if the table didn't mind, $19.50 was good enough. All agreed except Vlad. "A rule is a rule. He is out. Call the floor for a ruling. He is out. A rule is a rule, dammit," stormed Vlad.

"All right," said Dominic as he pulled a twenty-dollar bill out of his wallet.

"Can't do it," Vlad stated sharply. "Cards have already been dealt. You can't buy more chips once the cards have been dealt."

Vlad insisted Dominic could not play that hand. The floor manager said that he didn't want to ruin a friendly game, but he had to rule in favor of Vlad. Two players got up, threw their cards in, and left the game. All the while they glared at Vlad. Twice more the deal went around the table with no one but Vlad speaking. The smooth talker could not get anyone to engage him in harmless chitchat. Vlad stood up, picked up his chips, and left the table saying, "Rules are rules." So much for a friendly low-budget poker game.

The Old Man had another coughing fit. He got out of his recliner and found some nighttime cold tablets and downed them. It was only 6:00 p.m., "damn winter, no baseball," and using the closing words of diarist, Samuel Pepys, "And so to bed." The Old Man was a retired English teacher.

By 3:00 a.m. The Old Man was awake and unable to get back to sleep in spite of the nighttime cold tablets. His dreams had been invaded by the face of Vlad the Impaler.

The cold tablets might have done some good. He felt better. He had a good morning with the newspaper, the tenth viewing of a Perry Mason case, two crossword puzzles, and a good five miles on his stationary bike. Now he had Jeopardy! to look forward to.

His good day was still humming along as he started a new Lee Child thriller. He liked Jack Reacher as a somewhat tarnished hero. He thought, how could they have made a Jack Reacher movie of the six foot six loner rescuing the downtrodden by casting Tom Cruise?

Lee Child went a long way, but by late afternoon Vlad the Impaler was back on his mind. The Old Man wondered how yesterday's Cracked Aces went. Did Vlad have the audacity to show?

The Old Man replayed a game of six months ago. It was a Saturday afternoon. The little gnat was at it again. Weekends often attracted inexperienced, occasional players. Vlad would often show up and pounce on them. He tended to feast on those who had some form of physical handicap. Such players usually showed up once a month with $100 or $200. Sometimes a caretaker would accompany them.

Heyward came to the table using his walker as a casino employee carried his tray of chips. Heyward was a quiet guy. He wasn't a poor player, but he played slowly and conservatively. His deliberate pace annoyed

Vlad, who kept harping, "Come on, let's go. What the hell are we waiting for?" After that, whenever the opportunity presented itself, Vlad raised Heyward's bets. With about half of his stack gone, Heyward got into another hand with Vlad. Vlad raised pre-flop; Heyward stayed. Vlad bet the flop; Heyward followed. On the fourth card Vlad bet, and again Heyward stayed. On the fifth and final card Vlad bet; Heyward raised. They were the only two left by then.

Vlad then looked at Heyward but did not call the bet. Instead he tossed his cards on the table face up, showing two low pair. He had not called the raise. As a courtesy when one folds a good hand and shows that hand, the winner often shows his or her cards. Heyward smiled, showing only a pair of kings. "You bluffed me," shouted Vlad. "You damn bluffed me." Then he thought and threw four dollars in the pot. "I call."

Everyone at the table knew that Vlad had folded his hand. He offered evidence of that when he said, "You bluffed me," not, "You tried to bluff me." The dealer was stunned. He didn't know how to handle this. He, too, was intimidated by Vlad. All just sat there waiting for the dealer to toss Vlad's four chips back to him and award the pot to Heyward.

"I win," insisted Vlad. "I did not muck my cards. I did not throw them face down. I could still call." After a house ruling, Vlad was awarded the pot. "Rules are rules," said Vlad with a smirk.

"And ethics, not a lack thereof, should be a part of a two-to-four, low-level stakes game," shouted Andy sternly as he left the table. Heyward packed his remaining chips and without saying a word, shuffled away on his walker. Soon everyone else got up and left Vlad sitting by himself.

Vlad the Impaler stories were buzzing through The Old Man's mind. It was just like bad TV, the same old crap. Oh, how he had wished he'd been able to make yesterday's Aces Cracked. Things had been building toward an explosion. Just three weeks ago there had been another Vlad-ignited meltdown.

Gronnie was another of the mostly regular group of low-budget players. She was only a little less despised than Vlad. She was a stalky, somewhat overweight older woman. Her voice begged sandpaper to smooth it out. She usually wore a cotton shirt that resembled an old basketball jersey top. The arms and shoulders were bare with a wide shoulder strap on either side. She wore baggy jeans and battered tennis shoes. Her graying hair was cut short, and she worked several sticks of gum from side to side in her mouth, resembling a cow chewing her cud. Her personality was brisk to the point of being tactlessly gruff. What she had in short supply was patience. Vlad's provided the nitro to Gronnie's glycerin.

Vlad was up to his usual tricks. On that day he was using his delayed checking technique. If he was one of the first to bet or check, he just sat there hoping others would check after him. If a few did and he had reasonable cards, he would say, "I haven't acted yet." Then he would place a bet after his survey suggested the field was weak. He did that several times that day. On his fourth attempt Gronnie, who was about to check after the person next to her had checked, was interrupted by Vlad. "I haven't acted yet," he said and he bet.

"Hey, look, skinhead, that's the fourth time you pulled that crap. It ends here. You have the conniving habits of a coyote. I have heard about you pulling that crap before," shouted Gronnie as the gum she was assaulting flew across the table.

"What do you mean? I haven't acted yet. I can take my time. You are out of your mind. Dealer, call the floor."

Gronnie stood up and stared down at him, saying, "Little man, if it looks like a skunk, smells like a skunk, and raises its tail like a skunk, it is a skunk. Put your tail down, leave the table, and take your weasel ways with you." Gronnie had no conscience when it came to mixing metaphors.

Vlad turned red as the floor manager approached. After asking the dealer to explain what had happened, the floor manager asked Gronnie and Vlad both to leave the casino. Both did.

Gronnie had not returned since the incident. Vlad was back the next day. However, several players left the game when he sat down. Word of this spread. For the next two weeks, every time Vlad sat down the other players withdrew. They went to the poker board and asked to be put on the waiting list, saying they would not play if Vlad sat down with them.

The card club management was in a dilemma. Should they have forty or more players walk out the door on Cracked Aces day, or should they ban Vlad, who technically had not violated poker rules, only the rules of proper decorum? For the past two weeks all the low-stakes games emptied whenever Vlad sat in.

What happened yesterday? The Old Man wondered. He couldn't wait for next week's Aces Cracked. Would Vlad kill their game? Or had the impaler impaled himself? He surely would tune in next week to see.

To Enter, Press 666

The Old Man returned home after a four-day journey to watch the Twins' Class A minor league team. After collecting his mail and the newspapers from the neighbor, he plopped into his ever-inviting recliner. Then he checked his phone, a real one with a cord and numbers to push, for messages. Yes, he had given in to some technology. He heard from companies who wanted to reside and reshingle his house. He had guessed that their voodoo search had failed them. They got his phone number but failed to get that he lived in a townhouse. Which meant he had no control over his siding and roof.

He found a message from his sister. Then he smiled as he heard the voice of one of his former students. She said she was in town and to call her. Dinner would be good, and they could catch up on the recent changes in their lives. The Old Man cursed. How could he return a call? She had left no number. Then he swore again; he was disappointed. She certainly knew better than that. Didn't she remember that he was not addicted to every new toy on the market? After all, she was one of the group who bought him a voice messaging system because they got tired of trying to find him at home to get a message to him.

After reading through his four days of mail, comics, and sports pages, he turned on his TV. There was no Twins game, rain in Detroit. Saturday night TV was the worst of all. He had read that Saturday was once the most-watched night for TV; now it was the least watched. He wondered if that was because there was less of interest to watch or because even the big four networks ran only reruns during primetime on Saturdays now.

That left The Old Man with his easy listening music channel and his overactive imagination. "Damn cellophane phones; and yeah, the damned voodoo internet as well." He was sick of the restriction of real communication. Even his townhouse association didn't communicate with him because he didn't have an email address. The only time they sent him real mail was when they raised the monthly fee. They didn't even warn him when they resealed his driveway. He was trapped in his garage, no car for two days.

Everyone who sent him bills kept harping on automatic withdrawal. Wasn't that discrimination against him? He was told to drop typing in college because he didn't need an F on his transcript. How many times did he have to redial a phone number because he always got the numbers mixed up? He was a victim of a technological handicap.

His anti-tech mind rant was snapped by "It's Party Time," which livened up his easy listening music treat. Maybe that's what he needed, a party.

That idea was squashed by his recollections of the last cookout he had attended. Friends invited him to celebrate a family holiday. He couldn't believe it. Before the outdoor meal almost all of the guests sat in one of two circles. Just about everyone there had his or her head buried in a Star Trek Tricorder of one kind or another. They certainly didn't visit much with each other and when they did, someone would ask a question, sending all heads into a device to find the answer. When it came to devices, The Old Man dreamed of finding success in his A-vice or his B-vice. He hadn't developed a C-vice, and hoped to God never to have a device.

It seemed no one had a memory anymore. No one needed to remember anything. "It's on my phone." Like any other muscle, memory loses its function through disuse. The Old Man wondered about the lost art of conversation. All these people reading and sending emails, playing video games, and ever plugged in to other sounds of their addiction. The makeup of the group had the usual teens and their machines. What bothered him even more was the old folks in the group beyond the age of sixty who likewise had their heads buried in one device or another.

After the hot dogs, hamburgers, and slices of watermelon, the party guests returned to the voices of silence, which they evidently couldn't stand. So they plugged back into their mechanicals. He wondered how many of them were texting each other as some looked up and smiled at

192

another. That led him to his standard old joke about two people in a car talking on their cell phones. The Old Man asked if they were talking to each other. Considering the looks he got, he had either insulted those who heard him, or they had assumed that of course they were talking to each other.

The Old Man was really getting his blood pressure up now. He needed to relax; perhaps tomorrow or after church, he thought, he would go play poker. He enjoyed the game, not that he won more than he lost, but it was less expensive than other big boy toys like boats, ATVs, and snowmobiles. He didn't even like those environmental terror machines. At the thought of what the poker table had become over the years, his blood pressure re-surged. Most of the cheap tables he played at consisted of old fogies like him, but even most of them had the habit. If they weren't talking on the phone, they were playing a video game. Poker play was getting slower and slower as the table waited for someone to pull his or her head out of a phone.

Then there were those who were checking the weather report for next week's vacation in Glacier, the Apostle Islands, or the cheaper July season in Las Vegas. Most likely they were just showing off, wanting everyone to know of the jet set life they were leading.

That was irritating enough. Now they added more techno crap. Usually one or two players were plugged in to some form of voodoo; maybe they were listening to music or messages from their stockbroker. Whatever it was, they had to be awakened from their trance when need arose to make contact with them. Perhaps the dealer should have sent a text message.

The Old Man decided he would skip poker tomorrow. Maybe a ride in the country would be good. Maybe a drive to see the schools in which he taught; a trip down memory lane would be nice. He hoped his former students remembered him. Memory, oh yes, that modern day cell phone catastrophe. Memory would soon be a thing of the past. No one needed to remember anything anymore. "Phone number? I don't know; let me see. I'll check my phone." "Directions on how to get to my house from yours? I don't know. Let me see what I can do. Give me your address; I'll put it in the GPS on my phone. Then I'll be able to tell you." Memory was fading into the past. Maybe the cure for Alzheimer's was a super cell phone inserted into the brains of the elderly.

The next morning on the way to church. The Old Man smiled, as he liked the future. The night before he'd had a dream that gave him ample reason to offer up thanks when he got to church. In the dream he was approaching the pearly gates. He expected to meet St. Peter, who would quiz him about his life before possible entry into heaven. Instead he saw a cell phone that rang. He picked it up and hit "answer." A plastic voice told him that the entry was now all electronic. He should begin the process by pressing the proper function. The Old Man stood there. He didn't have a clue. After a few to fifteen minutes of pushing, stroking, punching, and brushing his fingers on the face of the device, he gave up. What the hell, he thought. Moving further up the road, he smiled. Certainly, the keys to heaven were not buried in the mastery of an automated phone system. Gaining heaven had always been and always would be trying to live a good life, helping others, being kind, generous, understanding, and compassionate. No, only hell would demand automated entry. He was saved.

Guilty or Not

The Old Man awakened from a restless nap in his ever-faithful recliner. Windy, rainy November loomed with no sign of a needed Indian summer. In spite of a flu shot, he felt like he was in the early stages of the damned menace. He ached all over. He fetched a blanket to drive off the chill. No use turning up the heat; he'd rather save the environment.

A return to his nap was inviting, but he didn't want to revive the dream he'd been having. He was repeating a sequence of dreams that had been haunting him over the years. In the dream he was back in basic training in the Army, having been recalled ten or fifteen years after his discharge from the National Guard. What sort of rat's nest in his brain kept sending him back to the military? Veterans Day? Radio and TV were filling the air with reminders of wars gone by. Did he feel guilty after all these years because he considered himself a draft dodger? The Vietnam War was some fifty years' history.

In the late 1960s he was teaching high school English and speech. His draft board told him he would not get another deferment; within six months he would be drafted. As a college graduate not about to make a career in the military, he knew where that would land him: the infantry and then on to Vietnam. Not for The Old Man. Canada? No, The Old Man hadn't had the heart for that. He didn't want to forever live north of the Rainy River, too much to leave behind. He considered the National Guard but was told he would be far down on any waiting list. On the other hand, what was there to lose? He drove twenty miles west of where he was teaching to a Guard unit in which his brother-in-law was a green first lieutenant. The first sergeant interviewed him. The Old Man left figuring that the effort was all for naught.

A few weeks later, his brother-in-law told him there was a good chance of getting in. Waiting lists were only a guideline. His brother-in-law said that the first sergeant was more interested in a twenty-four-year-old who had a steady job rather than seventeen- and eighteen-year-olds who were too full of hell and wild oats. Too many of them had already caused the first sergeant headaches. The Old Man got the call. Inside help no doubt counted.

So, it was the National Guard instead of the draft. It was six months of active US Army duty and at least five and a half more years in the Guard. Not much of a choice; it was the Guard or Vietnam. In The Old Man's mind, that made him a draft dodger. Over the years The Old Man was often asked why he never joined the American Legion. He told people he didn't serve in the military. Some of them knew he had served seven years in the National Guard. They said that qualified. Qualified him for what? He had dodged the draft.

Maybe that was why over the years he had avoided movies and TV shows that featured US wars. The Old Man made an exception for movies like Catch-22 and M*A*S*H. He also watched a highly successful TV version of M*A*S*H. However, those were anti-war features. Some even said anti-military, but he enjoyed the satire. Joseph Heller's novel was even better than the movie. No surprise there.

The Old Man again drifted off in his recliner. No dream this time, just the faint background of easy listening music from his cable channel. When he awoke an hour later, he felt better. He needed liquid. He heated up some tomato soup and sat back with steam coming off the mug in his hand. He kept thinking about his dream of reactivation into the military.

That sent him into his library/office in search of some Tim O'Brien to read. For years he had avoided O'Brien's recount of the fight within himself about crossing the Rainy River in order to avoid the draft. O'Brien never crossed. Instead, he ended up in Vietnam. Years later he wrote some masterful fiction (fiction, really?) about his tortured years. The Old Man avoided the book The Things They Carried for years. The reason was the same: The Old Man dodged the draft. Because of his English teaching and speech coaching, he had been forced to read O'Brien. The writing was superb, the stories gut-wrenching.

The Old Man carried one of O'Brien's books back to his recliner. Instead of reading from it, he poured more liquid into his system. He thought about Catch-22: the absurdity of Major Major Major, Doc Deneeka, Yossarian, Clevinger, and all the rest.

Yes, thought The Old Man, he saw such absurdity at Fort Jackson. When he first got to basic training, after the hell week in the induction center, he was going to be the best soldier in his unit. He did as he was told: he finished his work, polished his boots, kept a neat footlocker, learned to disassemble, clean, reassemble, and fire an M-16. He qualified as an expert marksman. Not bad for a school teacher who disliked guns. He was more accurate at slinging grenades than anyone in his platoon. He became a model soldier with ribbons on his chest.

That English teacher, a soldier? He was rewarded for all of this. He didn't need extra training in any of these areas. The map reading classes and all the other academic study was a breeze. He needed no extra time there. His reward was to relieve those on KP who had failed and needed more training with an M-16, the .30-caliber machine gun, or learning how to read a map. He spent more time on KP than anyone in his platoon. He was learning the value of being a good soldier.

The Old Man recalled even more absurdity. In basic training they used him, the school teacher, to tutor those who couldn't follow a compass, read a map, or pass written tests. The Old Man was pulled out of training to remediate those who failed the tests. Perhaps some sanity there; however, that morphed into insanity. Some flunked the written test three times. The Old Man was given a copy of the written test and told to take the trainees off into the woods and drill the answers into them, rote learning. In reality the trainees didn't need to learn anything, they only needed to pass the test. The Old Man produced a sarcastic laugh. He guessed public education had taken to the military method: it was not education that was important, it was scoring well on standardized tests. Learning was not a part of the equation.

The Old Man was not happy with the onset of his flu symptoms. The

197

recalling of his days of basic training was driving him toward depression. He sought relief and dialed up Jeopardy! It was not easy finding anything watchable on TV. Supper didn't sit well with his aches and fever. Reruns of American Pickers got him through the rest of the evening.

The next morning he felt better. Maybe it was only a twenty-four-hour flu. He thought of last night's TV shows. He had slipped some reruns of NCIS in there, but that show, with all its acronyms, sent his mind back to the military. He tried to get his mind off the military during his half hour stationary bike ride, breakfast, and two daily crosswords. By 10:30 a.m. he was back at Fort Jackson.

At Fort Jackson he learned the military way. By the time he was out of basic training and sent to Advanced Infantry Training—his National Guard unit was mechanized infantry—he had learned to take care of business. Instead of hanging around when his work was finished, he now got lost, to hell with the rest. In his barracks he found a room piled high with mattresses. It made for a good place to hide and catch up on some extra needed sleep. In the field he found ditches and clumps of trees to get lost in instead of standing around when he had completed his turn at whatever that day demanded. It sure beat being available for extra KP. This worked out so well for The Old Man that by the end of the cycle he was a squad leader. Yes, sir, one could move up in the Army by being selfish.

He shook his head and felt sad recalling the lack of skill so many of these kids had. The Old Man was twenty-four when he was at Fort Jackson. Most of those with him were seventeen to twenty. Most of them were from New York City, Boston, or Philadelphia. The instant sergeants, only a year into the Army and graduates of NCO school, were also younger than he. They were the platoon leaders. They had extra training, but those from the urban areas seemed lost in a swamp or the woods.

He recalled two incidents where he answered an instant NCO's summons. "Hey, school teacher, come here." The first time was on a night problem. His platoon was lost in a wooded area. Two guys had already suffered injuries after falling into fox holes that had not been refilled. On that moonlit night the sergeant and his trusted aides couldn't read a topographical map. They needed to find a way out of the woods in order for the platoon to reach its checkpoint.

"School teacher, can you read this damn thing?" His sergeant handed him the map and told him where they were supposed to end up, what the coordinates were. The Old Man was The Old Man already on that night. All of the forty in his platoon were much younger. He looked at the map, surveyed the area by the light of the moon and the Sergeant's flashlight. He located a hill in the distance. Then he found the same on the topographic map. He checked out other valleys and crests. He knew where they were.

"Okay, Sarge, this is where we are. Now this is where we are supposed to end up." He pointed all this out on the map. "We need to go this way and avoid the river and the swampy area. Once we get around that, we should be able to make our mark."

"Can you lead us there before 0200 hours?" asked the sergeant. So it was that the English teacher impersonated Sacagawea.

On another occasion, The Old Man's platoon was lost again, this time in a swamp on a cold, rainy day. Visibility was poor. Again, those words, "Hey, school teacher, come here. Can you read a compass and understand this map?" This time The Old Man channeled the Swamp Fox, Marion Campbell, and led the platoon to the dry landmark.

The Old Man sunk into his recliner after his five-mile stationary bike on the Reading Railroad. Good Lord, his interior monologue shouted. I was going back home to teach English. Those poor bastards were headed for Vietnam. If they couldn't find their way out of a swamp in South Carolina, how in the hell were they going to survive in a jungle with the Viet Cong shooting at them? Draft dodging? Hell no. It was the only sane thing to do. Why would I ever want to put my life in the hands of such poorly trained people?

Maybe it wasn't the draft he dodged but the Grim Reaper. Maybe it was meant to be. Thirty-seven years in the classroom and more than fifty years of coaching speech must have been of some value to society, to his country. He had several offers to get out of the classroom and make some real money. He had ample proof of his worth in the form of letters, notes, and personal thank yous from parents and students to support that.

After regaining control of his emotions, The Old Man began another crossword. There were no clues that took him back to the military. After lunch he took a drive. He liked November, the barren trees with all the leaves on the ground. The sun brightened the day. He was thankful. He guessed that was what Thanksgiving was all about. He had a good life in spite of some health issues, inherited arthritis, bad knees, and a divorce that, instead of ruining his life, kept him in the classroom where he thrived. Yes, it was a good life. He didn't dodge old age, though. The journey was still proving to be worth it. He couldn't find the guilt in that.

The Chrysalis

The Old Man sat in the front pew of St. Timothy's Church. Next to him was a redheaded woman in her early twenties. Fr. Klein went on and on about a woman whom he knew little about. He felt compelled to extol her imagined virtues. The woman eulogized rested easy in her casket. The beloved was the redhead's grandmother.

After the Requiem Mass and the requisite luncheon, The Old Man accompanied his young companion to Calvary Catholic Cemetery for the final rites and burial of Bergedha O'Leary. The Old Man had never met Mrs. O'Leary, but he was a friend of the granddaughter, Lynn. The Old Man comforted her as she said, "It's so sad. So few people saw my Mamó off. Most of the people here are from my work, the Heart Clinic. They are here for me, I guess, not Mamó. All that food back at the church will go to waste. I feel so sad. Mamó, the food, and, I guess, me. What do I do now?"

The Old Man put his arm around the girl and said, "One step at a time, little Irish. You will cry, mourn, and then come up fighting. The first step, the food, is already tended to. The luncheon staff asked me to get your permission to take the food to the Dorothy Day Center to be used in their free lunch program for the homeless.

"Step two, you will continue to live at my house as long as you wish. Step three, your gran's lawyer wants you to be in his office at 10:00 a.m. Wednesday concerning the will. We will then decipher the journey that follows, step by step."

Lynn let out an audible sob, and with tears trickling down her freckled cheeks, she gave The Old Man a clinging hug. Then the two headed for The Old Man's townhouse.

The Old Man had met Lynn at the Heart and Vascular Clinic, which he visited once a month at least to have his blood checked. His cardiologist had him on Warfarin, a blood thinner, for the past four years. Lynn worked at the check-in desk most of the time when he reported for the blood work. They got to know each other. She obviously knew more about him, as he had to answer the same litany of questions time after time: date of birth, Medicare, insurance plan, and once or twice a year a two-page questionnaire: address, telephone, email (which he didn't have), next of kin, emergency contact, medical history . . .

He got to know her little by little. At first she was only a pretty, red-haired girl with freckles who wore a uniform that seemed to be made for someone taller and much heavier than she, more like a hand-me-down from an older sister or something she found in the attic. Strange, thought The Old Man. All of the other clerk's uniforms, though modest, were much more up to date. When he first met her, he guessed she was eighteen or nineteen.

She always smiled and asked how he was. Did he have a good week or month since she saw him last? Once when he checked in, he had waited fifteen minutes without being called. He finally went back to her station and asked if there was a problem. "I don't know, sir, but I'll check and get back to you."

The Old Man returned to his chair across the lobby. He noticed her on the phone. A few minutes later, instead of signaling him to her station, she left the enclosed booth and walked over to him. She smiled. "I'm so sorry for your wait. The nurse who does your blood work was called next door to help with an emergency. She will call you for your test soon. Meanwhile, can I get you a glass of water or anything? I see you have your book with you, as always. It shouldn't be long." He thanked her and said no to the water. She smiled again and returned to her other check-ins.

Once when he had to give her his birth date, she blushed and said, "Mine is a month from today."

He returned her smile and said, "That was a lucky day, especially for me. I'm so happy to see you here when I come in."

Lynn blushed some more, looked away, and said, "Thank you."

Four weeks later, back for his monthly poke in his finger, he checked in with Lynn again. When all questions were asked and answered, he gave her a Mounds candy bar and said, "Happy birthday."

She offered an embarrassed smile and said, "Thank you." She held up the candy bar and added, "I guess this is one of the many reasons I like you."

During the next two years The Old Man got to know more and more about the little leprechaun. Once, because of other appointments, he had scheduled his blood work as the very last patient of the day. Lynn again checked him in. By then other clerks always deferred to Lynn when The Old Man arrived. She seemed fidgety today, nervous. She fumbled the words as she asked the procedural questions. As The Old Man turned to find his seat, Lynn stuttered, "Can you . . . I mean, could you, I know I have no right—I'm so out of line, but I . . . nee . . . need your help."

"Lynn, whatever it is, if I can, I surely will help."

"I shouldn't use information from your records, I know, but after all these years I know your address. You don't live too far from me, but I, I, I . . ."

"Lynn, are you saying you need a ride home?"

"Yes." Lynn let out a sigh of relief.

The Old Man, too, exhaled and said he would go sit down and read his book. "Whenever you are ready, come and get me. Don't rush. It is not every day I can offer help to a damsel in distress."

As The Old Man drove her home, Lynn said that she lived with her grandmother, her Mamó, Irish for grandma. Her Mamó needed the one car they shared for a doctor's appointment. Her Mamó had not been feeling well. She had called and left a message that the medication she picked up on her way home was making her drowsy, and she couldn't drive. Lynn would have to get someone from work to drive her home.

"I waited too long to check my messages, and everybody I know well enough had already left. There are a couple of guys left here, but I don't trust them. They scare me. Then I noticed your name on the appointment list."

"So you live with your gran?"

"Yes. My parents died in a car accident when I was five; a drunk driver hit them. Since then I have lived with my Mamó. I have no other relatives that I know of. Mamó talks about my mother, her only daughter, but she never answers my questions about my dad, my other grandparents, or uncles and aunts."

By the time Lynn finished that part of her history, they were at her gran's house. It was located on the west bank of the Mississippi River in a northern suburb of Minneapolis. The yard looked to be a couple of acres or more depending on how gentle the slope in the back was to the river. The house was settled amid a grove of maple trees that reflected the sun off rich red leaves in late September. The two-story mansion of old yellow brick was a rectangle with many windows on both floors. The roof featured a half third-story attic with two dormer windows facing the west. On the southeast corner was a turret featuring a green cupola that must have afforded a picturesque view of the river and the wooded bank on the other side. If not built for the view, the turret might have protected the castle with gun emplacements to prevent a siege by a river flotilla. The lawns were still a lush green under the fallen maple leaves. Numerous flower beds gave the place a neatly trimmed look. "Do you do the yard work?"

"Not anymore. I used to help Mamó with it until her health gave out. Now we use a landscape service in the summer and winter."

Lynn and The Old Man returned to his townhouse after the funeral. Lynn had been staying in the lower rooms of his townhouse: a bedroom, bath, and what could pass as a rec room. There was a sliding patio door that led to a grassy, tree-filled common area. Crying, Lynn had called him when she came home from work one day and discovered her gran collapsed on the back lawn. She told The Old Man what she found and then proceeded to cry and cry. Finally she said, "I don't know what to do. Can you help me?" The Old Man told her to call 911. She said she already did that.

The Old Man drove the mile and a half to her gran's house. Lynn was sitting on the porch in front. "Mamó's body is on the back lawn. Ambulance attendants and two police officers are already here." As the day had been cool and misty, The Old Man put his jacket around Lynn. He then checked to confirm Lynn's suspicion that her gran was dead. He told Lynn that they should go inside. He asked her if her gran had ever spoken to her about any arrangements she wanted when she died. Lynn only shook her head no and continued crying. "Lynn, did your gran belong to a church?"

"Yes, St. Tim's; she liked Fr. Klein."

The Old Man called St. Tim's and asked for Fr. Klein. He identified himself and told the priest about Lynn and Bergedha O'Leary. The priest arrived just as the authorities were leaving for a nearby funeral parlor with the body. The Old Man sat in what appeared to be a library off to the side of a room that years ago would have been referred to as a front parlor, where Fr. Klein talked with Lynn for some time. Finally he asked Lynn if he could call a relative to come and stay with her. Lynn returned to sobbing and then said, "I have no one, only Snow."

Fr. Klein asked, "Who is Snow?" Lynn got up and ran into the library and hugged The Old Man.

"She calls me Snow, the hair. I have been a friend of Lynn's for several years. Apparently I am one of the few men who know Lynn that her grandmother approved of or at least tolerated." Before he left, Fr. Klein gave The Old Man the name and address of Mrs. O'Leary's lawyer. The old woman had been prepared.

"I can't stay here," Lynn blurted out. "Snow, I need your help again. Can I stay with you? I know you have room. I can't stay here, not without Mamó. She always told me about ghosts. I know her ghost will be here to keep me in line." So it was that Lynn packed two suitcases and moved into The Old Man's lower level.

Not long after The Old Man had given Lynn a ride home from the Heart Clinic, the two would sometimes meet for supper or a Saturday dinner. They talked. The Old Man learned a more detailed history of Lynn. At first she used The Old Man's full, formal name. He laughed and said most everyone called him Old Man. Lynn laughed aloud at this. "You know, when Mamó first saw you out of the window before she would allow me to go to lunch with you, well, she always referred to you as 'that white-haired old man.' I told her that your white hair reminded me of snow; newly fallen, fresh snow. I can't call you Old Man. I'll call you Snow."

Snow it was.

During those many lunches and dinners The Old Man learned about Lynn and her gran. Apparently her gran hated men, at least most of them. Lynn grew up learning to fear males. The only school friends Lynn was allowed to invite over or whose houses she could visit were girls. Her gran wouldn't allow her to attend public school. She attended St. Tim's Catholic grade school. When she got to be of middle school age, Gran enrolled her in a small charter school that was known for its strict policies. The total enrollment, seventh through twelfth grades, was around 150, seventy-five percent of them female. The students wore uniforms. Lynn showed The Old Man pictures of her in uniform. He shook his head. The uniform was not unlike the attire Lynn wore to work and on their ventures to restaurants.

The restaurant thing with Lynn was always an adventure. Gran never ate out. She cooked anything simple that might be found on a northern European kitchen table. Lynn learned to love Mexican, Italian, and Greek places. This was Lynn's only attempt at rebellion from the rule of Gran.

"Mamó had money to eat out but never did. I don't know how she got her money. My grandpa was gone long before I was born. Mamó never answered my questions about him except to say he was in Ireland, most likely in a peat bog. She would only say, 'Himself was a match for the devil.' When we learned to use computers at school, I tried to find out about him. The only things I found that I knew to be true were his name, DeClan Patrick Timothy O'Leary, and his marriage to Mary Bergedha Murphy. Other stuff I found out about the DeClan O'Learys didn't seem to be him. I was always referred to men from Chicago, Kansas City, Pittsburgh, or St. Louis, once in a while St. Paul. I don't think any of that was about Grandpa. None of it was very nice, anyhow.

"You know, Snow, I have never had a date in my life. Mamó always made me dress this way. I don't have and wasn't allowed to have any clothes that made me look like a girl or a young woman. I only get to dress like an old lady of fifty years ago. Since I graduated, you're the only friend I have, other than a few women at work. No one ever asked me out on a date, or a movie, the prom, or to eat at a restaurant. Well, I guess you have, but you are not really a date, I don't think. Oh, Snow, what a mess I am."

When Lynn and The Old Man returned from the cemetery, he said, "Lynn, we need to get you some new clothes and an appointment at a salon. That is, if you want. From today on you belong to you. Your gran is not available to control your every move. If you want, and only if you want, we can start tomorrow."

Lynn got off The Old Man's couch and walked in front of the curved glass china cupboard. She looked at herself, then pulled apart the bun that held her hair in place. As if her fairy godmother had passed a wand over it, strands of long, rusty hair unfurled. It hung down to the middle of her back. She looked into the reflection on the glass and smiled. Shaking her head from side to side, she turned and said, "Yes, but I don't know anything about what, where, or how. Mamó's restricted style is all I know."

"Lynn," The Old Man laughed, "I think you just started. I am hardly one to advise a monarch butterfly on appearance. Let me call one of my grandnieces for help."

The Old Man made arrangements with his grandniece, Abby, to take charge. He filled her in on Lynn's background and situation. "Abby, she has lived a sheltered life. We can't have her going from looking like a 1930s farm wife to a twenty-first century cover girl. I suspect that under her disguise is a stunning figure that more than matches her face and hair."

Abby, with the help of a shopping center, salon, and The Old Man's credit card, turned Lynn into a somewhat conservatively remade Irish Colleen. Lynn would not go long without a date request. He pleaded for Abby's help in educating a twenty-four-year-old who had missed her debutante lessons. Abby assured her great-uncle that Lynn would not be taken advantage of by opportunists.

The 10:00 a.m. lawyer's appointment proved generous for Lynn. Gran had bequeathed all that she owned to Lynn: the house, the property on which it stood, all of its contents. Lynn was also informed that all Gran's monetary accounts had been changed to a joint account in both their names; hence, the cash and stock assets were liquid. He gave Lynn a check-book, a bank book, a savings book, and a credit card with her name on it. He gave her the phone number of Gran's stockbroker.

"But, how can that be? I never knew about this. Shouldn't I have signed papers?"

The lawyer smiled, "You did. You just didn't know you did. Didn't your gran from time to time ask you to sign some papers? Like the obedient child, now woman, that you are, you did. Mrs. O'Leary also made you the executor of her estate. You'll need help on what needs to be done. I'll be happy to continue in your employ if you wish."

Lynn turned to The Old Man. "Snow?"

"Tell you what, Lynn, for now let's just go home and talk about it."

Talk about it they did. The Old Man didn't want anyone bilking this innocent woman/ child out of her money. He suggested she use his CPA for seeing to her and Gran's tax filings. He suggested she retain her own stock-broker. He gave her the names of some of his former students whom he trusted to choose from. He also gave her a list of lawyers, former students as well. He suggested she set up appointments to talk to them, see whom she felt comfortable with. He offered to drive her to the appointments and go in with her if she wished.

Lynn and The Old Man spent a better part of two weeks talking about what she needed to do now and what could be put off until later. They spoke with The Old Man's tax people, who also managed an investment firm. They spoke with lawyers and other investment firms. The Old Man thought that if Lynn stayed busy, she would function better than if she sat around and contemplated a, "Oh, woe is me" situation. She had two weeks' compassionate leave from the clinic, only one of which was paid, but money was no longer an immediate concern. She had more now than she ever believed she would have. There was more on the way as she told him, "Snow, I can't live in that house anymore."

The Old Man wanted Lynn to be sure she wouldn't make decisions she would later regret. "Lynn, let's see to what needs seeing to at your riverside house. We need to hire a yard service to take care of the lawn and snow removal in the winter. You can continue with those your gran used if you want. From what I know about real estate, you'll get a better price in spring than now. If by March you want to sell the place, there is a relator down the block that has a good reputation. Let's cut off cable tv, telephone, and newspaper. We need to get your gran's and your mail sent here for the time being. Are you okay with all of this and ready to get to work on it?"

"Yes, Snow, I need to do something besides wondering about all the things I wish Mamó had told me. You know, we never had cable tv. We only had what we could get on the antenna on the cupola roof. Mamó never spent money, as she said, 'frivolously.' I guess that is why we found the shocking dollar figures in her checkbook, savings account, and stock portfolio. Mamó used to mend her old winter wool stockings. She shopped at Goodwill. As I got older, I raised enough fuss that she finally let me buy something at Ragstock. Oh, Mamó, whatever possessed you?"

On the following Sunday The Old Man asked Lynn if she wished to accompany him to church. He attended a quite liberal Catholic church near the University of Minnesota. He told her about its liberal ways, and then suggested that if she wished to attend the more conservative St. Tim's, he would accompany her there.

"Oh, Snow, if I had to remain at St. Tim's, I would stop going. When do we leave for Mass?" So began Lynn's newfound faith in going to church. Six weeks of Sunday Masses began, and at The Old Man's suggestion, so did volunteering for several committees, such as the one for social justice and if she wished, the committee for racial equality and LGBTQ+ rights. Lynn found a new life, friends, and in some ways, a home.

On March first she told The Old Man, "I want to buy a condo near the church. There is one I already looked at. I know I have the money for a down payment. Some of the people at church said that they knew I could get a loan. I want to put Mamó's house up for sale."

It was happening; Lynn was growing. She was moving from pupa to chrysalis and soon would be a full-fledged monarch butterfly. She found new friends her age. They helped her in all the ways a teenage girl would have needed help: clothing, dating, dining out, feeling comfortable in a twenty-first century society.

Lynn went through gran's house and picked out the furniture, rugs, paintings, photos, and heirlooms she wanted. After the house was sold, The Old Man's neighborly realtor found a highly acclaimed estate sales manager to get top dollar for all that remained. In Gran's later years she was frugal, but earlier in her life she had purchased the finest furniture, carpets, china, and silverware. She had cedar closets and cedar chests stuffed with fine linen, tapestries, and lacework. The garage behind the house had a 1965 Barracuda that was most likely a leftover from her husband. Lynn's grandparents had great taste when it came to spending money.

The Old Man worried about the now-wealthy Lynn. He spoke with her financial advisers and a few people at church. The Old Man relaxed as all the good people assured him they would keep watch over her.

One Sunday at church he smiled in awe at what he saw. Lynn was at home with friends, part of a community, happy, and one of the most helpful volunteers. The chrysalis now had wings. What a happy ending.

Or so it seemed. Four months after the riverside castle was sold, Gran made headlines in both Twin Cities dailies. The news articles said that Bergedha O'Leary was suspected in the death of her husband, DeClan O'Leary. The new owners of Bergedha O'Leary's house, in a landscaping renovation, had unearthed what authorities believed to be the remains of DeClan O'Leary, noted figure in a nationwide underground Irish crime syndicate. The story indicated that O'Leary had not been seen or heard from since 1971. Since Bergedha O'Leary never turned in a missing person's report on her husband, she was suspected of the murder. Having passed away about ten months ago, she could not be questioned. Lynn O'Leary, granddaughter and only surviving relative, was reported to have been questioned. That was the gist of the stories in both papers.

Lynn had indeed been questioned but could offer no help. She related her reclusive life with her grandmother. Lynn's parents, Paddrick and Bridget Cunningham, died in an automobile accident in 2001 and could not be questioned.

The Old Man again was at Lynn's side as she was devastated once again by news of her gran. "Snow, everyone thinks I'm the granddaughter of Lizzie Borden. The newspapers say my grandad was hatcheted to death."

"Lynn, look at me. Have any of your friends at church or work treated you any differently than they ever have?"

After a long pause, Lynn shook her head no. "I don't think so."

"So as before, you stand tall, smile, and believe in your gran."

This seemed to help Lynn. A few days later, Gran's lawyer contacted The Old Man and asked him if he would accompany Lynn to his office. When both arrived at the meeting and had exchanged pleasantries, the lawyer handed Lynn an envelope. "Lynn, your grandmother gave this to me a few years ago. I know its contents. I helped her write it. Since communication with a lawyer is privileged, I have not and will not reveal its contents."

Lynn opened the envelope. As she read, she burst into tears. The letter consisted of several pages. Lynn had not read beyond the first few paragraphs. The lawyer picked up the pages. After Lynn finally stopped crying, he said, "Lynn you need to hear the rest of this." After a glass of ice water and The Old Man's calming influence, the attorney read.

Sixteen years of being married to DeClan taught me much. I never got used to the occasional beatings he delivered when he was drunk. He was on the road, as he put it, so often. He usually treated me and your mother well, but as your mother grew older, he beat on me much more when he drank, and then he took to your mother a couple of times.

Still, he provided well. Look at the house we live in. His travels took him away from home as many as six times a year, sometimes for a week or two, sometimes a month or two. During his last road trip I found a suitcase in the garage attic. I was bored being alone so much. DeClan never let me have friends of my own, and he never seemed to have any. One day, when your mother was spending a week with her school friends at a lake, I decided to clean out the entire garage, attic and all. When I opened the suitcase I found a bag of paper money and a collection of newspaper articles that reported the deaths of some prominent people. The deaths were sometimes violent, other times questionable but ruled accidental, suicides, or death by misadventure. In the suitcase under a false bottom was a collection of pornography.

I burned the newspapers and the pornography in the fire pit out back. I realized that DeClan was a hired enforcer for a criminal element. No wonder we had so much money. I began to fear for your mother's safety as well as my own, as the frequency of his beatings were on the increase. It was time.

When DeClan returned from his last trip and your mother was away again, I used the hatchet he always kept in the garage. As he was on his knees, polishing his prized big boy toy, his Barracuda, I showed him an old banshee knew more than warning of the upcoming death of a relative. This banshee could use a shillelagh with a blade on the end of it to not just announce his death but to cause it. His life ended in the way he made his living.

I don't regret what I did. I had to protect your mother and myself from a man I thought was good and who loved me. As I look back, I don't think he loved me for me. He loved my looks. Everyone said I should be a model or in the movies. I told your mother that her father had moved to Ireland.

As years passed, I grew to hate the man and, I guess, men in general. That is why I was so protective of you. As you were growing out of child-hood, I could see that you were going to have my physical features. I wanted to protect you. That is why I kept you away from boys, dressed you to hide your physical gifts, and sent you to school where you would be sheltered.

I am not sorry for my actions. I hardly think they were sins, or if they were, only of the venial variety. I never wanted to hurt you, only protect you. I hope you can understand this. I do love you more than life.

I planted DeClan under the bed of roses at the top of the slope near the river. I did it for us.

"There is more," said the lawyer, "but I will leave the letter with you to read later. Give it some time. Bergedha lived her last years only for you. She had me help her write this letter when her health began to fail. She said, 'I think Lynn will be okay now. I think that white-haired old goat can be trusted. She likes him. He'll help her get by.'"

The lawyer continued, "Since Mr. O'Leary has been long dead and no one's well-being is threatened, I felt then and still feel no obligation to make any of this public. Lynn, whether you make any of this public is up to you. Here is my card. Call me if you want my help or have any questions."

A few weeks later Lynn invited The Old Man for dinner. "I am learning how to cook after all those years of eating Mamó's cuisine. I am taking it slowly. This is my third try at lasagna. I think I have it down now."

After a great lasagna, a tossed salad with vinegar, garlic bread, and Spumoni ice cream, Lynn said, "Snow, I am at peace now. I am at peace with Mamó, the people at work, and at church. I'm going to leave the last part of Mamó's story with us. Gran was right; she knew she was leaving me in the good hands of a white-haired friend."

Play Ball

From the Land of Sky-Blue Waters (Waters)
Hamm's, Hamm's, the beer refreshing

The pleasant ditty looped through The Old Man's head. He pictured the rippling blue waters bounding in, over, and around in the rocky brook. The brook wound through an evergreen forest. The recollection of the old Hamm's Beer commercial was triggered by Mike and Frank on American Pickers. Their camera crew captured the scene on one of the pickers' stops in the north woods. Mike said the scene reminded him of a Hamm's Beer commercial. He hoped that he and Frank might be lucky enough to find a Hamm's neon sign or a cardboard diorama depicting the blue stream, maybe one featuring the cartoonish Hamm's bear.

For The Old Man, those commercials represented baseball. Baseball was something he needed on the second day of an old-fashioned Minnesota blizzard, already twelve inches of snow with thirty-to-forty mile an hour winds. He had been slogged in for two days. Even if it ended that night as predicted, it was still a day or more digging out, or at his age, pushing eighty, being dug out.

The Hamm's bear represented a dream come true for The Old Man. The dream had nothing to do with beer; it had everything to do with baseball. The Old Man loved the game. Growing up, he listened to games on the radio. The Mutual Broadcasting System on WXYZ out of Detroit did some of those games. Some evenings the station came through clearly. He treasured the memory of listening to the Dodgers in the World Series with his grandpa and his dad.

Before the Twins, Minnesota had been Milwaukee Braves territory, but for The Old Man it was the Chicago White Sox, the Go-Go White Sox with Aparicio, Fox, and Minnie Minoso, and the Cincinnati Red Legs with slugging Ted Kluszewski and his cut-off sleeves. He remembered watching the White Sox against the Dodgers in the 1959 World Series on TV with his grandpa.

Then, in part because of the people who gave him the Hamm's bear, the major league Minnesota Twins became a reality in 1961. The brewery solidified the move of the Washington Senators to Minnesota by signing a lucrative commercial sponsorship. Yes, the Land of Sky-Blue Waters gave him the 1960s voice on the radio. "Hello again, everybody, and welcome to Twins baseball." Herb Carneal's words had brought magic into The Old Man's way of life.

January, only five weeks more to spring training. The Old Man realized now even more how baseball was a mainstay in his life. He was snowed in for three or more days and no baseball to rescue him from another long, lonely evening. He had spent much of the day reading, but he needed a little variety. TV didn't offer much these days, and they didn't run three hours of new American Pickers or Jeopardy! episodes each night.

Mentally, he made a list of the number of people he might have phoned on such a night. However, many of them had already kicked the bucket. Others were far younger and had lives of their own to lead. He needed a baseball fix. Lounging in his recliner he laughed aloud thinking of Sid Hartman, the iconic Minneapolis sports reporter who was making a valiant effort to outlive God. A few years ago Sid harped on why the Twins needed a new stadium. "If the governor doesn't get us one, the Twins will move to a city that will build a stadium. Think of all the old people who will suffer when the Twins leave. They won't be able to listen to the Twins on radio or watch them on TV. They will be lost," preached Minnesota's Methuselah. The Old Man laughed again. Now he understood how right Sir Sidney was. The Old Man was lost without baseball.

The Old Man thought about purchasing salted in the shell peanuts and old-fashioned, German-style hot dogs to prepare for the season. Baseball was the best of all sports for many reasons, none of which was more important than the 162-game schedule. Plus there were an additional thirty spring games, almost 200 days of pleasure. The Old Man didn't really care about the playoffs and World Series that much anymore. The World Series should be played in the daytime during the first two weeks of October, he thought, not dragged into early November's wind and snow.

The next day began at 6:30 a.m. as the noise of the plow in his driveway awakened him, another day closer to baseball. As The Old Man scanned the sports page looking for new baseball information, he remembered how angry his mother used to get. "Baseball, baseball, that's all you think about. What will that ever get you?"

He reflected on that. He even got out a yellow legal pad and started a two-column list. In one he recorded the positives that baseball had given him. In the other he jotted down the negatives. When he finished, he noted that the positives list was ten times as long as the negatives. On the negative side he could find only three things: a broken jaw from being hit by a pitch, a cracked left thumb from being hit by a pitch, and being struck out on a Sunday afternoon on nine pitches from Jim somebody or other.

The broken jaw was costly; he missed a month of the American Legion baseball season and later suffered from needed dental procedures. Only today did he feel the aftereffects of the thumb injury. He didn't miss any baseball games, but did have to change his batting grip. Today, however, his left thumb and wrist were a magnet for his arthritis. The three at bats, nine pitches only served to keep him humble; perhaps that was really a positive.

The positives were so many. Baseball provided something to look forward to at the age of seventy-six. It filled summer evenings and always provided new hope for next year. Baseball took him to Port Arthur, Ontario, as a Little League All-Star. His Little League team allowed him to pitch for a city championship. Little League also gave him good friends that he still had sixty years later. Babe Ruth League gave him another championship game to pitch. The game was good to him.

The Old Man thought about another old man and baseball, his grandpa. Baseball with him was certainly a positive. How many times did his grandpa come to see him play? Grandpa came to see The Old Man play second base in the State American Legion Baseball Tournament. That was more of a positive for the second baseman than for the grandpa who lost his hat at the game. How many baseball games did the two of them watch together? Amateur games on Sunday, Twins games, and they even watched the Minneapolis Millers in 1959 play an exhibition game against their parent team, the Boston Red Sox. In that game the Old Man watched the immortal Ted Williams hit a home run.

The Old Man could still hear his mother ask, "How are you ever going to make any money fooling around with baseball?" But he did make money off of baseball, a little. After college it was time to make money off of the game, umpiring. The Old Man umpired town ball and high school games for a number of years. He also did many softball games. The extra money came in handy giving a beginning teacher some "egg money" to spend on fun things. Best of all, as an umpire standing at home plate before the game, he got to call out the best line on the grand stage, "Play ball!"

The Old Man also made a few bucks in the summer coaching kids baseball and softball in a recreation program. He didn't get rich, but it did get him more "egg money."

Then, too, there were all those baseball cards he collected. At a penny a card, bubblegum included, he had over a thousand cards. He spent hours reading and rereading the backs. He looked at the pictures and saw how the players changed as they aged. He sorted them by team, traded them with his friends. He rode his bicycle eight miles to another town in hopes of finding a different series of cards. Years later he sold the collection for a few hundred dollars. "Yes, Mom, I made some money off of the game." But really, that was only a small part of what baseball gave him.

Baseball was a physical game. It provided exercise. He had played as far back as he could remember. At age six, he came home with a bloody nose. He wasn't yet proficient judging a fly ball. Maybe that should have been in the negative column. But it hardened his resolve—don't quit, get better, learn from it—an asset after all. The pleasures of the game were always there, playing, coaching, umpiring, winning, losing, and reading about it.

With baseball on his mind that afternoon The Old Man combed his library looking for baseball literature. Besides baseball, his other lifelong obsession was reading. Reading did make him some money. He made his livelihood teaching writing and literature. How many times had baseball played a part in getting kids into reading? For the reluctant and slower readers it was Ring Lardner; for others it was Bernard Malamud, who wrote The Natural. The Old Man loved the book long before Hollywood realized what it was. The Old Man extracted other books from the baseball section: The Dixie Association by Donald Hays, If I Never Get Back by Darryl Brock, and The Universal Baseball Association, Inc. by Robert Coover. He loved those books. Baseball combined with good literature was the best.

In spite of baseball being America's grand old game, it was a Canadian who proved to be the best baseball writer, W. P. Kinsella. The US certainly knew Field of Dreams, a movie and a northern Iowa tourist attraction, but how many read the book, Shoeless Joe, which fostered all that hoopla? The novel far exceeded the movie for reasons beyond the inclusion of J. D. Salinger. Then there were all of Kinsella's baseball short stories, more great reading and illumination of the game. These, too, came in handy for the reluctant reader.

The most valuable of all of Kinsella's writing was the Iowa Baseball Confederacy. In that novel Kinsella revealed to the world that baseball must have been conceived by Leonardo DaVinci. It is a game of infinite perfection. It features an orb, a solid circle, perfection. It features a round barreled bat, more circular perfection. The game was originally played on open fields, no fences. The dimensions of a baseball field reach infinity. If the foul lines are extended the ever widening expanse is infinite. If allowed it would span the universe and circle back to encompass itself. Perfection. The rules of the game ignore the fourth dimension, time. Unlike other athletic ball games, there is no time limit. An extra inning game could conceivably go on forever. In the novel the exhibition game between the Chicago Cubs and an amateur Iowa All-Star team lasted days and surpassed 2,000 innings with no end in sight. Baseball and literature at their best.

The Old Man wanted to tell his mother that baseball did get him somewhere. It got him to a happy state of mind at the age of seventy-six and could continue to do so, perhaps not forever, but long enough to get him where he was going.

The Old Man knew they always had a baseball game there. Anywhere else, the game was always called because of fire. He looked forward to the day when he could stand at home plate, see all the haloed spectators, and yell, "Play ball!"

That's Crazy

She loped out of the garage dragging a lawn chair behind her. She put it down next to the mailboxes under the crab apple tree that separated the two driveways. Then she looked over to the old man sitting in a lawn chair on the other side of his driveway. He had a legal pad in his lap. It looked like he was keeping track of something.

"Hey, mister. How are you? I'm Laima. It's spelled L-A-I-M-A, but it is pronounced like the bean. I'm going into the sixth grade. If you want to talk, you could move over here to this side of your driveway. I'm grounded. I can't leave our yard."

The Old Man moved his chair to where she had pointed. The little girl stood about four foot ten. She had long, thick, light brown hair formed in two pigtails sticking out on each side of her head. She wore hiking boots and cargo pants held up by suspenders over her plaid flannel shirt. She smiled but could not hide the light pink splashing on her face. The Old Man winced. Before he could ask, she said, "Calamine lotion. My mom says I have poison ivy, I think it might be poison oak, but poison sumac is the most likely. Hey, what are you keeping track of on your pad?"

"Oh, I just keep track of the different birds I see. How did you know I was going to ask about your face?"

"Your expression told me before you did. We just moved here four weeks ago. We have been unpacking, so I haven't been able to visit you. School starts in two weeks, and I'm grounded for that time. Don't you think that's crazy for them to ground me for getting poison whatever?"

"I think," said The Old Man, "that you got grounded for going to where the poison whatever was, not for getting it. Unless of course you are in training for plant recognition and flunked the test."

Laima laughed. "You're pretty smart. I like that. I think we will get

221

along just fine. My mom was getting sick of me in the house all day. Besides, I was tired of unpacking stuff, reading, and drawing, so I just pestered her. That's when she told me to get out and straighten up the garage. This lawn chair is as far as I got.

"My parents are from Lithuania. Both of my grandparents are still there. My last name begins with an L; it contains 37% of the letters in the alphabet, 37.74% to be exact. What's your name? My mom says I should call you 'sir' or 'mister,' but that's crazy. You must have a friendlier name than that. I asked my mom your name. She said she didn't know; she just refers to you as 'that old man next door.'"

"Well, Laima, most people around here call me The Old Man. I'm the only retiree on both sides of this street; the rest of the townhouse complex is mostly retired. So when your mother is not within hearing distance, you can call me Old Man, and I'll call you Little Laima; no, wait. In so many ways you are not little. Let's see . . . I'll call you L. L. Bean, how's that?"

"I like it, Old Man," Laima smiled.

So, L. L. Bean and The Old Man became friends and had long, regular lawn chair chats. One evening as an orange harvest moon rose in the east, Laima asked The Old Man, "Do you think about the moon? I want to go there. I just read The Martian Chronicles by Ray Bradbury."

"No, L. L. Bean, I never wanted to go to the moon. No baseball there. But I do remember watching the moon landing. It was summer, and I was tending bar at a golf course. Back then beginning teachers had to have summer jobs to pay the bills."

"That's crazy."

"What? That I tended bar or that I needed a second job?"

"No, that you are really that old. That's history; we study it in school. I like history and English, especially reading, but I really want to be a scientist. I am not sure yet if I will be an astronomer or biologist. I like plants and animals. Say, are you really that old? You were really there, the moon landing, I mean?"

"I was in the bar watching on TV, looking; no one ordered anything as they all watched."

On another visit The Old Man asked L. L. Bean why she walked the Crooked Creek to Lake Marie. "You must have been looking for something other than poison something or other."

"Oh, I was. I wanted to see what flora and fauna were there. I learned those words in science. I think I'm going to like science. I like the teacher, Ms. Brook; she's cool. That wasn't the first time I walked the creek. It was just the first time I met the wrong flora. I looked up all the poison plants on the internet. Now I know what to avoid. Still, I get the itch, not the poison itch, but the itch to explore. See I like words, too. I like to play with them. That's why I like to read. Bradbury plays with words, too. Maybe I'll write science fiction.

"Let's see, so far along the creek and the walking trails around the lake I have seen fifteen different species of birds. Do you have that many on your list?" She rushed on before The Old Man could answer. "I like the red-winged blackbirds best. I wish I could see a loon, but the lake is not deep enough for them. Once I saw a pheasant run across the path as it gave a weird call. That's when I realized I had heard that squawk often out there, but that was the only pheasant I actually saw. I've seen muskrats and their huts, and once I saw a fox, such a beautiful, graceful animal. And then there are so many deer. I've seen as many as five on one hike there."

"Be careful, L. L. Bean. In November when they start mating rituals the bucks may become aggressive. If you see one just stop and stay still until it leaves. It will charge you if it feels threatened. Those antlers are sharp."

"Thanks for the warning. I wish I could see an aggressive one. That would be just crazy." Before The Old Man could respond to that, Laima resumed her monologue. "You know, Old Man, I think there's a feral cat out there. I keep hearing one in the trees on the southwest corner. A cat in a tree, I wish I could see that."

The Old Man laughed. "L. L., you need to be searching those trees for a steel-gray bird with a long tail, not a cat. You are hearing a catbird, so called because it sounds like the meow of a cat."

"That's crazy. I'll look for one. You're even better than a history museum. Maybe you are a natural history museum, too. Ms. Brook taught us that, too, natural history."

The visits went on, weekends and after school. "Tell me, Old Man, what is the strangest animal you saw around here?"

"An iguana."

"An iguana?" responded L. L. Bean with her copyrighted, "That's crazy. Really? Don't they live in South and Central America?"

"Yes, they do. I remember seeing some of them that were five feet long in a city park across from the hotel I stayed in while touring Ecuador. It was in Guayaquil. The one near Lake Marie was only a two-footer. I assume it was the result of an unwise decision to own an exotic pet. Someone must have gotten bored with it and wondered what to do with it in winter. I saw it in early November. It just stood there shivering in the cold. A bunch of trail walkers like me were standing around staring at it. Iguanas are not aggressive. This one was too much in shock even to run. Someone had already called the DNR."

"Don't tell my mom. She'll keep me from going there at all. They don't want me to walk the creek anymore, but I got them to let me ride my bike on the creek and lake trails. They think that is safer for me than walking. If my mom hears there are wild iguanas there . . ."

Another history lesson had Laima ringing The Old Man's doorbell. "What do you know about the Kennedy assassination?"

"Which one?"

"There was more than one?"

"Yes."

"Okay, the president guy. I want to get all the information before class tomorrow."

He told her what he knew about all the news film footage: the grassy knoll, the hospital, Lyndon B. Johnson being sworn in on the plane, and the live TV footage of the Lee Harvey Oswald shooting.

"Boy, tomorrow I am going to be ahead of everybody in class. I can report from my own private history museum."

The next time L. L. Bean came calling, she had a towel with something all wrapped up in it, a bird. "I just saw a flock of crows over at Lake Marie.

They attacked this bird. It fell right out of the sky, about fifteen feet. I rode over and picked it up. It seems to have an injured wing. I wrapped it in a towel. Mom makes me keep one on the bike along with a first aid kit. I'll bet Ms. Brook could fix it. Could you keep it in your garage for me till I catch the bus tomorrow? I'll go home and get our old birdcage. I know my mom won't let me keep the bird at home. You know, the old country. Mom worries about lice too much."

"You have a birdcage, Ms. Bean?"

"My parents gave me a parakeet four years ago. The guy at the pet store assured them it did not have lice. It was blue and yellow, so pretty. I hated to see it caged up, so I often let it fly around the house. My mom got mad. She had me cleaning up bird poop all day long. Once, when I let it out, I forgot to close the patio screen and Keetie flew outside and never returned. My folks were upset with me, and I was grounded.

"Mom said that the bird would die come winter, but I told her not to worry. Birds have instinct; Keetie will fly south. They don't rely on their bird brains all the time." The Old Man told L. L. Bean he would keep the cage in the garage, and now she could add a starling to her bird list.

In early April, L. L. Bean pumped The Old Man for what he knew about 9/11. The Old Man told her he was teaching that day. Word had come over the intercom asking teachers to keep students in their rooms. The Old Man said his room had a TV set, and they all watched the news clips of the Twin Towers. He told her of all the tears and fears of the kids. School was dismissed early with no school for the following day.

Laima had no "that's crazy" that day, only tears. After the tears and a glass of ice water Laima reached into her flannel shirt pocket, pulled out a slip of paper, and handed it to The Old Man. It was an essay contest entry form for a nature camp in northern Minnesota, a 500-word essay on why the study of nature is important to the world's future. The winner would earn $500.

By the time all the tears dried, L. L. Bean had regained her unbound enthusiasm and told The Old Man she would enter. She had to win, because the winner would get $500 for the camp. "I have to win because we can't afford the $500. I just have to go to that camp." The Old Man perused the entry form closer. He read the fine print. The total cost of the camp was $1,500 for a three-week stay. He said nothing.

During the next month The Old Man told L. L. Bean about the time he found evidence of beaver on the creek. He noticed all the sharp-ended stumps from saplings. As he stood on the walking bridge over the creek, a guy who lived next to the nature preserve told him that it was the work of beavers who had come up from the Mississippi River. They had a good start on a dam before the DNR trapped and moved them seventy-five miles north. Laima almost swore, "Darn, I missed them. I would have camped out there at night to watch them gnaw, drag, and build. That would have been crazy wonderful. Maybe I will see them up north when I win the nature essay contest."

Two weeks later Little Laime Bean joined The Old Man on his driveway as he checked his mail. She had tears in her eyes. She showed him the letter. She had won the essay contest for the summer nature camp. Then she showed him the line that said the $500 would cover one-third of the fee for the three week camp. "Mom says we don't have the money."

After a glass of lemonade and some freshly baked chocolate chip cookies that The Old Man had, Laima regained her composure and smiled. "You know what? I'll get a job this summer and earn enough money to go next year. I don't need to win a contest to go."

Two weeks later L. L. Bean ran out to the mailbox as The Old Man came to collect his junk mail and bills. She sang out with joy, "Look, Old Man, a letter from the camp. They said that an anonymous donor sent in $1,000 for me and with the $500 I won, I can go. That's crazy! A donation? $1,000? When I get back, it will take a full month to tell you everything. I hope I don't get poison whatever. I'll talk to you later. I gotta pack my clothes, backpack, fishing gear. Oh, so much to do."

L. L. Bean dashed into the garage. Her mother was standing there watching. Then she nodded and smiled toward The Old Man before she followed her daughter inside.

The Old Man considered himself lucky. He had a good friend who provided him with many reasons to vacate his ever-faithful recliner. He wouldn't miss the money, even if L. L. Bean had never gotten around to asking about important stuff like baseball. His time with her was priceless. But if she ever asked about baseball, he had much history to tell her. He had actually been there in person for the historic events. He was there at the Old Met in Bloomington for the sixth game of 1965 World Series. He saw Jim "Mudcat" Grant hit a home run and pitch the Twins to victory over the Dodgers. In 1991, he sat four rows behind home plate in the Dome and watched Jack Morris grit out a ten-inning complete game victory over the Braves to capture the World Series. Well, there would be time for that.

Not only was The Old Man a winner for knowing L. L. Bean, the world was also a winner. An exceptionally bright, enthusiastic, and charismatic little girl held all the hope for the future that Ray Bradbury had. With a driven scientist with a thirst for knowledge like Laima, hope for the world's future did exist. Such brains and enthusiasm were needed now more than ever. And that wasn't crazy.

Missing

The Old Man suffered a severe whack to his head. After a few days in the hospital he was released with no apparent damage beyond the rattling of his brain.

A few days later, still a little wobbly, he noticed a flyer that must have dropped out of his morning paper. The flyer was an application form for an English language investigator. The Old Man was puzzled. What was it all about? he wondered. Being a little bored and these days even more cloudy concerning the world around him, he decided to investigate. He filled out the application.

The next thing The Old Man knew he was being interviewed for the position of Private Investigator for the Committee to Bring Suit Against Those Who Are Leading the Charge In the Ruination of American English.

"Sir, heretofore, you will answer to the name of Curmudgeon. The position for which you applied is of grave importance and long overdue. The first thing we wish to hear from you is a sample of what you think needs to be addressed in regard to the sad case of American English."

"High Inquisitors, I will begin with the case of American writers, both novelists and news reporters. For example, I will quote from a recent novel. 'When did you first notice that the girl went missing?'

"'Went missing.' What the hell does that mean? 'Went missing.' Did she leave a note that said, 'I am going to the supermarket, and then I am going missing?' Going missing, going missing. Went missing? No one 'goes missing.' People are kidnapped, get lost, disappear, hide, suffer from amnesia or Alzheimer's disease, but they sure as hell don't go missing."

"Mr. Curmudgeon, there is no call for such language. However, you are correct. From where do you think such an expression originated, Mr. Curmudgeon?"

"My first encounter with that expression came from the British. The quaint Brits often use a novel way of expressing things. That is fine for them. No doubt American writers, not having the imagination themselves, have plagiarized from the Brits. While I recall the original speakers of the language using that term for years, I do not recall seeing it used by American writers until about twenty years ago."

"Very well, Curmudgeon," boomed the lead inquisitor. "That does show us something of the skills needed for this endeavor. Now, sir, if you are able, give us another example."

"Another example, yes, let me see . . . what about American television dramas, situation comedies, newscasts, and sports reporters lacquering the country with, 'It is what it is'? What the hell—sorry, Grand Inquisitors. What exactly does that mean? Why not tell us what 'it' is? Be clear about what is means. Do not leave the public the task of reading the mind of the speaker or writer."

"Excellent, Curmudgeon. Now, to what do you attribute the cause of such behavior as you have placed in evidence?"

"As in the first case, as I already stated, the lack of imagination. The second cause is obfuscation. The writer or speaker wishes to confuse the public or keep the public from knowing that the author or speaker has no idea what is meant. The statement is used to befuddle.

"No doubt the blame for this lays in the worlds of politics and mass media. In the 1960s and '70s congressional hearings often became public television fodder, which eventually led to today's reality TV. The Watergate hearings, the Iran-Contra Affair hearings, and others that followed, including the public obsession with Roger Clemens defending his 'misremembering' the various contradictions he made before a Senate committee, all of these gave birth to the proliferated use of such glitterarrie and misleading terms. For example, such phrases as 'at that point in time,' or 'at this point in time,' instead of a clear and simple 'then' or 'now.' I suppose the coiners of such phrases were either trying to impress an ignorant public with their supposed erudite language, or they were stalling for time to come up with a suitable excuse for their behavior. Today con artists and politicians continue to use such phrases because they tend to impress an ignorant audience.

"As for 'misremembering,' Mr. Chairman, I simply submit that the users of such are trying to disguise lies in which they have been caught. In my mind, people remember, forget, or lie. The very term 'misremember' is a true oxymoron. Perhaps the emphasis should be placed on moron. To an educated public, 'misremember' means, 'I am trying to cover up your having caught me in a lie.'

"Furthermore, politicians have a tendency to damage the credibility of a perfectly useful word. For example, Mr. Chairman, the word 'transparent' for years has meant to see through things clearly. Webster's puts it in two ways: 'so fine in texture as to not conceal what lies beyond,' or as 'to not conceal.' Today the word is used by politicians to accomplish the very opposite, concealment from the public. Instead of a 'transparent statement,' what the public hears is, 'what I wish you to misinterpret with the help of my spin doctor is . . .'"

"I see. Now tell us, you old goat, what you mean by the title 'spin doctor'? That is not a term with which we of the committee are familiar."

"Good sirs of the committee, 'spin doctor' is a new political cabinet appointment. Think of the term 'surgeon general.' Today's politicians require a wordsmith, spin doctor, to do one of two things. One, interpret clear statements made by others into a twisted, jumbled message in which the original meaning is lost or reversed. Two, make outright lies or ignorance stated by superiors into a maze of lexicon from which no sound thinker can escape with the truth."

"Very well, you old goat, sorry, I mean Curmudgeon. How did this country get itself into this mess?"

"In my humble opinion, I am sorry to say, education."

"Education, you numbskull, sorry, I mean, Curmudgeon. Is not education the institution that this country uses to make the world safe for democracy? Is this not the institution in which you spent a half a century wallowing?"

"Yes, your Royal Eminences, education has failed us. I am part of that failure.

"In addition to the reasons given, another reason for the rotting of American English is the people whom the 'educated public' elected to such positions as mayor, governor, and even a president or three.

"Perhaps the root of this starts with elementary education. Elementary teachers used to be guardians of the language. One did not get out of the sixth grade unless one could demonstrate the proper use of 'good' and 'poor', adjectives, and 'well' and 'poorly', adverbs. We learned to do things well or perhaps poorly. We learned that things could be good or bad. We learned that 'he' and 'I' were to be used as subjects of sentences, while 'him' and 'me' were used as objects. No third grade teacher would abide by such a statement as, 'Me and him went to the store.' Sore knuckles discouraged such behavior. Today most high school students and many of their erudite faculty members live in ignorance of the standard use of such words.

"We used to learn that the word 'number' was used for things that could be counted, as in the number of people. The word 'amount' was used for things that could be amassed, such as the amount of money. A phrase such as 'the amount of people in the room' would envision a picture of people stacked like cordwood, a pile of people.

"I'll not even get into the totally oxymoronic 'very unique.' One of a kind cannot give us a comparison.

"Who added the 's' to the word 'anyway'? Years ago, 'anyways' was used as a method of identifying speakers who were ignorant or educationally deficient.

"To recapitulate, gentle people of the committee, the deterioration of the language began in elementary school. I do not fault the teachers as much as I fault administrators and legislators who do not value language."

"Ergo, Mr. Curmudgeon, you do not fault education beyond elementary schools?"

"I certainly fault higher education as well. Students are being graduated from colleges and universities by the thousands who have no more than a substandard command of the language. I once had a student teacher in English whom I wished to fail because she consistently used substandard English in the classroom. I was told it would do no good as it would not prevent her from being granted a degree; furthermore, she had already secured an English teaching position in another state. Not having standard command of the English language would change nothing."

"So you fault elementary and higher education for the demise of the language?"

"Let us not forget the media. Newscasters, emcees, and sportscasters contribute also, kind people of the committee."

"For example, Old Man."

"Troy Aikman, Troy Aikman, sirs, sirs."

"We fail to understand your redundancy."

"I, too, fail to understand such redundancy. Your Eminences, the football analyst, Troy Aikman, he is prone to use the double subject, usually a noun followed by a pronoun. He may say something such as, 'The dog, he gnawed on the bone.' For years Troy Aikman, Troy Aikman has done this on national television with an audience in the millions. His superiors continue to pay him an obscene amount of money (note I did not say 'number of moneys') without correcting his annoying habit of using substandard English. Lately, the practice has been adopted by Cory Provus, Minnesota Twins radio broadcaster."

"Mr. Curmudgeon, you present some excellent investigative skills. However, you need to provide us, to use a sporting term, with a knockout punch."

The Old Man, still a bit groggy from the blow on his head and the pressure of the interview, scrounged through the cobwebs of his mind. A knockout punch, sporting term, sports, baseball—yes, baseball.

"If it pleases the committee, one of the most instrumental cabals causing the ruination of the American English is Major League Baseball. Not only is it undermining the language, it is plotting the ruin of our national game.

"Let us start with two terms with which baseball has used to malign players and fans: offense and defense. As long as this old Curmudgeon can remember, baseball has used terminology that is uniquely appropriate to it. In order to score runs (not points), a team has to be at bat. In most other sports a team controlling the ball scores the points. In other sports this is called the 'offense.' In baseball, scoring runs is done mainly through hitting the ball with a bat. Hitting is supported by base running. Thus, a team at bat, using hitting and running, score runs. Note they are at bat, not on offense.

"Sometime before the turn of the century, baseball, along with scheming sports writers who would rather be associated more with football, basketball, or hockey insisted on using the term 'offense' when the proper baseball terms were 'hitting' and 'base running.'

"On the other side of the coin (an item used to start football games), sports writers used the football, basketball, and hockey term 'defense' when writing about preventing the other team from scoring. These writers were only referring to one of the methods of keeping the other team from scoring. They use the term 'defense' when they are referring to fielding. When they said the team had a good defense, they meant fielding. In actuality the defensive part of baseball is dominated by pitching. Seventy-five to eighty-five percent of preventing the other team from scoring is pitching. Pitching is the most defensive part of the game. Yet when using the term 'defense,' sports writers make no mention of pitching.

"Major League Baseball itself began using this mainly football-based terminology. Instead of speaking more precisely about hitting and base running, they jumbled it into one term, 'offense.' Instead of being precise about preventing the other team from scoring, they did not credit pitching as the core of the defense. The term 'fielding' has all but disappeared.

"Further evidence of this is using the term 'defender' instead of the proper term, 'fielder.' Instead of saying a player is a good fielder, they say a player is a good defender, a hockey and soccer term.

"They have further savaged proper baseball terminology by using such phrases as 'a good-hitting catcher.' There is no such thing. A catcher, when being a catcher, cannot use a bat, and therefore cannot hit. A catcher can use a mitt, throw a baseball, wear protective gear, and line up outside of fair territory. However, a catcher can only use a bat when becoming a batter, not when functioning as a catcher; hence, an offensive catcher does not exist.

"Major League Baseball has now further bastardized the game and its language with what it has done to the intentional walk. By definition, a walk is a result of a batter not swinging at four pitches outside of the strike zone. Baseball has done away with the pitcher throwing any pitches when intentionally walking a batter. Now the batter goes directly to first base; they say he was 'intentionally walked.' This cannot be a walk, intentional or otherwise, by definition. Baseball needs to address its issues in terms of imprecise language. If no pitches are thrown and the batter is awarded first base, it is a 'put,' not a walk.

"If America accepted this lack of precision in airline pilots and surgeons as they do in the use of the English language, far fewer of us would be alive today. As a former English teacher I resent the country's regarding my profession as one of so little importance. The attitude is, 'If it is somewhat close, who cares?'"

"Thank you, Curmudgeon, the committee will make a decision on your selection anon."

A few days later The Old Man received a telegram saying he was disqualified as a candidate for the post of English language investigator. The reasoning was that he was a former English teacher, therefore, part of the problem, and he could not be part of the solution.

After mulling over his blow on the head, a vague recollection of a long interview with somebody or other, The Old Man took action. He wrote a note and posted it on his neighbors' door:

Please collect my newspaper
and mail for me.
I AM GOING MISSING.

The Old Man

The Old Man dozed on and off, the radio playing easy listening music. Some called it elevator music, but he was sure old Otis himself would be proud of the designation. He was dozing off more and more during the day. At eighty-four, aches, pains, and the loneliness of people his age gave him an understanding of his grandma's advice, "Don't get old." He was still living in his own apartment in a seniors-only complex. He worried about how long he could continue to do that.

As he dozed, his fleeting dreams were haunted by the theme of Father's Day. Perhaps the radio station had aired a commercial to guilt someone into buying things for dear old dad, things that most dear old dads didn't want or need. If dear old dad wanted or needed it, he already had it. If he couldn't afford it, chances were his kids couldn't either. Then again it was the thought that counts, or so he had endlessly heard. However, for The Old Man there never had been thoughts of that nature. That he had deciphered this meant that he was now fully awake.

He glanced at his nearby calendar. Yes, it was early June. The calendar had marked Father's Day as June 16. He wondered if the celebrating of that event and others like it was a creation of Hallmark or others to sell cards and gifts. No doubt the economy owed much to such events. Christmas, Easter, and Halloween could not by themselves sustain those commercial enterprises.

Yes, it must have been the radio that planted the theme in his head, yes. But what did it mean? Did it have any meaning for him anymore? His dad had been dead and buried for thirty-some years. He had given cards to his dad, gifts. But what did it mean? Had he done so just because he was supposed to? He guessed that was all there was to it. He was expected to.

He got out of his recliner and checked the newspaper for the time of the Twins game. Now he had to get his supper. Today it would be the sloppy joes that he had made on Sunday. Sunday was the only day he really cooked anymore. Chicken breasts, pork loin, or Italian macaroni hotdish usually lasted for a couple meals during the week, better than a cold cut sandwich or a can of chunky soup.

As the hamburger with a tomatoey, smoky taste warmed, he thought about his dad. He remembered when he was five or six and wanted to go fishing, his dad took him to Rascal Lake and rented a boat. The boy wanted to catch a northern, so his dad rowed him around the edge of the lake three times. His dad had no motor. The Old Man now realized the physical effort his father must have endured to make him happy. Those old wooden boats were not easy to move. The boy did snag a two-foot long, skinny northern pike. A great day for the boy, but a great deal of labor for the dad. Perhaps that was a good reason to celebrate Father's Day.

The Old Man was seventy-nine years too late to thank him for the fishing outing. As he ate his sloppy joes, supplemented with good Gedney baby dills, he wondered what his doctor would say about consuming so much salt. As he once told his then eighty-seven-year-old grandma, who wanted to go out in her garden on a hot summer day to pick raspberries, "Why not? What is the point of being eighty-seven if there is no fun allowed anymore?" The Old Man remembered the hell he had received from his aunts for allowing Grandma to put on her bonnet and fill with berries the tin can that she had tied around her neck.

The Old Man smiled and reached for another dill pickle. Another smile followed. He should have given his dad a Father's Day card for the great dill pickles he canned each summer. Gedney had a ways to go before they matched those. Then there was his dad's canned beef, better than the sloppy joes for his sandwiches. Yes, his dad gave The Old Man many legitimate reasons to honor his father. His dad worked two jobs much of the boy's growing years. The part-time work, baking doughnuts from 4:00 a.m. to 7:00 a.m., came before his regular job. In other years he worked from 6:00 p.m. to 9:00 p.m. piling lumber after his regular job. This allowed his dad to clothe his eight kids, feed them, and see that there were Christmas gifts and a few summer picnics. There were many reasons for celebrating Father's Day. The Old Man felt depressed. He had never really said thanks.

As he cleaned up his supper dishes and grabbed the two chunks of his daily chocolate ration, he began to feel even worse. In eighty-four years, he himself had never received a Father's Day card. He had never had any children in his seven to ten years of marriage, as he put it. He always said "seven to ten years" because it was over after seven but not legally ended until the tenth. After the divorce he often regretted not having children. He recalled telling his wife that if they had children, he felt he would have to quit teaching. He said he didn't think he could spend eight hours a day meeting the needs of his students and have anything left over to properly give enough to their children. After the divorce he regretted not having had children. At least he would have had something more than good memories to show for his married years. But he knew it was selfish to think that way.

His ex-wife wanted to travel and live all over the world, Europe, Asia. He told her he would go wherever she wanted. She told him no; she couldn't be responsible for his leaving teaching. She said she knew how much he loved it and how good he was at it. She left for England, and he remained in Minnesota to continue teaching.

Even with the nap The Old Man had a tough time lasting through the entire Twins game. The Twins were at home and helped him stay awake by avoiding a bottom of the ninth. There was not much else left in his life other than a Twins game to bring him happiness.

That night his dream was still on Father's Day. In his dream, people asked him about his children and grandchildren. They kept bugging him about how many kids he had. In the dream he gave the answer he had often given in real life: "A few." When pushed for an exact number, he laughed and said, "Four or five thousand," and waited for a reaction. After the attempt at humor failed, he said that he was an English and speech teacher who retired after thirty-seven years but continued to coach speech for twenty-seven more. He told them that the official count was somewhere between four and five thousand kids in his life.

The next day was his house cleaning day. Oh, he had a cleaning gal who came in every two weeks, but he tried to keep up on his cleaning chores a little so he could have more time to visit with her. Some days she got little cleaning done in her three-hour stay, but she seemed to enjoy his stories. As he pushed the noisy vacuum cleaner, he thought about his nonexistent children. He remembered that in an education class a point was made that a teacher was in loco parentis. What did that mean? He shut off the vacuum cleaner and got out his two remaining dictionaries. The Oxford American Dictionary defined the term as "in the place of parents, responsible for child protection." Protection, interesting word, he thought. He had stood in for parents; he had been legally responsible for the safety of those in his charge. He knew that in the last twenty-five years of teaching, laws had been enacted to require teachers and coaches to report known or suspected cases of child abuse. They were legally required to report erratic or self-destructive behavior or hints thereof.

Well into the afternoon he decided to forgo his usual nap and read. He still read mystery novels, but today he browsed through his poetry books looking for poems of parenthood. Robert Frost, Emily Dickinson, Carl Sandburg, and T. S. Eliot offered little on the subject. He missed his collection of five thousand-plus books. Surely if he still had all of it, he could have found something. Instead he reread most of the Robert Frost collection. That still left several hours before the Twins game. They were now on the West Coast; it would be a late game. Maybe he could make it through the fifth inning.

He didn't cook that evening. He was still chewing on in loco parentis. Ice water, Bing cherries, and salted in the shell peanuts preceded the two Dove dark chocolate bits for his supper. He always like to read the message on the inside of the Dove wrapper. One of them said, 'Help the children.' He guessed he had done that. He had protected his children. There was the girl who ran into his room to hide from her mother's abusive boyfriend. He stood between the girl and the husky aggressor who could have ripped him apart. Instead the man retreated from the room. He reminisced about how he went to Sandy's aid. She was a sophomore whose locker was directly opposite his classroom door. She was shy, naïve, and not one of the brightest of his kids. She was also tall and pretty, the perfect prey for the likes of a bullying, sexist male whom he observed for several days getting into Sandy's personal space and putting his suave moves on her. She was visibly uncomfortable. The Old Man intervened and told the hulk that since he didn't have any classes on that floor, if he saw him again he would personally make trouble for him.

The Old Man didn't see the kid around after that. He asked Sandy if the boy was bothering her elsewhere in the building. She said no. She said her friends told her that the boy said, "That skinny," here she stopped and mouthed the word "bitch," "was not worth it." Her friends told her that the boy's cronies said he didn't want to mess with, "that guy up there." The Old Man smiled.

Two home runs by the Twins in the first inning against the Angels added to the smile. The Old Man dozed off in the fourth and woke up in the eighth with the Twins ahead four to one. He headed to bed hoping his dreams were about baseball rather than Father's Day.

His dreams were not about baseball or Father's day. A restless night of tossing and turning was punctuated by jerking awake from dreams that were more like nightmares. In each one he was in some type of trap or predicament that he couldn't extricate himself from. When he was faced with the worst of it, he woke up feeling helpless. He eventually drifted off and found himself in another dangerous place.

The next morning, working the daily crossword in the newspaper, he rehashed his trap dreams. Maybe he had been wrestling with Father's Day issues. When he was a kid, who had he always gone to for help when he needed it? His dad. Kids went to their parents for help at least until they were teenagers. Teenagers, if they went for help at all, often turned to teachers or coaches. Many of his students had come to him when they found themselves trapped. Vicki came into his office crying because the counselor had told her to forget about college; she would flunk out anyway. The Old Man told her to follow her dreams. He then quoted John Greenleaf Whittier, "The saddest words of tongue or pen is that it might have been." She did follow her dreams, was admitted to a private college, and got her degree.

Then he thought of Elaina, the Mexican girl he had in class while teaching in South America. She, too, came in tears and asked what she should do. Her mother and her mother's new boyfriend wanted to send her back to Mexico to live with her sister. "My mother and her boyfriend don't want me around, and if I go back with my sister, her husband will come to get in my bed again." He advised the girl to tell her mother and her sister. She said she told her mother, and the mother called her a liar. Elaina said she could never tell her sister; how could she hurt her sister?

The Old Man had informed the counselor and principal of the private school. It was a few days before Christmas break. When school resumed four weeks later, he found out that Elaina's mother had pulled her out of school and asked that her transcripts be sent back to the school she had formerly attended, apparently back with her sister.

Maybe he didn't deserve a Father's Day card. He failed to protect that time. But what could he do in a foreign country, and the girl had been sent to another country?

Elaina's story led him to Jenny's tale. She asked to speak to him privately during his prep hour. At the time The Old Man was about forty years old. He could still hear her words, "I have come to you because you are the only one around here who will listen and not be judgmental. I can't go anywhere else. I think I'm pregnant. I don't know what to do. There is college, my parents, my boyfriend's parents. I don't know what to do." The Old Man just sat there for a few minutes, both in silence.

Finally, he asked the girl to list what she thought she might do, to write down her options. The girl did. Then he asked her about the pros and cons of each option. She made a column for each. After some silence, Jenny said, "I guess my first step is to find out." He offered her money if she needed it to find out. She said, "No, both of us have money to find out." She then smiled and left. About two weeks later she said there was no problem.

He didn't solve the problem directly; however, he listened, which helped her sort the issues and pursue her own solution. The Old Man guessed that was a parental responsibility: listen.

The Old Man's summer was moving along. To pass the time he sorted through some old yearbooks; he ruminated on some of his speech teams and plays he had directed. He looked at senior pictures and marveled at the memories, how much those seniors had changed and grown from grade nine. Some of those he remained in contact with over the years, but the years saw those numbers dwindle to only a few. He had outlived more than a few of them.

Yearbooks nudged his stream of consciousness to thoughts of his "goody file." He moved to his old oak desk, which his aunt Mary had rescued from the Standard Oil junk pile when they cleaned out some old offices. That was sixty-four years ago. He located the wrinkled manila folder and began to revel in the jewels of his teaching career.

First were the letters from college deans and admissions offices. The letters were sent to inform him that so-and-so had listed him as the most influential and inspiring high school teacher.

The second pile contained letters from parents for his work in helping their children to achieve excellent writing and speaking skills. One single mother said, "You turned Marci's life around. She was a lost, angry teenager who hated authority figures and inflicted her anger on any and everyone since her father's death several years ago. I was so worried about her. She was forced into an independent study with you because of a scheduling conflict. You would not put up with her crappy behavior; you told her to use her excellent brain. You cajoled her, pushed her, nurtured her. You told her you cared about what she became. You both won. I remember the day she told me, 'Mom, I didn't know learning could be so much fun.' She was so happy when she came back from a reading at a local bookstore with the autograph from the author she did her project on." Marci was a success. She had turned into a star basketball player who led her college team, graduated, and became a teacher and coach.

Another letter thanked him for having taken a mother's sad, moody, depressed ninth grader and somehow convincing her that in spite of being a terrible speller who didn't know that punctuation marks existed, that she could be a good student. The letter said, "Not only did you guide her into being the editor of the school literary magazine, but you got her to join the speech team. The shy, scared, quivering-voiced daughter of mine won a speech conference, first place. She went from baggy sweatpants and sweat-shirts to hide herself to wearing clothes that allowed the world to see the beautiful, confident girl that she is today."

The old codger smiled and thought, Maybe that was my best effort. The last he heard of the girl was that she wanted to pursue a PhD in linguistics.

He guessed the dictionary had missed a great deal in defining "par-ent." All of the dictionaries listed biology first, then mentioned rearing and responsibility for. Didn't fostering come into this? Wasn't that a vital part of raising children? After all, that was such an important part of his grow-ing up, becoming a man, a teacher. Fostering. That was what he got from his best coaches and teachers. They convinced him he could do things, be somebody he never thought he could be. They would not accept less than his best effort to be and do; they convinced him he could. Yes, fostering.

Perhaps instead of *in loco parentis* he was a foster parent.

As he got up out of his curved back oak chair that was also retrieved from the scrap heap, an envelope fell to the floor. His aching knees and back didn't make it easy, but he rescued the envelope and took it with him to his recliner. He needed a nap now so he could make it to the end of the Twins game that night.

Comfortable in the recliner, he opened the envelope. Inside was a card. He opened it and read:

Dear Sir,

I am sitting in my room, the night before my first college classes. I just wanted to say thanks. I know I wasn't your top student, and your classes were so hard. I never had to work so hard in any other class. I worked hard because that is what you demanded. You told me, actually all of us, that we could do it. You made us work and learn. I did it. I only got B's from you, but all the kids said that a B from you was like an A from anyone else. I took all of your classes I could.

I know I'm not so smart, but in your classes I felt smart. You made me feel smart. I want to be an elementary teacher and make kids feel smart.

Thank you so much,

Tara

A big smile on his face was sprinkled with a few tears as he drifted off to sleep. He drifted so deeply into his sleep that he never awakened.

He had received a Father's Day card over thirty-five years ago. It was on his very last day that he finally recognized it.